The FOURSOME

One Man's Faith Matched Against Doubt, Ignorance and Pride

The FOURSOME

One Man's Faith Matched Against Doubt, Ignorance and Pride

Terry Dodd

Printed in the United States of America

Publishing services by Selah Publishing Group, LLC, Arizona. The
views expressed or implied in this work do not necessarily reflect those
of Selah Publishing Group..

ISBN 1-58930-050-5
Library of Congress Control Number: 2001099347

THIS STORY IS FICTION and theological statements incurred in these pages that are not wholly consistent with the Gospels are neither beliefs of the author nor are they thereby suggested as being worthy of consideration with respect to Christian truths.

ACKNOWLEDGEMENTS

THESE ARE MY PASSIONATE THANK YOUS for everything these people have either done for or meant to me: My wife, Judy, for her forty-plus years of support and quiet Christian witness through her love not only for me, but for her fellowman. Our three adult children, Wendilynne, Jason and Martin, and our son-in-law, Kevin who each in his or her own fashion contributed in ways they will never fully know to my passion in writing this novel. Our precious grandchildren, Abigail and Karsten, whom I am anxious to have read grandpa's words of faith when they are of age to understand and to accept Christ for themselves.

My mother, my two brothers and their wives and children, and my wife's family, all of whom I have lovingly had in mind during various moments in writing this story. Jack Larimer, my best friend of forty-five years. The many supportive pastors, including Warren Lathem and Dan Dunn, as well as staff, congregational members and small men's groups at Mt. Pisgah UMC, and especially Allen Hunt, the senior pastor of my church who sagely suggested using a disclaimer such as found at the beginning of this story. The continuous efforts of my agent, Becky Hardy. My editor, Ann Fisher, who being Jewish said of the novel, "I'm not converted, but it's interesting."

To Chris Cupit and his family, Tommy Lyman, and Rivermont Golf Club, the golf course model for my story. To Anita and Garlen at Selah Publishing, who made a beautiful book of my manuscript. And lastly, to the many publishers who expressed no interest whatever in this work, I forgive you.

And I thank God, for I work for Him and am accountable to Him in all that I do.

ONE

Paul Clayman leapt wildly from his vehicle mere seconds before the inevitable crash. His bicycle met the massive, lone backyard tree of his Dover, Delaware home. "Bulls-eye!" he said in a gleeful tone born partly of boredom with school, but mostly over anxiety with family. The twelve-year old slipped quietly into the house through the back door, intending to quickly climb the stairs of the small, two-story home he shared with his dysfunctional family. That make-up included his mother and step-father, Naomi and Peter, plus his aging and ill, immigrant great aunt.

The adult threesome were arguing as usual and on this occasion occupied the kitchen, which was near the back door. Thus for Paul to avoid the unpleasantness he had to dart unobtrusively down the basement stairs to his secondary retreat.

The youngster usually pulled the stairway door shut behind him when he felt the need to burrow below ground, but that would have given away his presence. There were no significant barriers to the kitchen voices carrying to his ears as he probed disinterestedly through his various well-worn toy collections.

His aunt was speaking to his mother. "It's Passover, and if only once you would serve a Seder dinner or even light a menorah, maybe Pauli would learn something useful about his Jewish heritage. I could be dead in a week and then who'll be your conscience?"

"Don't threaten, Lila," Naomi said. "My conscience doesn't need yours to drive it. As for Pauli, he knows he's Jewish. And why pretend we're religious when we're not? As I recall, 'do as I say, not as I do' didn't keep your own family from splintering."

"Well, even Peter-the-profane here manages to make that effort," the aunt said, spitefully.

"Hah!" Naomi said, pointing to the uninterested Peter, who was reading a newspaper. "He takes Pauli to church twice a year so he can tell his friends he's raising my son as a Christian. Then just last Easter the poor boy comes home from Peter's hour-of-penance and asks . . . for God's sake, 'Was Jesus really a Jew?'"

"There!" the aunt said, vindicated. "He knows more about the gentiles' savior than he does about Moses."

"Who're you to talk?" Naomi said. "You yourself called the visit a mitzvah."

"Oy! I'm afraid the boy will need more than a few good deeds by a pretender. He'll need Jacob's Ladder to reach faith. Well, his lack of religious training won't hurt him any more than Peter's belt buckle, or your three divorces." The aunt was just warming up to the argument and added, "I'm too played out to help on this battleground. And mark my word, one of these days he'll find out about the abortion, too!"

At those remarks Pauli's eyes glazed over as if subconsciously shifting his thoughts from drive to neutral. Within a year the aunt died and young Paul was left to wrestle with Satan rather than with God.

Two

Paul Clayman, now in his late twenties, lay dreaming about a long-past episode in his first year of college. Oddly, he had never before dreamt about the emotionally draining experience, but for some reason his mind was busy vividly re-creating the scene. Six years after the 'basement revelations' and numerous subsequent conflicts a determined, religiously skeptic, but enthusiastically-independent young Clayman had accepted a full scholarship at the furthest geographically-removed university to make him an offer. He would study English and business at Florida State in Tallahassee. "Tallahassee!" everyone had said. "Where or what is that?"

In his dream he saw himself standing in the same familiar classroom where he had taken a particular mandatory Humanities course. On a whiteboard he saw the title of the joint comparative religion project he had been assigned to with a fellow student, "Faith Appreciation." As the dream unfolded the actual project was once more clearly and accurately presented.

Clayman had reluctantly chosen to do the lion's share of the research in over-viewing eighteen of the twenty assigned religions and cults. This was so he could avoid any connection with either biblical Christianity or Judaism. They had each completed their part of the assignment, but not until the oral presentation of their papers was Clayman privy to his partner's work. The dream re-presentation continued.

The student partner was summarizing and made a point of comparison between Judaism's zealous dispensation of the law and Christianity's grace from God, and quoted from the book of Hebrews. Clayman once again clearly heard the words so confusing to him: "'Therefore, when Christ came into the world, sacrifices and offerings you did not desire, nor were you pleased with them.' Then Christ said, 'Here I am—it is written about me in the scroll—I have come to do your will, O God.'"

Then came Clayman's partner's second and much more disturbing biblical quotation: "With Christ's coming God set aside the first—or Old Testament—to establish the second—or New Testament, made holy through the sacrifice of the body of Jesus Christ once for all."

As Clayman tossed in his sleep the dream presenter glided to the write-on board and continued his presentation by drawing a graphic of ice, water and steam. Finishing the illustration he re-gripped the dry-erasable marker and enclosed everything in a circle, saying, "This simple example illustrates the concept of the Christian godhead, symbolic of three persons in one; God the Father, God the Son, and God the Holy Spirit."

Suddenly, Clayman abruptly stood in the dream. "That's a contradiction!" he shouted. "It's a contradiction!"

His dream partner remained calm, saying, "No, Paul. It's an *apparent* contradiction. It *is* a paradox and it *is* mysterious, but it is *not* contradictory. God is not both one person *and* three persons. God is one essence, but in three different persons." Clayman's partner then closed his presentation to the class amid the bizarre and strenuous objections of his project-mate, saying, "They're all made of the same stuff, but are different. And they all exist at the same time, unlike the common elements in my board illustration."

The dream-Clayman shouted once again, "No, no. I can't accept it!" At that point the dream faded.

THREE

THE FOLLOWING MORNING at his modest-sized, but well-appointed apartment where he lived by himself, Clayman had awakened thirty minutes earlier shaking his head over elements of the dream which had filtered back to him. He smiled, not only because it was merely a dream, but also because he didn't really care about the subject. He walked across his living room toward the front door carrying a half-eaten banana in his left hand. Without pausing, but still with an amused smile, he used his right hand to snatch his company-logoed golf cap from the fireplace mantle. He exited the apartment and strode purposely to his car, anticipating the upcoming round of golf.

Fifteen minutes later the young, auburn-haired distributor of promotional products was seated in front of his wooden locker, changing shoes at RiverTree Golf Club. "Ready to test the old handicap today, Mr. Clay Man?" bantered the shoeshine man as he peered out from behind his window-barred, shoe storage domain.

"'Test' is right, Sammie. But since it's been three weeks since my last round, how successful I'll be only the golfing gods know."

"Well, I doubt God'll bother himself with it . . . but play your best."

Clayman's disturbing dream of the previous night was suddenly triggered by Sammie's response. He brushed the dream aside, but not the shoe attendant's remark. *That's a rather personal statement to make to a member!* He might mention that fact to management, he thought, but he knew Sammie had been at this club for more than twenty years and the club's private ownership considered their locker room man nearly as tenured as the head professional. Then the thought of his golf game intruded. *You're too thin-skinned, Clayman.*

His change completed, Clayman headed for the pro shop, his obvious enthusiasm for the day's round betrayed by his whistling. "What can you tell me about the three guys I'm playing with, Joey?" asked Clayman of the young female assistant behind the pro shop counter as he signed his play ticket.

"Two of them can peel your skin from you and leave you standing," she said with an impish smile. "As for the other one, he'll only worry you to death."

Clayman had recently begun a proactive search for his internal self. Externally he continued to exhibit his personally perceived version of Renaissance Man. Both efforts were understandable, he reasoned, the result of having to become his own mentor at an early age. He knew his weaknesses just as surely as he was confident of his considerable talents. Golf for him was a wonderful, if irregular, distraction from long hours laboring for the fulfillment of his ego as an idea man in the business of selling imprinted everythings. "Tell me about their strengths and weaknesses," he said.

"You haven't met any of them, Mr. Clayman?" Joey asked.

"Nope. Since I joined the club two months ago I've only played three or four times. I don't really know anyone I'd feel comfortable asking to play." Clayman thought for a moment. "Except for my girlfriend Sheila's father, Wendell Levin."

"Oh, I know him. Nice guy. He has a regular foursome."

"Right. So, I asked your boss to put me in with the earliest available Saturday morning threesome and here I am, live meat, fresh for skinning." Clayman was eager to return to the game he had only taken up relatively late in life for many golfers, during college. Since moving to Atlanta's north side three years ago he had played golf occasionally at area public courses, but Sheila's father had recently volunteered to sponsor his membership at RiverTree and he could find no argument. For a reluctant athlete he was a quick study, and he could usually play to his eighteen handicap.

Sheila Levin. He almost said her name aloud as he suddenly thought about her. Was she really his girlfriend or not? Exactly what was a girlfriend these days? They weren't living together. They hadn't even slept together! Oh, they had professed their love for one another . . . in between arguments over religion. Why couldn't two young Jews iron out a little thing like religion? *The so-called Trinity, that's why!* He recalled his dream from the night before. That's what his college project partner's illustration had been all about. Now, where had that come from after all this time?

Of course! From the echo of Sheila's tantrum during their argument earlier in the week. He recalled their near-public squabble.

"Look," Sheila had said, continuing to argue the controversial point over her grilled salmon at their favorite Italian restaurant in Roswell, an Atlanta suburb, "It's very simple. Refusing or neglecting to evangelize Jews is anti-Semitic."

Clayman sat back, dropping his fork onto his plate for effect. "Evangelizing a Jew *by* a Jew?" he asked, incredulous at the irony.

"You're not paying attention to what we've been argu—talking about," she said. "The *Messianic Jewish Manifesto* makes the point that if Christianity is Jewish--and it certainly is because it has its roots in Judaism and the Jewish people—and if anti-Semitism is un-Christian—which it is because that would otherwise violate everything Christian and would have to be regarded as sin—then neglecting to make Yeshua's message known to unsaved Jews is just as anti-semitic, whether by Gentile Christians or by Messianic Jews."

"What? *That* is patently ridiculous!" said Clayman. With that he had refused to say anything more during the remainder of the dinner—other than polite conversation—and then he took her directly home. No apology. No conversation. No kiss. Great evening, he thought.

"Mr. Clayman?" Joey said.

"Oh, I'm sorry. I had a long week. You were going to fill me in on my foursome."

Both the assistant pro and the new member had easily established a professional rapport during their short acquaintance. "Sure, Mr. Clayman," she said in a voice barely loud enough for anyone in the pro shop to hear. "Let's step over to the practice green and I'll check it for you."

As they walked to the nearby putting green the assistant said, "All three of the guys in your foursome are about as new to the club as you are. They came in during the Fall membership drive."

"Drive? Is that what it was? I thought of it more as a gimme putt, what with the big discount on initiation." As they neared the practice putting green he laughed and tossed up one golf ball, and then another, juggling them with one hand. Joey ignored what she considered Clayman's obvious attempt to impress her.

Nuts, I've lost it! he thought. Juggling used to work for him on the college campus, from the classroom to the front porch of the sorority house. Juggle three erasers, three cans of Coca-Cola, or his favorite ploy in any grocery store's produce section—four borrowed oranges—and young women seemed to love it. Not Joey. *Oh yeah, this isn't the campus.*

"Lots of competition up here," Joey said. "Fourteen close-by courses have either recently opened or are under construction." She took the two Maxfli brand golf balls from Clayman's hand and dropped them onto the practice green. She motioned for him to demonstrate his putting stroke. As he did so she said, "You've got a wonderful mix of talent and personality in this foursome, Mr. Clayman. Now, take Lucas "Luke" Santan. Rhymes with 'sun tan.' He's an "A" player, a solid eight-handicap. He has maybe fifteen years on you. Keep an eye on him when he misses a shot."

"Verbal, is he?"

"Oh, yeah. And a club flipper."

"That part's no big deal. I've been known to execute an occasional full-gainer with a sand wedge myself."

"That's chump change. This guy would make Tiger Woods' shot reactions look like genuflection. Santan is the only golfer I've ever heard of to be asked to actually resign from a club because of his attitude on the course."

"Resign?"

"Oh yeah. From Shadow Pines. In fact, he's RiverTree's first-ever probationary new member. On the flip side though he can eat you up with his game."

"What's he do?"

"He's a math professor at Georgia Tech. He's a believer in whatever he can observe with his five senses."

"Sounds like my kind of guy. How do you know so much about him?"

"People fascination."

This girl has it all together, Clayman thought. Unlike Sheila, who was into patchwork these days. "Gotcha. Who else is playing, Joey?"

"Roland T. Randall. He signs his name 'R.T.,' but some people call him Rollie. He hates that. Really nice guy, though, but a little short on self-esteem. He's a 22-handicapper, little older than you. Problem is he takes anyone's and everyone's swing advice. And he thinks equipment makes the game. If the game could be bought, he'd own it. Uh-oh. The pro would kill me if he heard me say that. You know what I mean." She moved her bangs to one side of her forehead in response to a gust of wind.

"What's his business?"

"Ad agency. Not like what you do. You know . . . public relations. That's a contradiction, though."

"How's that?"

"Well, he must be a creative type, yet he's the ultimate materialist and copycat. Just moved here from Winston-Salem. Don't think he's attached to anyone."

"A thinker is he? Interesting. If he isn't my partner, I'll try to share with him some little observation about his back swing. He just might start thinking about it. What about our fourth?"

"Thomas Danikov," she said in five distinct syllables. "Tommy Ray to most. A class guy, but also a real character. Laid-back, mid-fifties, clean-liver, built a graphics and print brokerage business from scratch. He's an eleven or twelve-handicap player."

"What's with the 'character' bit?"

"He's a long-time Atlanta resident. Played at another local club for years, but he joined here after finally dropping his membership over discrimination at his former club. Not about *him*: he's Caucasian, Russian descent, I think. Takes some fiber to resign from a club and give up your regular golfing buddies over perceived discrimination against *others*. Think you would ever do that, Mr. Clayman?"

"Couldn't and wouldn't. I'm Swiss."

"You are not. You're Jewish."

Clayman smiled and stroked the second Maxfli with his putter.

Apparently embarrassed at her outspokenness Joey quickly recovered, saying, "Well, you know what I mean. But now Danikov is a real contrast to Santan. Both are strong individualists, but they come from opposite directions. Santan runs over people, maybe even Danikov if he wanted."

Clayman walked over to the golf balls, followed by Joey. He then removed his cap for a momentary head scratch. "Anything else?" he said.

"About Mr. Danikov?" Joey said. "He's not really very outgoing. In fact I think I'd characterize him as passive on most things. With him, personal conviction is enough. I hear he's a self-educated student of the Bible, though not vocal about it." She quickly glanced back at the pro shop and then said, "Well, ought to be a fun round for you, Mr. Clayman. I gotta go. Good luck. Oh, yeah. Put some splints on your wrists. Too much hand action." She reached out and took one of his wrists in both hands, making an imaginary splint. "Substitute more shoulder movement for wrist action."

"Thanks. Any stock tips? Just joking. I appreciate your insights. As far as categorizing me, I'm a part-time seeker of truth. Now, can you hold off any more rain for the day?"

"You got it, Mr. Clay Man," she said, exaggerating the two syllables of his name. With that she darted back to the pro shop.

Clayman had another forty-five minutes before his 9:56 tee time, the earliest he could get for as late in the week as he had called the pro shop. Standing just off the practice green he withdrew some #30 sun block from his golf bag and liberally applied the gel to his face, neck, ears, legs and arms. He knew that without it even the early June sun would turn his fair skin as red as fresh shrimp boiled in beer. He had proven that point to his mother countless times as a boy passionate about spending his summer days at the public swimming pool. His recalled that his defense never varied. "Mom, I don't *need* sun tan lotion, I'm brown enough." She never smiled at his attempted humor, but stubbornly insisted. The thought of his unhappy boyhood and how it was brightened only by the fleeting mid-Atlantic Summer brought an involuntary smile to his lips.

Satisfied with his preventive measure he capped the lotion, tossed it high into the air with his right hand, caught it left-handed and deftly dropped the tube into the open golf bag pocket. The three-hour credit elective course FSU offered in Circus has been the most fun class he took in four and a half years of college.

He drove his golf cart down the hill to the practice tee and hit a handful of balls, getting mixed results. Rather than dwelling on that for the moment he exulted in the typical late spring Atlanta warmth with still-tolerable humidity. Clayman then involuntarily made a brief effort to analyze his day's swing, a general self-improvement effort that was little better than dreaming. Dropping his five-wood, six-iron and pitching wedge back into his bag he slid into the golf cart and steered it back to the pro shop.

He was still early and he wanted to introduce himself to the others in the foursome before heading to the first tee. The three were all inside the pro shop. Picking up a handful of tees from the large glass bowl placed for that purpose, Clayman smiled at Joey after the head pro had made the introductions, saying to the pro, "These guys look like a bunch of bandits. If I don't make the turn with 'em, call the sheriff."

"Go get 'em, Clay Man . . ." Joey said, and then noticed the head pro's stony stare. Her broad grin instantly faded. "Uh, Mr. Clayman," she said, correcting herself loudly enough for her boss to hear.

The two carts with the four players lurched off to the first tee. Right on time the starter signaled that their foursome was up. They obligatorily shook hands for the second time as they stepped up to the "blues," the second longest of the four teeing areas on each of RiverTree's eighteen holes. This was a club whose membership director— until recently— typically characterized it by saying, "Our golf course is our club's signature feature." Until this year that had always meant as opposed to the dated club house and locker room facilities of the private, thirty-year old subdivision club. The past year's prolonged membership drive and the resultant initiation fees had fattened the capitalization budget for many long-overdue facilities' upgrades, which had been successfully accomplished.

The first hole was a 396-yard par four with a narrow, but deeply cut stream bounding most of the left side of the fairway before cutting across the fairway less than 100 yards short of the green. A thick stand of pine trees beckoned from along the entire right side length of the fairway. Luke Santan spoke up. "We need to make a game, gentlemen. The cart manager placed my bag and Randall's on one cart and Danikov's and Clayman's on the other. That doesn't mean we have to play cart partners, however."

Danikov swung his three-wood once and then said, "Have a particular game in mind?"

"Well, my usual game is 'two and one,' Santan said. "Automatic press when one team is two down. Team 'trash' on birdies, sandies, greenies and polies. And the first team down by two gets a tee-of-choice on the next hole. That O.K. with everyone?"

Danikov laughed as he looked at the other two. Clayman shrugged with amusement, while Randall had a questioning expression. Danikov turned back to Santan and added with mock sarcasm, "What, no barkies or squares?" Turning to the others he said, "Translation, guys: automatic press is a new two dollar best-ball bet added for the balance of the current nine holes every time one team is down two on each nine. 'Trash' is worth a dollar each for the team with every birdie. Likewise for an up-and-down for a par from a bunker. Of course, a greenie is a closest-to-the-pin tee shot actually on the green on par-threes, providing you don't three-putt. A polie is especially designed to give the better player an advantage in that a holed putt longer than the length of the flagpole is also a piece of 'trash'. I think we can drop that."

"And the 'barkie' and the 'square' you apologized for?" said Randall, as he wiped his practice swing's club face of damp, freshly cut grass.

Danikov gestured to Santan with his palms up and head shaking. "Come on. Hitting a tree and still making par, plus an additional penalty for three-putting? That's sucker 'trash' for high handicappers playing with lower handicap players. As for the one time 'tee choice' bit, that's new to me, but I'm certain you wouldn't scam us. Right, Luke?"

"It's no big deal," Santan replied.

Clayman finally spoke up. "All this with full handicaps, naturally."

"For the match, of course," Danikov responded, "but handicaps don't figure into the 'trash' game. We'll use Santan's eight handicap as the base. I get four strokes, Randall fourteen, and you twelve. Gimme a ball each, men, and I'll throw 'em up for partners."

Randall turned to Clayman, saying, "Whatever. I don't think I can lose more than my week's lunch money . . . unless I choke like a 'fifties Ford."

Clayman laughed. "Good attitude . . . if you're my opponent." He thought to himself that this group ought to have some fun, which was why they were all there. "Here you go, Santan-man. I'm playing Top Flight XL-4s, fresh off the discount shelf. Which one of you low handicappers gets to carry me today?"

As Santan prepared to toss the four balls into the air Clayman offered a suggestion. "Wouldn't it be simpler to match youthful exuberance against wily experience instead of invoking this ritual appeal to the golfing gods?"

Danikov frowned at the use of the all too-common expression.

"Yeah, it would," said Santan, unsmiling, "but that's not how it's done."

"Well," said Clayman, "we certainly wouldn't want to change any traditions." The two younger players winked at each other and performed a casual high five as Santan tossed the four balls into the air.

Danikov, eyeing the results said to Clayman, "Well, looks like you didn't jinx the toss after all. You still have me for a partner."

Slightly embarrassed, Clayman rebounded. "Pretty good decoy move, huh, partner?"

Randall countered also. "It's only right the high-handicapper got the 'A' player. I'm up to the challenge, too, partner. You believe in taking prisoners?"

"Not in the game of golf," Santan said in all seriousness. Bored with the small talk, he added, "Let's tee it up." He tossed a wooden golf tee into the air to determine which team had first tee honors. The tee landed with its tip pointing closest to Randall. "We're up, Artie," he said. "Lead off."

"Actually, it's R. T., not Artie, but I answer to anything but Rollie. Absolution, however, is thine with birdies, Captain." Randall laughed at his joke as Santan smiled thinly. The other pair glanced at each other with raised eyebrows.

Randall overswung with his huge, new nine degree Taylor Made, bubble-shaped, titanium driver and pulled his tee shot badly. As it went sharply left into the parallel water hazard, Santan said, "Nothing lost. Our Irish friend 'Mulligan' is with us on the first hole. Swing easy and finish high on this one."

Randall swung at the bonus shot and did nearly exactly as he was advised. He was rewarded for faithful execution by a shot that was pulled just far enough left to cling to the fairway two hundred yards off the tee. Santan then hit a three-wood shot squarely and was straight and long, leaving himself only one-hundred and forty yards to the flag, for him a nine-iron shot to the green. The group congratulated him on his drive.

Clayman hit next and pushed a solidly hit driver far enough right to catch a fairway bunker. His first-tee bonus drive—with an identical swing—caught the same trap. The moment the second ball lit in the sand he turned to the others, bowed, and said, "Any questions about how to execute that shot, class?"

Everyone laughed. Danikov proceeded to tee up for his turn saying, "Don't give it a thought, partner. What other sport allows a grown man to play in the sand in public?" He connected well with his three-wood, though the trajectory was a little low. He safely hit the center of the fairway. The tee shot wasn't quite as long as Santan's, but it drew equally low whistles and compliments from the others. As was the case with Santan, Danikov saw no need to take a second-shot 'Mulligan'.

As they stepped toward their respective carts, a small portion of the leaden sky suddenly turned golden and a breeze freshened as a rainbow made a vivid, if surprising appearance low off the horizon in the direction of the first green. Santan growled and said, "Jesus Christ, I thought the rain was through. Looks like the freakin' rainbow is just takin' a coffee break."

Danikov was only a few yards away sitting in his golf cart and instantly responded to Santan's remark by clapping his hand over his heart as he said, "Thank you for that. Jesus is in my heart, too." Santan stared at him for a moment, obviously irritated, but said nothing.

Danikov then added, "I think a rainbow is a blessing, Luke. That's the way Noah took it after the forty days of rain."

Santan laughed derisively. "Old Testament Noah?" he asked. "Well, you can pray for good shots if you want. I'll make my own."

Danikov looked at him with amusement. "You know, my new friend, I don't usually witness on the golf course . . . or much of anywhere for that matter, but you just set me up. I'm personally offended by your taking the Lord's name in vain. As for the rainbow, what I meant is merely that in Genesis we're told that they remind us of God's faithfulness to his covenant with man."

Santan looked irritated. "Pardon my language, reverend, but I don't care any more for religion than I do for politics, on or off the golf course. They both make too much of faith and too little of reality." Santan got into his cart, but didn't press the accelerator. "Let me ask you a question, preacher," he said as he looked back at Danikov calmly settling into his own cart. "Exactly what is your cause that you see fit to bring it up on the golf course?"

Danikov was surprised by Santan's challenge, but not put off. "The greatest cause of all: the salvation of mankind," he said. The other two uninvolved occupants of the carts each looked away and rolled their eyes, but said nothing as both carts leaped forward at the same instant.

Driving bumper-to-bumper, Santan retorted over his shoulder from the lead cart, "Man should not proscribe how God should run the universe. —Neils Bohr."

Danikov responded first by laughing, then shouting loud enough to be heard, "God does not throw dice. —Einstein."

As both carts pulled off the path perpendicular to the shortest drive of the group, Clayman couldn't help but remember what Sheila had said about the notion of salvation when they first met. At her insistence, they each shared something of their individual beliefs. What had been her cornball way of putting it? Oh, yeah. If it's hard for believers to be saved, which is only because of God's mercy, what chance do those have who reject Christ? That had impressed him. Not for the message—he wasn't really searching—but for her genuine concern for him. He remembered that she looked great. And soft. He liked spending time with her in spite of their inevitable mini-arguments.

As the two carts rolled to a stop, Clayman jumped out and said, "Gentlemen, I feel like the burden of an umpire has been placed upon me. How about some neutral ground for the sake of the match? Let Tommy Ray's faith be further inspired by the spectacular presence of a rainbow, which the scientific-minded Luke can argue is merely an arc consisting of prismatic colors formed by the refraction and reflection of rays of light from drops of rain." He was proud of himself for his intermediary effort and added, "There, now isn't that better? Let's play some golf."

Neither answered, both hitting their cart's respective accelerators at nearly the same instant as Santan waved off Clayman's defusing remarks and Danikov reacted with a dismissing smile. Each of the two apparent antagonists seemed satisfied that he had made his point.

Clayman and Randall both cleared the creek with their second shots, but both were also wide right and into the sand on the slightly doglegged-left hole. The former ultimately made a center-green approach and finished with bogey five while the latter three-putted from the green's apron for a double bogey. Santan lipped out his ten-foot birdie attempt after a crisp iron shot to the green, settling for a par. Danikov managed to make his six foot par putt following a green side sand blast from the left bunker. That ended the hole.

Stepping up to the second tee, Clayman said to Danikov something designed for everyone's ears, "Nice piece of work, partner. They tied us for low ball, but your sandie drew first blood."

Santan issued a brief smile and said to Randall in a voice also calculated for their opponents' ears, "Don't worry, part-ner. Dog that craps fast doesn't crap long." The other three men all chortled at Santan's golf-worn cliche.

Clayman stole quick, successive glances at each member of the threesome and thought the round might well prove to be a lot of things, but boring wouldn't be one of them.

About an hour later, as the foursome walked off the sixth green with Danikov and Clayman having won the hole and being the first team to break ahead of a one-hole lead, Santan announced, "We're the first team to be two down so we'll be playing the 'green' tees this hole, boys."

"Here it comes," Danikov said resignedly to Clayman as they dropped their putters into their bags. "When he mentioned his cute little option on the first tee I shouldn't have let it go, but I didn't take him for an opportunist."

"Big deal," said Clayman as he powered the cart. "Heck, you and I each get a stroke on this hole. Randall, too, of course." Danikov still shook his head.

"Gather 'round," Santan said on the tee of the most dif-ficult hole at RiverTree. Even though the seventh hole was a short 507 yard par five, it was a solid test starting with trouble in the form of water on the immediate left and for the entire length of the hole and also crossing the fairway at about mid-length. Never mind the thick stand of trees to the right, plus one turtle pond, five bunkers and a fairway that dwindled to less than twenty yards in width before ending with a two-tiered green.

"My tee choice is simple enough," Santan said. "I'm moving the 'blue' markers wide left." With that he physically removed the two blue tee markers, which were almost always positioned on the far right of the monstrous-width tee box, and repositioned them thirty-yards away at the never-used far left side of the tee box expanse. As he did so he chuckled to his partner who was trailing him, and said, "Danikov's gonna hate this shot."

Danikov moved to address his ball, at first fretting over the shot. The otherwise straight-away tee shot to a very narrow fairway with water to the left was now much more ominous. The new angle started the shot over both swamp and water and even scrub trees, but also required a sharp draw if not an outright hook to bring the ball back into play. To make matters even worse the fairway ran downhill to the creek from right to left, for the longer hitter. "Piece of cake for a duck hook, partner," Danikov said to Clayman. "Unfortunately, I own a fade."

"Ain't that the truth," said Santan, grinning.

Danikov could not keep his tee shot in play. Clayman was unnerved by that and dumped his own drive into the creek. Neither could recover sufficiently and Randall's ball was not needed as Santan made a perfectly played birdie four. Clayman offered the eulogy, saying, "With the automatic press we lost two bets there, partner."

"I know," Danikov said, "It's called a thumping."

Clayman had not heard that word for a while and it registered with him. *Thumping! That's what my 'Christian' stepfather called it when he knocked me around out of range of Mom's eyes and ears.* Until he was sixteen anyway. He wouldn't likely forget that day. That's when the teenager had been popped on the head for the last time. They were in the basement workroom and in reaction to the unwarranted thump the young Clayman had grabbed the nearest tool available. Waving the long-handled screwdriver under his tormentor's nose, Clayman vehemently said, "Never again!"

FOUR

THE FOURSOME completed the first nine holes of play and then—with Danikov and Santan each driving—they wildly raced their electric golf carts, bumper-to-bumper, down the concrete cart path a quarter-mile to the halfway house. Near the bottom of the hill where the narrow path most closely paralleled the street, Danikov, who was leading, glanced to the left to see how close he was being followed. He wasn't. Suddenly, Santan's cart was abreast on the right, having banged over the curb and onto the street.

With Randall caught up in the excitement of the moment and actually urging him on, Santan nosed his cart back onto the path at the club driveway, clipping a sign which read "No Carts On Street" and drawing a blaring horn from an oncoming car. In the meantime, Danikov had slowed his cart enough to avoid a collision as Clayman first cursed Santan and then shook his head and laughed at the preposterous situation.

Both carts pulled into the designated "half way" parking area, with Santan's cart still at the head of the two-cart caravan. Randall jumped out and wiped his brow in mock relief saying, "I guess we have the 'pole' for the start of the second race, boys. That is, if we both don't crash and burn on the way to the starting line." Everyone laughed and the tension dropped away.

Clayman popped into the pro shop to see Joey while the others walked the few steps to the halfway house to replace the spilled water cups and to pick up turkey and cheese sandwiches-to-go. "How's it going, Mr. Clayman?" asked his earlier tutor.

"Weird, Joey. We're going at it like it's the club team tournament. Danikov and I are down some trash and a couple of bets after losing two of the last three holes, including a sucker deal on number seven, but even that's not the whole story."

"What do you mean?" she said with a quizzical look.

"I think I'm witnessing a match that's beyond either golf or personality."

At that the head pro raised his head from the desk of his small office next to the sales counter. "What's that all about?" he asked.

"Get this," Clayman said. "The highlight wasn't Santan's bending his $400 Warbird driver after pushing his tee shot into the breeze *and* the creek on the five hole, or even his belittling poor Randall for missing a two-and-a-half foot putt on the same hole."

"Things got better than that?" Joey asked, looking amused and pushing her bangs to one side.

"Oh, yeah. Santan and Danikov are jousting over who or what's in charge of their souls."

"Religion at RiverTree. Story at eleven," she quipped. "But tell me, where does that leave you and Randall?"

"Actually, as near as I can figure it, we four are Doubt, Ignorance, Pride and Faith. Can't say it isn't interesting though."

"That's pretty exciting," she said as she looked around. The head pro was still in his office, but appeared to have returned to his paper work, so she continued. "A RiverTree foursome with action hotter than either golf or the bet itself. Looks like you have more than the weather to watch out for on the back nine."

At that moment the head pro barked, "Joey! Can I see you in my office for a minute?"

An hour and forty minutes after they had teed off on the tenth hole, the group was about to hit to the par three seventeenth green, RiverTree's signature hole. Danikov and Clayman had recovered from their losing front nine, actually going up by one on the match and evening the trash points through the sixteenth hole. Clayman had been playing well and his handicap strokes on ten, twelve, fifteen and sixteen had more than made up for the opponent Randall's strokes on the same holes, plus one additional stroke on number eleven. "Let me lead off again, Captain," said Clayman. "I own this hole."

"It's all yours," said Danikov, happy to have his partner playing well and feeling positive about his game.

"You know," Santan said softly to Clayman, as he stood next to him while they selected their clubs for the tee shot, "your partner probably doesn't have to tell you that even though this is the third easiest hole on the course, you can easily make six or seven if you can't steer it straight down the mountain."

"You're trying to get into my head, Luke, but I'm all plugged up."

The hole was a magnificent sight even on a cloud-covered day such as this. It was beautifully forested on three sides, but highly deceptive. They all walked out, nearly simultaneously, and peered down from the blue tees toward the amoeba-shaped green in the narrow valley below. The vertical drop of 120 feet was over only 165 yards of mostly impenetrable juniper scrub. The hole was all tee and green with no significant fairway other than a few square yards in front of and to the right of the green.

In spite of his denial, Clayman was thinking when he should have been on automatic pilot. His thoughts were compressing. Sand on the left, sand on the right, five if way short and death if long, right or even left.

He panicked on the downswing and shanked a sick, short-lived shot into the right-hand undergrowth. Then, momentarily incensed by Santan's own ingenuous "pshaw" comment, Clayman nearly hurled his eight iron after the ball. Struggling for composure, he found it, re-teed, and hit a second ball to near right of the green. Turning to Danikov, he said, "My wheels came off. It's your race."

Danikov moved hesitantly forward to the tee, aware of a sudden, cool breeze. He had two clubs in his hands. Since the tenth hole, black clouds had continued to build as a light rain had alternately peppered them and withdrawn. He stood, waiting. The breeze, which had been blowing with them, suddenly stilled. *Now!* He dropped the longer of the two clubs he had in his hands to the ground as he quickly moved to tee his ball. His routine address waggle completed, Danikov swung his nine iron in as consistent an imitation of his generally trustworthy swing as possible. As he did so, the fickle breeze kicked in once again, this time against them.

What would otherwise have been a pin-high shot onto the green had its forward advance stunted by the unforseen one-club wind gust. The ball ended up on the green, but slightly right and way short, better than thirty feet away. He had obviously left himself a long, but uphill putt to a hole which was situated no more than twelve feet from the back of the green.

Clayman was relieved and said in sing-song fashion, "It weren't purty, partner, but at least we're dancin'!"

Randall moved from being on-deck to the batting box. "Not bad," he said, "but it's no greenie if we're inside you or you three-putt." Turning to Santan he said, "Let me test that wind again." He plucked some grass from the fringe of the teeing area and threw it up and into the air, carefully observing the minimal breeze's action. In order to get a second opinion he glanced up at tree top level to see what sort of wind activity their branches betrayed. "Correct me if I'm wrong, professor," he said to Santan. "With the drop in elevation this hole starts out as a three-club reduction, then you add back one club for hitting into a tree-top breeze. If that formula is correct then with my length I come up with hitting a seven-iron."

"Fire away!" said Santan, nodding his approval, but not expecting much of a result. Randall fired as commanded, but with a too-quick swing and slightly too much turf, although the ball was launched right on line.

Clayman was the first to predict the result. "Unless your afterburner kicks in, that'll hit the cart path."

With the dramatic descent of the seventeenth hole, the top four-fifths of the snaking cart path crossed the "fairway" three times before a fourth and final cart path crossing. This juncture was ten yards short of the green and brought into play a newly poured concrete finish to the otherwise asphalt-ribboned runway. Randall's shot fulfilled Clayman's prediction, striking the concrete cart path and sending the ball forty yards skyward in a mostly forward-advancing carom that left the scarred missile in the left hand bunker.

"That's O.K.," said the owner of the shot as he turned to face Clayman, saying, "I still have *my* man covered." The sky directly over and behind them was rapidly moving from gray to charcoal while a small portion of the sky on the forward horizon quirkily revealed the second—if fleeting—rainbow of the day.

The breeze stilled and sprinkles began falling as Santan moved to the tee. He dropped one of the two clubs he had been holding. "There's your good luck omen again, Danikov." With a smirk he pulled his cap down ever so slightly, yet briskly, as if to punctuate his comment. As he addressed his ball he said, "How about I knock a hole in your ark before the rains come?"

Santan took his pitching wedge back smoothly and struck the ball squarely and firmly, finishing well-balanced and with the smirk still on his lips. The just-washed white ball soared in a beautiful arc that showed plainly against an increasingly contrasting sky, dropping softly onto the back of the green. It bounced a foot forward before spinning backwards on the second touchdown to within seven feet of the hole. "Timber!" he said as he froze his completed swing a few extra, unnecessary seconds.

The two carts wound their way down the hill in a light rain. The sun was now completely hidden, and some faint, rumbling thunder could be heard while steady, if light rain beat into their faces. Randall did not like playing in inclement weather and he made his point to his cart partner using an illustration. "I once directed an outdoor photo shoot in a North Carolina tobacco field. While we were shooting, a sudden hailstorm hit. Not only was the field flattened by golf ball-sized hail, but our equipment was ruined and my car was damaged to the tune of five thousand dollars. If that warning siren goes off, I'm outta here."

Santan was driving and did not turn his head at the remarks, but he said without empathy, "Not before this match is settled, you aren't."

Clayman purely shanked his next shot, ending up no closer to the green than before the shot, and out-of-bounds by inches. Disgusted with his turn of play, he retrieved the ball and, without comment, slowly and deliberately drew back his right arm and proceeded to throw the ball high and over the back of the green towards the eighteenth tee. He then slammed his club into his bag.

"Are you in-your-pocket, partner, or is that your drop?" Danikov dead-panned, grinning at Clayman from across the green, trying to loosen up his teammate. Clayman was forced to look up and smile ruefully, shaking his head.

Randall barely dribbled his sand shot onto the edge of the green, and then with a nearby rake calmly erased all evidence of his previous appearance. Santan held the pin for Danikov's furthest-away putt as Clayman walked up to the green, obviously still keenly interested in the next-to-the-last hole's net results. The rain was now falling harder and all but the player about to putt were holding upraised golf umbrellas.

Danikov was the only one who hadn't been wearing either a hat or a cap for the entire round. He now retrieved one from his golf bag just before walking up to the green. He pulled the hat tighter as he crouched behind his ball, lining up the long and undulating path his putt would have to delicately negotiate. Clayman said from nearby, "If I were a praying man, I'd say a word or two over this putt, partner."

"That wouldn't help," said Danikov as he stepped up to his ball. "God is not a micro manager."

"A lot of football players sure as hell seem to think he is," said Randall, standing several yards to one side and hoping to 'freeze' his opponent by distracting him.

"The only way you're going to hole out from there," said Santan, joining in with Randall's needling, "is for me to concede the putt." Then he shook the pin within the cup before withdrawing it and added maliciously, "Frankly, you'd do better praying to me than to your god."

Danikov stopped his pre-put routine, straightened up, and turned slowly in Santan's direction. He looked him directly in the eyes and said, "Is your atheism so fragile that you have to belittle God?"

"I was trying to be humorous," said Santan, "but if you don't find it so, then I take the position that it wasn't entirely inaccurate." Santan started to walk away, but then as an afterthought he stopped and said, "And another thing, Mr. Righteous—since we're on the subject—a lot more people than you think are practical atheists. Oh, they may profess to believe in God—including millions who are churched—but since they still go their merry way they're simply closet atheists. If you called them that, they'd be horrified, but that's still calling an atheist an atheist. Putt the goddamned ball!"

"C'mon, guys," said Clayman, "we're here to play golf, not argue religion. Knock it in, partner." Clearly upset, but controlled, Danikov was trying to refocus. Calmed, he wiped the steady, but still lightly falling rain from his face and resumed lining up the putt from his standing position. He tried to imagine exactly how the ball would roll. Grasping a positive mind's-eye picture of his interpretation, he then bent to his work.

Danikov stroked the Titleist smoothly and firmly with his usual metronome touch and it rolled directly over his spot mark. The ball agonizingly continued its course over the thirty-plus feet of its pilgrimage. At that point the projectile was precisely on target. Pumped with the player's new-found adrenaline, however, the ball caught too little of the right side of the hole and veered sharply left to finish a little over eighteen inches away, a distance barely outside the length of the putter's leather grip. He would have to putt again.

Abruptly and arrogantly, however, Santan said, "Good three!"

More surprised by the concession than upset with the miss, Danikov picked up his ball and snatched his company-logoed golf umbrella, retreating to the same nearby cart to which Clayman also quickly strode. The light rain continued unabated, but golf was still definitely playable. Randall putted lamely, but was reassured by Santan since only the lowest net score on the team counted.

Randall, too, scrambled to protect himself from the rain with the umbrella that lay upside down near him. A gust of wind caused it to skitter away from him on a zig-zag angle. But Randall was far more concerned at the moment with the approaching blackness and faint lighting of the skies.

Not Santan. He briefly eyed the one-cup fall of his right-to-left curving, seven-footer and said, "Hear those bells in the distance, boys? That's the sound of school letting out." Danikov and Clayman refused to acknowledge his comment by so much as looking at each other. Within seconds the ball was softly touched by Santan's putter and it ran unerringly to the front of the hole, then entered and fell, center-cut.

"Birdie, boys," Santan said, greatly exaggerating the plural sound. And with only a moment's hesitation he added, "The match is dead even, partner, and we chalked up a piece of 'trash' in the bargain. One hole left. Let's close 'em out and that'll be all for Team Jesus." Santan walked leisurely through the rain toward the cart, picking up his open umbrella, but then closed it before walking in the rain to his cart, seemingly enjoying the moment as none before.

"Right on, man," Randall said quickly, skipping Santan's offer of a high five as he anxiously ducked into the cart, scanning the skies as he did so.

The foursome rode the two carts down the short, but steep path from the seventeenth green to the eighteenth tee, parking front-to-back and touching. All four stepped out of their carts and stood huddled together under two umbrellas, peering alternately at the skies and the scorecard on one of the carts. The sky was roiling, and low thunder could now be heard as the rain pelted them more aggressively. Randall looked nervously at the unstable skies and said, "Let's beat the siren and finish this match at the gin table."

Clayman was enjoying both the golf and the match itself, although he was uncomfortable with some of the repressed feelings that were continually being dredged up by the two primary antagonists. The confusion he had felt since childhood over the advertised rewards for faith had not abated for him in the least as an adult. Maybe he could end discussion of these troubling issues if the game was called on account of rain. Yeah, right, he thought, but he did nod in agreement with Randall.

Danikov shrugged, but his face clearly registered little enthusiasm for the idea.

As Santan was about to vigorously protest, a tremendous bolt of lightning suddenly spewed from the now-menacing skies immediately overhead. The resultant bolt of brilliant and discharging electricity first struck a hardwood tree not four feet from the huddled foursome. The one-inch thick bark on the tree was pierced some twenty feet up from ground level, peeling a three-inch strip from its trunk like a ripe banana peel. The inner surface of the stripped bark was left as smooth and splinter-free as if it had been treated by a belt-sander.

The bolt's nearly 50,000 degree heat and energy was barely lessened by its encounter with the tree as it spectacularly halved itself before finding competing electrical grounds. The newly birthed twin bolts hungrily attached themselves to the two unsheathed metal lightning rods being held upright in the center of the tightly bunched foursome. All four men fell to the ground like fifty-pound sacks of grain thrown off a truck.

FIVE

Within moments a groggy Randall looked around to see the other three sitting near him and said, "We were struck by lightning, right? Well, it must have knocked me unconscious because I just dreamed I was dead."

Clayman tried to run his hand through his hair and said, "Look closely." He paused, then added, "You are."

"What do you mean?" Randall said, shaking his head. "We're talking, aren't we? You and the others are here with me. We're still on the eighteenth tee . . . hey, wait a minute . . . no, something's wrong with this picture. Where are the golf carts?"

"I rest my case," Clayman said.

Danikov jumped in. "Don't worry, Artie. Since the dead don't necessarily know what death is, I'm confused also, but one thing is certain: this isn't life as we've known it. You're right about one thing, though. We were all struck and felled by lightning. Frankly, I have to tell you I'm disappointed."

"Disappointed?" Randall asked.

"Absolutely," Danikov responded. "I would have expected to be in heaven. Now, since we're not in hell either, I don't know what to make of it."

With that, Danikov stood up and then turned and faced back up the steep, canyon-like seventeenth hole and shouted, "God loves you!" The others also stood as they looked at one another other, perplexed. Danikov cupped his ears. He shouted again and listened once more. Same result. No echo. He turned to the others and said, gravely, "Gentlemen, I'm going to pray for our souls."

Santan's first words upon their change of status came at precisely that comment. "Pray if you want, but keep me out of it."

"I'm out, too," Randall said. "I'm scared to death, but not that scared. I don't see any flames."

Clayman made it unanimous among the three. "I'm assessing," he said, "especially since we're still on the golf course."

"Father in heaven," Danikov began as he bowed his head, "my friends here are a stiff-necked lot, but it's not my job to worry about that. Give me the courage to confront my own difficulties." He paused, raising his head with his eyes still closed, but then dropped his head again with a deep sigh and continued, "No, Father . . . that isn't right. It's much more important that I ask you give Marilee and our grown children and grandchild the courage to deal with the loss of a husband, father and grandfather. And . . . in Jesus' name I ask that the families of my three associates also be consoled. Amen."

"Now for the other perspective," Santan said, intently scanning their surroundings. "What I see is what is real. We may well be 'gone,' but as Clayman has observed we also happen to be standing where we were in chapter one, the same golf course. Under the circumstances one out of two ain't bad."

"Hey, look at this," said Clayman, happy that Danikov's prayer effort lasted no longer than it did. "I can't lift this ball washer handle. My hand passes right through it. For another thing, however, we aren't actually 'standing' on this turf. It's simply where we *are*. And precisely where we *were* . . . on the eighteenth tee. Look, I'm Casper the ghost." With that he floated away several feet and then back with no apparent effort.

"I don't understand this," Randall said, his voice suddenly quavering in denial. "No!" he shrieked as something of their situation apparently settled in his mind. With that he tried to 'run' toward the eighteenth fairway, but could only drift in that direction. After fewer than twenty yards he met with some sort of invisible barrier and his progress was instantly halted. He tried again and again, up and down and alongside the near borders of the tee with the same result. Finally, straying off towards the seventeenth green he met no obstacle, but as he drifted further from the group his eyes widened and he rushed back to his only haven . . . the others. He collapsed as close to the ground as he was able. "Help me," he wailed.

"Get hold of yourself, Randall," Santan said. "It's a simple situation. We all died at the same instant in the same place and in the same freak fashion. Everyone has to be somewhere and this is where we are."

"And exactly where do you think that is?" asked Clayman. He was amused by Santan's self-assurance. In that respect, Clayman reluctantly thought of his despised stepfather who—on the day Paul had left home for college—had encouraged him to become self-sufficient and avoid dependency upon anyone or anything. That had surprised him. As a youngster, Paul hadn't known what his stepfather believed in. The day he left for college he still didn't know. If he were honest with himself Paul didn't know to this day what *he* believed in, let alone his alienated stepfather.

Santan answered Clayman's question. "Let the obvious speak for itself. We're in some kind of spirit form and we can talk to each other. How it is that we're apparently confined to a single golf hole is beyond me, but under the circumstances who the hell cares? Maybe we can figure out some way to continue the match."

"What?" exclaimed Danikov, throwing his hands up into the air. "You treat the most traumatic moment of your life with a call for a tee time? How about we give things a little more serious thought?"

"I guess no one's pushing us," Santan said with a shrug, still searching their surroundings with his eyes. "So what's your take, preacher?"

Ignoring the intended disrespect, Danikov said, "A little earlier . . . well, actually in another life . . . you and I used quotations from famous physicists rather than religious figures to make our points about faith or the lack of it. I understand that faith isn't necessarily counter to science, Luke. First of all, you'll have to grant that death is obviously not the oblivion you thought it was. And as for the manner in which we were dispatched, would you be interested to know what the Bible has to say about lightning?"

"Lightning?" Santan asked incredulously. "No, I can't say I would, although I doubt very much that your scriptures contain any direct comment on such a common phenomenon."

"Pardon the pun, but you're dead wrong," Danikov said. "Jesus himself said, 'For as the lightning that comes in the East is visible in the West, so will be the coming of the Son of Man.'"

"What does that mean?" asked Clayman.

"It simply means that Jesus' return will be unmistakable and that unbelievers will suddenly realize they've chosen the wrong side. Right now you're all much closer to needing to make that choice than you were just moments ago."

Something caught the periphery of Santan's eyesight, but he continued to pan the area as if he were still searching. "First of all," he said with disdain, "that's a bunch of crap. You can call me by any label you want, but I've always lived for the present without reference to some god or divine moral law. I see no reason, even now, to change my position. And I'll can sum up my argument with a single brief point."

"Before you do," Danikov asked, interested in having engaged his adversary in any sort of dialogue about faith, "let me ask you whose authority do you think you're now under?"

"Authority?" Santan's back had been turned to the others, but he whirled to face the threesome, a sense of 'gotcha' on his face. "Mine, as before!" he said. "But I'll tell you something that *has* changed: I'm rapidly becoming fed-up with your apparently never-ending proselytizing."

"My friend," Danikov said, "the fact is that I barely care about you, but sometimes things present themselves and you have to respond in the best way you can. I think you know there's a God, but you simply don't like him."

"Now exactly why would that be?" Santan asked, challengingly.

51

"Because God is holy and you're not."

"And you are?"

"Certainly not. Not only is Man not holy, but he is inherently hostile to God."

"Now that's a different sound bite coming from one Tommy Ray Danikov."

"Don't credit me. God Himself has said as much."

"Well, for Christ's sake, you're a broken record."

Danikov took a symbolic deep breath and then responded as he felt he must, "Let me go on record right here. As a declared unbeliever asserting the name of Christ, you nevertheless have no common ground with the Godly. Christ can be with those outside the Church *only in name* and not in reality."

"Short but formal now, are we? But those words don't sound like yours."

"They aren't, but I agree with them."

"Well, I don't think I've just been forgiven," Santan said, mockingly, "but I do know one thing for an absolute certainty, which is my point."

"And what would that be?" Danikov asked, bracing for his next defense.

"Thank you for asking," Santan said, an obvious swagger in his movement. "What would you say to having a little company? I suggest you all turn around and watch the foursome about to tee off on seventeen."

With that statement everyone did quickly turn—or rather, pivot, since they couldn't push against the ground—to see four golfers stepping up to the tee on the hole the spirit foursome had most recently played. "I don't believe it," said Clayman, instantly brightening. "Come on. Let's check it out."

All moved instantly and, without walking, traveled the short distance up the hill from the eighteenth tee to the middle of the seventeenth green. The entire foursome could clearly see that the figures were live players. Live golfers in our dream? wondered Clayman. As the first player swung at his ball the spirit foursome moved as one to the back of the green.

"This is incredible," Clayman said. "We're dead, yet as if by instinct we made a collective, natural reaction by moving out of potential harm's way. You know, maybe Santan is right! I find myself more excited about some form of a golf game than about our plight."

"I don't know what to make of it either," Randall said, "but let's don't fight it."

Danikov offered no comment, but he was just as curious and keen on watching as they were.

The golfer's tee shot was launched into cloudless skies. The ball soared upward and then obliged gravity by plummeting downward, landing short and right in the green side bunker. The second golfer pulled his shot sharply and it bounded steeply off the left side of the deep rough-covered plateau on which the green had been constructed. The third player's tee shot lit a few feet short of the green's soft up slope and stayed there, plugged. The final tee shot was headed for the back center of the green as Santan humorously shouted, 'Fore!' and then playfully headed directly for the ball's flight path.

He put up his hands up as if to catch the missile. Passing through him the ball bit into the grassy carpet, took one short hop forward and stopped. Santan laughed uproariously and then began dancing in circles like a stereotypical native American Indian, whooping and hollering. "This is *my* man, boys. Pick yourselves a player. The bad news is we're dead. The good news is the match is still on!"

Six

Having evened the match on the last hole played before they were felled, both Randall and Santan were eagerly anticipating the game's vicarious resumption. From the expression on Danikov's face, however, Clayman gathered that the most spiritually mature member of the group was pondering the greater meaning of the moment, including some sort of accounting for the *live* foursome's sudden and surprising appearance on the tee above them. As for Clayman he was more than merely curious as to what this new foursome's arrival might possibly suggest for either the spirit foursome's amusement or existence.

The other three spirits of the foursome could so far be fairly easily labeled, but Clayman wondered exactly where he sat. Fence sitter? No one likes neutrality by others. That's why no one thinks much about umpires and referees, he thought. Their hearts aren't into the game, only their minds.

Following Joey's initial pegging of the others Clayman had fleshed out thumbnail sketches of his own by asking individual questions of the three between shots and argu-

55

ments. That's the sort of thing he did all the time in his promotional products business: identifying customer problems he could then solve through the presentation and sale of his broad range of custom decorated product lines.

Randall lived up to his pre-billing, Clayman thought. As a talented, but insecure account executive for an ad agency Randall apparently thrived in working with controversial accounts, including his largest, a North Carolina tobacco company. His agnostic philosophy concerning religion was easily transferrable to business, and selective "can't know, don't know" served him, his company and this particular client, very well. All business biases could be rationalized through accountability to senior management. All he required was assignment. Clayman's assessment of Randall was that of a cue ball waiting to be struck by a project manager's stick.

On the other hand, Randall's playing partner seemed to wear his position on most things taped to his forehead. He saw Santan as aggressive bordering on cunning, and Clayman painted him as owning a personal philosophy of life which simply could not accept an invisible means of support.

His own partner, Danikov, was not without taint either, in spite of his altruistic club membership move and his apparent Christian commitment. He was known to be openly chauvinistic, apparently having little patience on the golf course with female golfers regardless of their abilities. From Clayman's perspective perhaps this trait was more closely a result of his Russian ancestry than to his apparently successful thirty-year marriage to the same woman. Then again, Danikov's wife did not play golf.

How did he, Clayman, fit in with his analysis of the group's individuals? An honestly written self-description would have portrayed himself as a disenchanted Jewish product of a dysfunctional East coast family. If his pal Joey knew his favorite religious-skeptic story, she probably couldn't wait to prattle to others about it. He'd told the story often enough, simply to get a laugh. What he never told anyone was that it was symbolically *his* story.

He had written the story for a college senior short story course. He developed the tragi-comic story line during the Vietnam war setting. A spiritually confused field soldier managed to find a Buddhist priest willing to give him a Christian baptism in a Jewish synagogue. Clayman had always favored covering all the bases in order to avoid being positioned at the wrong one. Even now he wasn't far removed from that notion.

O.K., so much for the spiritual reverie, he thought. How long had that introspection taken? They were in a new world and he had neither watch nor clue. Did the others really think their time would be well spent by focusing on a vicariously competitive game of golf? But then, what was time to them? Clayman was a pragmatist. People and circumstances considered, what would be his objection to continuing the match? Absolutely none. For closure on the matter he turned and asked, "How does Santan the Seer see this shaking out?"

"No rules," Santan responded, throwing out his hands, palms up. "Our living responsibilities are over. Don't you see? We don't even need rest. Recreation is us."

"Pun unintended, I assume," Danikov said, who had been conspicuously quiet to this point. "Actually," he continued, "I object. Frankly, I think we're in a perilous situation. I've been thinking . . . in fact, praying . . . and I feel certain our condition isn't permanent. God gave man free will, but He doesn't insist that we make right choices. That's up to us. I suggest we prepare to make those choices."

"My will," Santan said, "is that you shut up."

Danikov ignored him, saying, "Since we arrived as a group it could well be that to go forward on our spiritual journey we must leave together, but . . ." he paused, ". . . of one mind concerning salvation."

Both Clayman and Randall flashed pained expressions, but Santan held up a hand and said, "No, no, children. Let him talk himself into a corner if he wants. Do you know the odds against four very different-minded people arriving at a unanimous opinion about anything controversial, including even a preference for bagel flavor?" Santan shrugged and raised his right hand and arm in Clayman's direction, as if to say, "You of all people can see the truth of this."

Danikov smiled, a little condescendingly, and said, "You're deliberately missing the point. While it may be surprising to you I have never been much of one for overt witnessing, much less evangelizing my beliefs. Nevertheless, I think we would be stupid to ignore the facts of our circumstances, and even more stupid not to consider how we might be able to impact them."

Clayman had an inspiration. Maybe he could both cut to the chase and reduce the Santan-Danikov adversarial relationship certain to continue its development. "Tommy Ray," he said, "I never heard of a strong believer in anything who didn't want to share. You're gonna tell us your story sooner or later. Go for it."

Both Santan and Randall were about to protest, but Clayman rephrased the invitation. "Like you said, Luke, let him have his say. We may want the floor at some point ourselves."

Clayman's surprise move didn't leave much room for Danikov except to take advantage of the opening. "O.K.," he said, almost reluctantly. Composing himself for a moment he then launched into the short version of his Christian memoir.

"As an adolescent I came to a nominal belief in God and Christ Jesus. For many years following I simply labeled myself a Christian, but hadn't actually committed myself to God. Then one day I was doing some writing for a project and for some compelling reason, I decided to include a Biblical comment or two. When, surprisingly, none came to mind I was unable to satisfactorily complete the project. I decided to do a little research."

"You went to the Internet, huh?" Clayman said.

"No. Back then we had things called 'books.' Remember those? This was ten years ago. Ironically, I bought a Bible. I had never owned one before, in fact had never actually read from one. I quickly found a couple of useable passages and finished my project, but inside the Bible I also found a leaflet schedule for reading the 3,000 pages of text in one year. I don't know why, but I actually did that . . . which, incidentally, I repeated for each of the next three years, along with a lot of other Christian and some comparative religion reading."

"That's still a pretty narrow perspective," Randall said. "The Christian Bible isn't the only spiritual book in print," Randall said.

"True," said Danikov, "but except for the Bible all others are simply attempts to immortalize mortal man's thinking. Anyway, to finish the point, I hadn't finished reading the sixth chapter of Genesis, much less the Gospels, when scripture spoke to me and I wept."

"Wept over what?" Clayman asked, incredulous.

"Over what I realized God was saying to me through His Word, 'My spirit will not contend with man *forever,* for he is mortal.'"

"*That* broke you down?" Randall said, derisively.

Danikov paused and looked at Randall, his emotions tumbling for the first time since the accident. "Yes," he said, his voice cracking, "that's exactly what happened, brokenness before God. I finally realized that I couldn't see the stopwatch of God's patience."

Clayman was getting more uncomfortable with each sentence. "End of story," he said.

"Not quite. You're in sales, Paul, so maybe you can appreciate how that experience really set me up for the close. That came within a month or so as I was prompted to go to the book of Matthew. A single verse there, stacked on top of all I had been studying and thinking about to that point, drove me to my knees in surrender. Then and there I accepted Jesus Christ as my Lord and savior. Simply put, salvation means acceptance of Christ's death for our sins, his resurrection and promise to return."

"I don't really want to know what you left out," Clayman said, "but the salesman in me has to ask." He then shouted in exasperation, "WHAT was the verse!"

"I thought you'd never ask. They were Jesus' very words: 'Every one who will acknowledge Me before men, I will acknowledge Him before My Father in heaven.'"

"God," Santan said. He immediately and visibly winced at his initial word choice, but then shrugged it off and finished his statement. "I hate pious wannabes. Perhaps you'd also care to make a symbolic burnt offering."

"Luke, you know very well that we're under the New Covenant and not the Old, but I'll seize the opportunity to throw in a short Sunday School lesson. As all of you know, Old Testament-time Jews honored God and the Law by symbolically transferring their sins to an animal, which they sacrificed."

Clayman observed that Santan was shaking his head, probably storing up rebuttal arguments. Randall, on the other hand, was inattentive and marked time by slowly drifting from one side of the group to the other and back. "So that's how the 'sin' thing works," Clayman said, marginally interested only because he hadn't actually heard it put that way before. "A co-worker on my first job out of college once said to me, unkindly, "You Jews had your chance and lost it when you killed Jesus."

Danikov shook his head and closed his lips tightly, saying, "All mankind is guilty of that offense, not just the Jews, but that's how the change came about. With Jesus' death He wiped away the old covenant requirements for sacrifice and replaced them with the new covenants, or New Testament."

"The original replacement theory, eh?" challenged Randall.

Danikov nodded. "You could say that."

"While you're grinding your way through your personal tribulations," said Santan, who by now was also anxiously floating from one side of the group to the other side and back, "we're suffering the loss of the next live foursome to appear for our pleasure."

"So be it," Danikov said, looking at Santan. "This is a golf course. We won't run out of golfers." He turned to face the others. "To finish my story, I finally came to understand what it meant to accept God's grace, though certainly not being worthy of the offer."

"So, for want of grace," Randall said, sarcastically, "the kingdom is lost?"

"It's O.K. if want to mock me, Artie, but it's also true. You're a thinker, so consider for a moment that man's downward spiral from rejecting God is inevitable. The next thing a person does is to make up his own ideas of what a god should be and do. Then he falls into sin of various kinds, whether vile or simple. Finally, the person grows to hate God and actually encourages others to do so."

"If God knows all this, then why doesn't he prevent it from happening?" queried Clayman.

"He doesn't owe us that. When people reject God he allows them to live as they choose," Danikov replied.

"Time!" said Santan, making the universal symbol with his hands. "Thanks for the sermon, pastor. Your time is up and church is out, but I do have a practical question. What do you really make of our situation?"

"My personal opinion? Well, we're isolated, grouped and restricted, yet we have the ability to react to limited external stimuli in the form of live golfers. Personally, I think we're being asked to find our collective way to or away from the Lord."

"Oh," said Randall, "leap and the net will appear? First of all, I think it's a bit late for changing our spots even if we were so inclined. We're like dead. Secondly, this may be nothing but a dream phase of some sort. We may merely be experiencing something like phantom television reception, which is always a short term phenomenon. We could be on our way to hell. Would that be courtesy of your god?"

"God doesn't send anyone to hell," Danikov said. "We send ourselves." Then, in moment of reverie he added, "I wish I had a Bible to present to each of you."

"I'll bet you do," Santan said. As he spoke, out of either boredom or frustration, he tried to sit by bending his legs under him, but only managed to tilt slowly forward, as if he were in a low gravity environment. He recovered without humor, though the others tittered. He redirected their attention saying, "People love using biblical cliches to make their case. One in particular comes to mind, for example, that's patently ridiculous."

"Which verse is that?" Danikov asked, warily.

"The one about it being more difficult for a rich man to enter 'the kingdom of God' than for a camel to pass through the eye of a needle." Santan shook his head. "Another example of the Bible's hyperbole."

"I'm sure you grasp the point," Danikov said, "that the rich, with most of their physical needs met, often become self-reliant. And if you considered the verse in the context of the time, you would understand Jesus' analogy."

"Oh, really?" Santan asked.

"Yes. Camels were sometimes penned in a narrow structure called a 'needle.' The camel couldn't enter the needle's low entrance, or 'eye,' except by being forced to its knees. Once inside, the camel would not kneel of its own accord in order to escape. That is, the camel would not 'humble' itself. By the same token, a rich man finds it exceedingly difficult to humble himself in order to enter the Kingdom of God."

"So," Santan said, "I rest my case. Biblical verses *can* be used to make a case for almost any point." Santan turned toward Randall and said, "I'll bet even Artie here could use scripture to argue the case for agnosticism, although I don't want to hear it."

"Partner," Randall said. "I'm hurt." He pointed to his own misty form and said, "What am I here, talcum powder?"

Ignoring Randall's attempt at humor, Santan said, "I'm not your confessor, Randall, merely a golf partner. What I'm telling Danikov is that all one needs for any belief is a set of statements. I have my own beliefs and they're as valid as his. And I'm hardly alone in embracing such a concept."

"You're right about many people making such assumptions, but consider this," Danikov said as he whisked himself in deliberate succession from Randall to Clayman and then to Santan, his palms turned open and up. "What you're saying is that everyone who adheres to one of the many arbitrary religions in the world feels that his faith represents truth. I'm telling you that if any faith doesn't recognize Jesus as lord and savior, it's flat wrong."

"Dammit, man," Santan said as he faced Danikov, "don't you see that you're the epitome of arbitrariness when you label all other views of religion as arbitrary? Suppose some group accepted your Christ along with other saviors. That's what I would call tolerance, not what you preach."

Danikov put up two hands in front of him, palms out as he said, "Tolerance, yes. I agree. Truth, however, no. Christ put it very succinctly: 'I am the way, and the truth, and the life; no one comes to the Father, but through Me.' He didn't offer any options."

"But that's all predicated upon accepting scripture as truth," said Santan. "If you buy the so-called Gospels of Matthew, Mark, Luke and John, of course you can make your case. And right there is where your group's real problem comes in: Christians aren't satisfied with their own story. They want to impose their beliefs on the world."

"One of the diseases you're afflicted with is being a generalist. As I said, I have never personally felt the need to proselytize. But let me make a distinction between belief and faith. They're hardly the same. Belief itself lacks emotion and imagination. Faith has to do with holding onto a belief."

Clayman didn't see the need to arbitrate, but neither could he ride the bench. "I understand that part," he said. "In fact, another person's differing beliefs are a big part of my breakup with Sheila.

"What sort of differences?" asked Randall, relieved to see both a change of pace and another player in the discussion.

"I didn't offer her any support for her recent conversion to her incomprehensible new belief. Now get this: Jesus as the Jewish savior!" Clayman wafted his head from one side to the other for emphasis. "It wasn't good enough for her that most religious Jews would concede him to be a great teacher or prophet. No. Now I ask you to imagine the paradox here: A 'Jew for Jesus?' I put the question to her just that way. You know her answer?"

"I can guess," Danikov said, "but tell us."

"She said she was simply worshiping the Jewish messiah. The *messiah*, no less. I don't get it. She said I could call her either a Jewish Christian or a Hebrew Christian or even better, a Messianic Jew. And to top it off, she accused me of being anti-semitic!"

"Before you explain that," Randall said, "exactly what's the connection between the Jewish Messiah and the Christian Savior? Sounds like a matter of semantics."

"I can explain that," said an instantly brightened Danikov, "'Christ,' is the Greek word for 'Messiah,' thus Jesus 'the Christ'."

Danikov continued his story in light of Clayman's surprising perspective and Randall's own minor contribution. "I've read something of the Messianic movement and the rebirth of the Messianic Jewish 'remnant.' I was fortunate enough to have been invited to attend several MJ congregational services with friends in Atlanta. It may seem weird to you but it really isn't a stretch to say that Messianic Jews may be the ultimate Judeo-Christians, but they don't call themselves that."

"Why not?" said Clayman, interested primarily because of the enigma Sheila had presented.

"Well," Danikov said, "because of all the anti-Semitism the word 'Christian' has meant to the Jews, as well as the Muslims, in the 11th and 12th centuries. That's one reason why the word 'crusade' in most of the middle East is a sure fire way to raise both fists and rhetoric against Christians, or Americans in general."

"Not that I'm all that much interested in the details," Clayman said, "but I just can't figure it out. Hey, I'm a Jew by birth, not by faith. What do I really care?"

"You should care deeply," said Danikov. "It's your soul you're risking. The Messianics call Jesus what the disciples called him, by his Hebrew name, Yeshua. Messianics believe the same as Christians, that there's no way of salvation other than through the atoning sacrifice of Jesus, or Yeshua."

"Well, merely for the sake of argument," Clayman said, "what's wrong with worshiping the God of Abraham, Isaac and Jacob?"

"Nothing at all," Danikov said, glancing at the other two to see if they were paying any attention. Randall appeared only mildly interested. Santan again appeared totally disinterested, but Danikov knew he missed nothing. He continued. "Listen to this. It's nothing short of miraculous that of all persons who have ever lived you can have a relationship with that most illustrious, most famous and most awesome of all. Incredible as it sounds you can have a personal relationship with the creator of the universe. Think of it. God is there for you through His only Son. And Paul, whether you know it or not, you are wrestling with God right now."

"Wrong!" Clayman said. "I'm wrestling with you. I don't even think about God."

"Don't you? Well, you're not the only one who has ever wrestled with God. Two thousand years before Christ the God of Abraham and Isaac didn't find Jacob a willing inheritor of God's covenants with Jacob's father and grandfather. Jacob was worldly until he went to the mattress with God."

"The mattress," Clayman dead-panned.

"Yeah, the mattress. The 'mat,' like in the book and movie, *The Godfather*. Only this was over holy matters, not greed."

Clayman fidgeted and said, "I remember snippets of my Jewish mother's faded traditions and the hollow Christian beliefs mouthed by my stepfather." *Will I never get over family?* "You mean of the three only Jacob, the grandson, wasn't a good guy?"

"No, I don't mean that at all," said Danikov. "Scripturally revered as they are, none of the three were born holy. And Jacob was the worst of the lot before his transformation. He not only deceived his father and conned his brother, he entered into an ungodly conspiracy with his mother."

"Ungodly?"

"Well, Jacob and his mother tricked the blind father, Isaac, into conferring the eldest son Esau's birthright onto Jacob."

"I didn't know that."

"Yup. Of course Jacob finally came around to God's way of thinking."

"How's that?"

"Jacob's Ladder."

Jarred for a moment by the two best-remembered words from the worst day of his childhood when he first decided to keep his distance from both Christianity and Judaism, Clayman didn't immediately respond. After a moment he said, "Do you know something about Jacob's Ladder? I didn't know the phrase had any real meaning."

"Yes," Danikov said, "It's a wonderful story found in the book of Genesis."

"Yet another story," Santan said. He turned to Randall and said, "Is this going to be our life from now on, listening to Bible stories?"

"It's Clayman's question, Luke," Danikov said. "Cut him some slack. Then I'll go along with working out some kind of game." He turned back to Clayman. "Jacob was on the road one evening when darkness overcame him and he camped for the night taking a stone for a pillow. He had a dream that brought about a dramatic change in his life."

"So tell me," Clayman said, trying to disguise a spark of interest, "but don't expect me to scratch an itch I don't have."

"You're the one doing the asking," Danikov said. In spite of both Santan and Randall being restless, they were paying *some* attention. Danikov resumed his story. "Jacob saw a staircase resting on the earth, with its top reaching to heaven, and the angels of God were ascending and descending on it. Above the stairs stood the Lord and he said, 'I am the Lord, the God of your father Abraham and the God of Isaac.' In the dream the Lord was heard to further say He would give Jacob and his descendants the land on which he was lying. Finally, the Lord repeated the covenant that God had made with Jacob's father and grandfather."

"That's where the supposed blessed lineage began. Right?" Randall said. "With old Abe himself. Great story."

Danikov bristled slightly, saying, "It's much more than a 'story' and it isn't 'supposed.' It's God-given scripture. That stairway Jacob saw in his dream is referred to as Jacob's Ladder. It was Jacob's life's bridge between heaven and earth."

"Is that all there is to it?" Clayman asked. "What about the 'wrestling' part?"

"You need to do some more wrestling on your own before I fill you in on how Jacob actually went to the mat with God's angel and survived."

"Save it. My curiosity isn't that great."

"That's exactly what I mean. You need to be pinned a few more times."

Randall had had more than enough of the subject. "Excuse me, but since there are only four of us in our little world, can I get in another word?"

"Just a minute, Artie," Clayman said. "I have one more question for our Shabbat school teacher. What's your take on why Sheila doesn't like the 'Good Teacher' label for Christ I offered her for the sake of compromise."

"She must have told you why she objects," he said.

"Actually, yes," Clayman said. "In retrospect I give her credit for her argument on that point. She said that the 'good teacher' label damns Jesus with faint praise by putting him in the same class with prophets of every other religion."

"Well said!" Danikov said, fairly beaming through his faint lips. "Since Christ made a lot of claims, such as having come down from heaven, possessing the power to know men's minds and hearts, the authority to forgive men's sins and to raise himself from the dead, if he couldn't back up his claims he must be either a liar or a lunatic. In either event he simply couldn't be merely a 'good teacher' or prophet."

"Prophecy!" Santan said loudly, finally joining the argument. "Another word for ambiguity. Respected people have pointed out that some of those prophesies were fulfilled by a number of others, including Martin Luther King, Jr. "

"It's true that a few of the prophecies have been fulfilled by others," Danikov responded, "but nothing close to all forty-eight major prophesies, like Christ. That's getting a hit every time He came up to bat, thank you."

"Now just a minute," said Randall, "let's back way up. You glossed over Santan's much earlier point. What difference does any of this really make to us anyway? I mean we all arrived here in the same train crash."

"But," said Danikov, suddenly beginning to sound a little weary from having to fend off his attackers from every side, "that's the point. We may not be leaving here on the same train. "

"Well, rabbi," said Santan in an even more patronizing tone than before, "I'm certain the invisible bricks keeping us here will no doubt yield to the righteous." Santan seemed inspired to further agitate Danikov, saying, "Maybe you'll share with us the answer to this commonly asked riddle: with so much rancor and hate in the world, most of it inspired by competitive religions, where's the justice?"

"Hear, hear," Randall chimed in. "If Buddhists, Muslims, Hindus, Jews and a host of Christianity-claiming cults all swear by the rightness—if not the divinity—of their beliefs, who's to arbitrate? How can you be so dead certain everyone else is going to hell for not conforming to your Christian absolutes?"

"Here's the bottom line, Artie," Danikov said, finding renewed strength. "The Bible offers no hope that sincere worshipers of other religions will be saved without personal faith in Jesus Christ. Not Buddha, Confucius, Muhammad or any other religious leader, including Moses, has ever been capable of saving anyone, including themselves. They all died and were never heard from again. Faith in them or in their teaching will not gain anyone salvation. Faith alone in Christ alone is the only way."

"That doesn't sound very enlightened," Randall said.

"God doesn't grade on the curve," Danikov countered. "When Nicodemus stole out in the night—to avoid being seen by his fellow Pharisees—to ask Jesus what He meant by being born again, His answer was, 'No one can see the Kingdom of God unless he is born again.'"

"I see," said Randall, sarcastically, "Who you gonna' call?"

"Exactly," Danikov said. "As for man's tyranny, man was given free will in order to see if he would use it to obey God or His most powerful, fallen angel, Satan. God doesn't insist upon our salvation: only the opportunity for it, through Christ."

"Remind me to ask you some time about that 'fallen angel' bit," Randall said, "but for the moment remember that we were talking about Clayman's woman problems."

"O.K.," Danikov said, "you're an analytic sort. What do you think Clayman's girlfriend was really trying to share with him?"

"What is this, a pop quiz?" Randall asked with exaggerated annoyance.

"Let's take another approach," Clayman said. "So, Mr. Witness," he said, pivoting effortlessly to address Randall and sensing an opportunity to lighten things a bit, "aside from the prosecution trying to frame you with my former girlfriend, what's your personal take on this discourse?"

Randall had actually been thinking of that very point so he framed his thoughts aloud. "Think of a colony of ants living a full and busy life on the old ant farm . . . 'judge', entirely oblivious to an outside world. What's real for them is what they can drag home and eat. If they could worship, it would be to some sort of leaf or insect god because that's the limit of their exposure."

"But Man is not an ant," Danikov said. "Ants don't reason. Though each individual human being is different from all the others, each of us is also part of the same organism. God's creation made in His image."

"No sale!" said a suddenly defiant Randall. "Man sets up his own gods and his approach to him or them according to perceived personal needs. Why else would so many exist in the world today? I think Santan has it right. With so many choices, there can be no absolute truth. We need to work and grow and believe in *ourselves*."

Santan weighed in to reinforce the surprising Randall's point. "Not only that, Danikov, but I think you're a little schizophrenic on top of being hypocritical. One minute you claim to keep your own counsel and the next minute you place us all in the same sinner's pew and set up a pulpit for yourself. You're so good at pointing out our weaknesses that you've overlooked your own."

"Good point," Clayman said. "Though my match partner here is obviously well-intentioned, he is definitely inconsistent in his own claim of not being much of a—what's the term—'witness.'"

"Thank you for your reluctant support," said Santan, hiding his much greater satisfaction. "Your partner here is too confident of his own righteousness."

Danikov was taken aback, but said nothing. He pondered Santan's hurtful, but telling remarks.

"All of this is boring," Santan said. "Let's get back to the match. What do you say, Randall?"

"I second the motion, Captain."

"Third it," said Clayman with a laugh. "But exactly how are we going to make golf go in our brave new world?"

"We'll need a little player-selection twist," Santan said. "Randall and I will take the players with both the best and worst tee shots on seventeen. Your team will take the other two. We'll switch that order with the next foursome off the tee. Anytime someone wants to use another base for selecting partners, fine by me. Suggestions, anyone?"

"Yes," Danikov spoke up. "Gentlemen, this 'situation' you all find so boring merely deals with what remains of your existence in eternity. That's pretty serious short-term thinking, but if that's your collective choice, I'll go along for now. Consider my efforts to place Christ on your plates tempered for the time being." Then he added, head down in one of his hands, the fingers of which were pulling at imaginary chin whiskers, "By the way, you're right about one thing you said a moment ago."

"Oh, really?" Santan said, finding the statement itself amusing, coming from Danikov.

"Yes. There is a verse in Luke about he who exalts himself being humbled, and he who humbles himself being exalted. I apologize. Not for presenting the Word, but for my inconsistency in doing so."

Clayman smiled at Danikov. "Don't be too hard on yourself, partner."

"It didn't sound like an apology to me," Santan said, taking a practice swing at an imaginary golf ball with an imaginary golf club. "I have a suggestion on a more important subject. Since these spirit forms we've inherited have us apparently hung up on one hole, let's stay with our best ball play, but raise the ante to two points a hole."

"Looks like we're back at the game," Clayman said, relieved in the change in direction of the group, "but what's the difference? It's not like we can stop off at the bank on the way home to deposit winnings."

"Well," Santan said, "man's usual method for determining success is to keep score. This approach will make the chance to score more interesting by potentially doubling the action on a given hole. The opposing team has the option of accepting or refusing."

Danikov shrugged and said, "That is indeed the world view, but it also sounds like a game you've been hiding in the bushes and waiting to spring. I'll go along with it only if the others buy in, at least for a while."

Neither of the other two objected.

SEVEN

CLAYMAN AND DANIKOV whisked themselves over to where Randall's player had found his ball in four-inch deep rough on the steep down-slope left of the green. Clayman was trying to dance for joy over said player's misfortune. "I like our position, partner," he said. " Even if this guy has a backhoe in his bag he'll never get the ball to within thirty feet of the pin."

"Doesn't matter," Danikov said. "Their team's best ball is already on the green in one."

"I knew that," Clayman responded. They both quickly moved to where one of their own team members was about to play his shot from the right hand bunker.

"Maybe he'll get lucky," Clayman said.

"You don't get lucky with sand explosions," countered Danikov. "Besides, I've watched his practice swing. He has no confidence in it." As if on cue the player took a weak swing and managed to advance the ball a good two feet, leaving it still in the bunker and well short of the edge.

While the real life player then set about trying to limit the damage with a second sand shot, the spirit pair abandoned him and sped to their remaining hope on the hole: the player with his ball a few feet short of the front of the green.

The opposing spirit team was there ahead of them. As the player took a short back stroke with an eight iron, probably intending to land the ball about half-way between himself and the hole and run it uphill and onto the green, Randall began jumping up and down. He comically waved, shouted, and made faces at the unobserving player. Clayman was irritated and said as much. "Randall, that's cheating. You wouldn't do that in real life, why would you try it now?"

"Loyalty to the team!" Randall said emphatically. "Maybe you could stand to be a little more pro-active yourself, Pauli-boy."

Santan grinned, but then the grin quickly turned sour as the player's topspin-heavy shot came out hot. As the ball landed on the edge of the green with almost no hop, it began a fast forward roll. "Damn!" he said. "He's got it right on line. He'll have a putt for par."

"Maybe a shorter putt than you think," Danikov said as the ball continued its unerring procession. "Run, baby, run!" he shouted. The ball never wavered from the line, and the pace was perfect, dropping dead center into the hole for a birdie. The Danikov-Clayman team whooped and whooshed to the hole, first trying unsuccessfully to retrieve the ball and then attempting to congratulate their player. Again they were unsuccessful. They settled for personal jubilation.

Santan turned to Randall and said only, "You jinxed us. Now the best we can do is a tie." By the expression on his face Randall had taken the comment as undeserved criticism. He was only having a little fun. This wasn't a life or death issue, was it?

Santan and Randall's 'A' player's ball was a full ten feet short of the hole, but it was straight up the hill. The player stepped up to his ball. "Smooth but firm. Smooth but firm," Santan repeated into the player's ear, only a foot away from him. The player took two practice swings to set both his rhythm and the length of his swing. On the second practice swing his putter hung up momentarily on the green's surface. He took a third practice stroke, which was much smoother. "That's it," Santan said. "Get it right."

But he hadn't. He repeated the earlier stutter stroke and the ball came up a full foot short of the hole. Santan went into a rage as Randall winced and moved off. "Damn you, you dumb son-of-a-bitch!" Santan cried out at the unhearing player. What followed Santan's profanity Danikov found so comical he laughed at loud, at the same time prompting Clayman to join in with the fun.

Apparently needing to give immediate physical vent to his anger over the missed putt, Santan had headed for the nearest tree, intending to butt it. Instead, he jerkily passed through the tree. Then, not fully comprehending what had happened he again tried to vent his ire against the tree, this time slapping at it with a round house swing. Same result. Both Danikov and Clayman were by now laughing without restraint. Completely ignoring their reaction Santan paused for a momentary reflection as he was standing immediately adjacent to the totally unaffected tree. As if to catch up with himself, he then attempted to lean back against it. Instead, he once more passed through the tree. To Danikov's and Clayman's amazement, Santan also began laughing. Only then did Randall find humor in the situation.

EIGHT

THE FOURSOME PULLED ITSELF TOGETHER and congregated near the back of the seventeenth green, waiting for the next group to arrive at the tee. Clayman posed a question for all of them: "Is this how it's to be for the rest of eternity? One never ending, vicarious golf match, punctuated by religious discourse?"

"What's wrong with that?" Santan responded. "The first part, anyway. We died, but here we are, in continuous pursuit of a sport of passion, absolutely independent of either weather or tee times. Of course my team is one down at the moment, but we'll shortly rectify that."

"You don't think this spirit condition is permanent?" Clayman asked.

Santan shrugged. "I don't know. But you gotta live for the moment because there's no guarantee of tomorrow. I think even Danikov would agree with that."

"Since you brought up the subject, Luke, don't you think we're somehow accountable for our time on Earth? I mean, did you live such an exemplary life that you aren't worried about the consequences?"

"Man is responsible to himself," Santan said. "Man punishes man. What happens, happens. And when it's over, it's over."

"I've spent my life confused by religion," Clayman said. "Now, in death, I'm even more confused. You know, it's strange, but when I first met Sheila I was crazy about her. She had it all together and that's what I needed: stability. Then come to find out, she brought her own baggage. While we hit it off for a while, everything kept coming back to her greatest concern."

"Evangelizing you," Santan said, his tone one of sympathetic irritation.

"Not exactly," Clayman said, for some reason trying to scratch the back of his neck. "It was more a matter of trying to reconcile her Jewish identity with her newly found interest in Christ. You know, Danikov talked about my wrestling. Well, Sheila told me she had wrestled with her problem for a long time before finding her answer . . . such as it was."

"She accepted Christ as the Jewish messiah," Danikov said softly. "Why is that a problem for you?"

"As I already said, I found it odd. But, you know, that didn't really bother me one way or the other. I would as soon have forgotten it, but how do two people grow in their relationship when they have major points of difference regarding their spiritual beliefs? Even if one of them doesn't believe much of anything."

"For me the answer is fundamental," Santan said. "Don't worry about someone else's perspective. I used to carry a clipping by astronomer-philosopher Carl Sagan. I can recite it from memory the way Danikov does with scripture: 'I would love to believe that when I die I will live again, that some thinking, remembering part of me will retain awareness. As much as I want to believe this, and as aware as I am of the ancient and worldwide cultural traditions that assert an afterlife, I know of nothing to suggest that it is more than wishful thinking. I require both logic and proof for my decisions.' Ditto, Luke Santan."

"Santan," Danikov interjected, putting his forefinger to his lips and then releasing it, "you omitted one tiny qualifier in that quotation. Sagan prefaced that last sentence with eloquent, but desperate longing by also saying: '*I regret my lack of religious faith, but* . . . I require both logic and proof for my decisions.'

"Whatever," Santan said, irritated by Danikov's precision on the quote. "But if ever I choose to serve a god, it will be a god of my own making. The point is that man's refuge in religion is due to his unwillingness to think of himself as merely elemental. Not much different in concept than when people thought the Earth was the center of the universe."

"Since you brought up the subject of serving God, follow me on this," Danikov said to Santan. "Suppose you were the Creator of the universe. Sticks and stones, and even plants and animals still lacked something, so as the Creator you chose to make a being in your image. You gave him a mate, and through the generations you sent messengers to your children with instructions for keeping faith with you, their father."

"That's humorous," Santan said.

"Stay with me," Danikov said. "After a while, your gift of free will allowed your children to turn away from you in their belief of self-sufficiency. As a result of this apostasy, or falling away, you cleaved a part of your very essence to be given physical birth by one of your mortal children."

Santan looked to the others for support. "This is a fairy tale," he said.

They both shrugged, as Clayman spoke up. "How would you describe the reality of being on a golf course in spirit form?" Santan did not respond.

Danikov continued. "As the Creator, Santan, you provided for your Son to become the people's savior, but even as the Son of the Creator's teaching took hold with his disciples, many more rejected him. Sadly, in your imaginary role as the God of the universe, you allowed your son's persecutors to crucify him, as you also promised to raise him from the dead. With your Son's resurrection a reality you offered—purely out of compassion, for they did not justify your action— the unworthy children unconditional forgiveness, if they but asked the Son for it. Seeing that you wanted to offer them even more you added the incentive of eternal life. How sad for you then that so few of your created people actually desired to honor the Father through choosing to accept His saving grace through His living Son."

"What's your point?" Santan asked.

"That man is consistently presented with the opportunity to either worship God freely by expression of faith or reject Him by rebellion of will," Danikov replied.

"That's heavy," Randall said. "Let me throw some of my own hazy philosophy into the mix. All religions and cults have their own celebrated texts that are admittedly written by fallible man, maybe even men with an axe in need of grinding. In my opinion, all religious thinking is flawed. Their 'truths' are often impossibly multi-faceted or ridiculously dogmatic. And since we can't know absolutely about any of them, the only logical conclusion is one of universal default."

"I know what you're trying to say," Clayman said. "Sheila's and my arguments over 'this faith, that faith or no faith' is ruining . . . uh, ruined . . . our relationship. It simply couldn't survive all the chewing and gnawing."

"You may have learned more than you realize because at least you've pretty well analyzed the situation," said Danikov, becoming even more animated by the discussion's direction. "

"Not so," Clayman said. "I'm only reporting the facts. I told her I thought she was a victim. Even for a non-religious Jew I couldn't accept her 'sea change' on such a fundamental Jewish point. She obviously didn't convince me, but then I think I've made cynicism my faith." Clayman was suddenly aware that, for some reason, he had shared far more of himself than he had ever shared with anyone, including Sheila! Imagine that, he thought: Paul Clayman actually opening up to strangers! He suddenly felt highly vulnerable. Now in near-panic he attempted to change the subject. "Looky here, boys," he said, pointing back up hill from their position on the green, "fresh meat on the tee."

NINE

"Artie," Santan said, addressing his game partner in an aside such that the other two could not hear him, "you've always prided yourself in choosing winners, haven't you? I mean, you're intelligent, observant and flexible."

"Well, I try to be."

"We would have won that last hole and the live match, you know."

"I hope we would have."

"No, it's more fundamental than that. I'm the best player in the group."

"And modest," Randall chided.

"Like they say, 'It ain't braggin' if you can back it up. I always play to my handicap. But you carried your own weight, too. Now this vicarious match. It's different. It's only part of a bigger picture."

Randall was still a little heady from Santan's compliments. "What do you mean 'bigger picture?'" he asked.

"If Danikov is right about there being safety in numbers when we finish our turn at the golf fountain, *if* in fact it ends, we don't want the group fragmented. As I see it, we know exactly who we are because of where we are. If our future is in anyway linked to some sort of group consensus, then we need unity—or at least a majority—on our point."

"Do *we* have a position? *My* position is basically *no* position."

"No it isn't. You believe in yourself, just like I do. And I know beyond a doubt that everything in the universe is ordered according to physical, mathematical and chemical laws."

"Come on, partner. I respect your knowledge, but I can't pull your whole wagon. Don't you think the evolutionary solution for man is just a tad flawed by its own huge leap of faith? I don't have much faith in any sort of faith. Man simply can't know all the answers either for or against the question of a God, living or otherwise."

Santan nodded his head in agreement. "Precisely. If we can't know, we don't know. Therefore, religious faith is nothing but dogma. We're of the same opinion. My point is that we came into this situation together and if that's the only way we can move out . . . well, I intend to lead us. But I need your help."

"Really? But what can I, or you, do? We're not exactly in control of anything here, you know."

"We can do more than you think. I'll share that with you later. We'll make a hell of a team. Don't worry, I'll take the initiative in bringing the others around."

"Thanks, Luke. People usually expect my help. They rarely ask for it. You know, there are a lot of things on Danikov's religious buffet that bother me. One of them is his notion that God simultaneously attends to hundreds of millions of human beings who may also be addressing him at the same time."

"Good point," Santan said, attempting to clap Randall on the shoulder. "Tell you what, I have a little proactive idea to try out on this next group. Watch things closely and give me your reaction."

The foursome was about to hit their tee shots. Before anyone actually teed off, however, Clayman posed a question for the group. "Suppose," he said, "we don't agree as to whose shot is best, worst or in-between? And trust me, it'll happen."

Santan shook his head and said, "Would you like to tell us about your solution, Mr. Game Analyst?"

"My privilege," Clayman said, pointing at Santan for exaggerated effect. "We rotate the deciding opinion between the two teams. Conscience should outweigh preference." Agreement was unanimous and Clayman-Danikov would be the first to officiate, if need be. The live players had already hit and the relative quality of their individual shots was clearly on display. Danikov and Clayman had best and worst. The two middle players fell to Santan and Randall.

Danikov turned to his partner to comment on the player foursome's relative abilities. "Based on their swings, all four of these real-lifers look to be high-handicappers. A bogey four may well be a winning score."

None of tee shots were on the green, but all were in play. Then came the second shots. Both Santan's and Randall's players each wasted a shot by burying their wedges into rain-softened ground and fluffing their balls barely forward. As a result, their second approach shots put each of pair on the green in three, but still nowhere near the hole.

"Now it's our guys' turn," said Clayman. The first Danikov/Clayman player reversed the trend and flew his approach shot well over the green. A third shot by the same player was barely chipped back onto the putting surface. Their number two man topped a too-quick chip shot from near the huge, green side, remote-controlled fan, which on more humid days stirred up enough air to keep certain airborne fungus from settling in and turning the green into salad. The fan wasn't running this day, however, and the ball ended up only two and a half feet right of the hole, an easy putt.

The live players roared at the gratuitous shot. "Great execution!" Clayman exclaimed to Danikov. "He can tap it in from there for a win. We can take this one to the bank, Tommy Ray." They both grinned broadly.

The player with the fortunate miscue was ready to finish off his bogey after the other three had all two-putted for double-bogeys. He confidently lined up the short, uphill putt and drew back his putter, intending to give the ball the simple, short stroke required. Randall was watching Santan, who was standing at the edge of the green, away from all of them. He had expected to see a combination look of resignation and frustration on the face of the man who, only a few moments ago, had been so self-assured. Instead, he was surprised to see Santan quietly turn his back before the putt could be stroked.

Then, the precise moment the player drew back his putter the huge, green-side fan whirred to life. The player flinched, causing his putter to strike the green before the golf ball, moving the ball forward less than a foot. Exasperated by his fortune, the player jabbed his remaining putt, barely managing to hole it. He gestured wildly toward the fan as his live opponents merely laughed. The hole was halved.

Clayman protested, but Danikov knew that would be to no avail so he merely commented to Santan, "Some break. The fan cost us a win."

"Yes, it was and did," said Santan, nodding to Randall. "Good job, partner. Say hello to the first carryover of the post-flesh era."

"Well," Randall said, "that was pure luck. What's the 'pro-active point' you didn't make?"

"It wasn't luck," Santan said.

For a moment Randall looked at his partner dismissively, but then curiosity entered his thoughts, followed by incredulity.

TEN

As Santan wafted back and forth near the green waiting for the next group to appear on the seventeenth tee he cornered Clayman, saying, "You know, Paul, you could have become a bitter man over your family situation and your girlfriend's state of mind, but you didn't. I guess that's because you're philosophical about it. Tell me, what does fulfillment and happiness mean to you?"

Clayman would have expected such a question from Danikov, but not from Santan. How had he overlooked empathy as a part of this spiritual hit man's character? "That's a trick question to keep me off balance for the next hole, isn't it?"

"Hey, we're not actually swinging the clubs, you know," Santan said. "I'm just curious. I think I already know what's important to Randall. As for Danikov he might as well tattoo 'God on board' on his forehead. But you, I don't know. In real life you appeared to be a fence sitter. Any changes?"

Clayman reacted to Santan's perceptive words. "Since you ask, I missed not having a mentor in my life. Someone I could have gone to discuss life's big decisions. Someone like a live-in father or a caring uncle, or anyone I could have talked to for that matter. Not just for the big decisions, for the little ones as well. Not to make my decisions for me, understand, only to explore the possibilities. I became my own mentor, but I'm not a very good listener."

"I understand," said Santan. "New subject. What do think about the holocaust? Were Hitler and his subordinates emissaries from hell?"

Where is this guy coming from? He's all over the place. "That isn't my concern, never has been. The Holocaust merely reinforces my skepticism. I'm not the only Jew who feels God owes him an explanation. That's why some Nazi camp Jews put God on trial and found him guilty."

"Well," Santan said, "I'm not Jewish, but if I were, I'd feel the way you do. Personally, I don't believe a just God would permit near-genocide."

"You're dead wrong on that point, Santan," Danikov said, overhearing them and abruptly joining the discussion without invitation. "What do you think the Egyptians had in mind for the Israelites before Moses led them out of Egypt?"

"If your God felt compelled to cause that saving exodus," Santan said, "then where was he during the Nazi persecution?"

At first Danikov appeared to Clayman to be upset by Santan's repeated baiting, but he was merely pausing to think. "God found a way to end it for Germany's Jews," he said, "just as he did for the Israelites before them. And this time it took him only five years, not forty."

"I'll bet that was comforting to the families of the dead," Santan said.

Randall jumped into the fray. "O.K., Danikov, let's get back to your Bible, which you enter as evidence for your argument for being a believer. A world court would not necessarily find that irrefutable. Other manuscripts exist that are considered by their adherents to be just as holy, but without any reference whatever to the historical incidents you treat as if they were absolute."

"Thank you," said Danikov, pointing to Randall. "First of all the holy Bible is not merely Christian. Exodus, for example, is a book from the Torah of the Old Testament. Those first five books of the Old Testament outline humanity's fall from grace. But on a broader scale, the Bible's writing is the work of more than forty authors from every walk of life, from fishermen to kings, from peasants to scholars."

"That's part of the point. It's not necessarily reliable, man, it's just old," Randall said.

Danikov was quick to respond. "You're dead right about one thing. The Bible wasn't written overnight. In fact, it was composed over a period of roughly sixteen hundred years. And we can trust the Bible because the Bible has been proven trustworthy. A couple of days before our real life match I read on a web site that no other ancient document comes close to the reliability of the New Testament."

Randall feared he might be treading foolishly, but he couldn't help himself. "O.K., Your Resident Scholar," he said in an accusing tone, "what's the basis for that truth-in-religion statement?"

"When you studied Plato in school did you question your teacher about the reliability of *The Republic*?" Danikov asked.

"Didn't need to. The documentation was presumed reliable."

"Thank you. Two factors mark the reliability of ancient documents. The number of manuscript copies in existence, and the time between when the document was written and the oldest existing copy. Try me. Name any ancient document you want."

Santan spoke up, confidently. "Homer's *Iliad.*"

"Good choice," Danikov said. "That's number two with almost 650 copies and a five-hundred year span between the time it was written and the oldest existing copy. The New Testament has more than 24,000 manuscript copies still in existence from 125 A.D., only twenty-five years from when it was written between 40 to 100 A.D.."

Randall resigned himself to his losing position on the issue. "So, pastor, can you use me as your set-up man if you ever take this revival show on the road?"

"Let's back up," Santan said. "Clayman made a good point about questioning a God who allows even a free-will people to repetitiously and horribly suffer for thousands of years. Now, had man been in charge, I would have understood. We do ourselves no ultimate good, but we nevertheless fight for the hope that one day we may."

Clayman looked to Danikov for a long-barreled rebuttal, but was surprised.

"Believe what you want," Danikov said with an impatient tone. "And that goes for Clayman and Randall as well. I've known the light of God for a long time, and I'm content in my own beliefs. You're all entitled to yours. Maybe I'll have to leave it with praying for you." Danikov looked expectantly back up towards the seventeenth tee.

Eleven

Suddenly, as the next live foursome was about to tee up, the clouds began racing across the skies, turning from benign grey to threatening black. Rain quickly began pouring down on the real-life players and the clouds rumbled with thunder, appearing to spook them. Anticipating their next reaction, Santan shouted loudly enough for the players to have heard him—if only he hadn't been in spirit form—"Shoot, you wimps! It's only rain. You won't dissolve!"

No sooner had he uttered his irritation than lightning framed the picture, driving the flesh-and-blood foursome to their carts and the shortest path down the hill en route to the club house. Turning to the others Clayman said, "Now what do we do to occupy ourselves for the remainder of—" His words were effectively muffled by a series of lightning bolts, which triggered some knee-jerk ducking by the spirits. In light of the foursome's "condition," of course, they were not impacted by one of nature's most vivid demonstrations. They heard the familiar siren sounding, warning golfers off the course.

Simultaneous with the multi-branched lightning, however, Clayman had felt a strange tug at his consciousness. The effect on his mind wasn't unlike that of a fishing bobber being nibbled as it sits in otherwise undisturbed waters. He tried to analyze it, but after several minutes gave up. "Did you guys feel something weird during the lightning strikes?" Clayman asked. Before they could reply, the treed and grassed golf course images before them began whooshing by as if on a huge, muted outdoor tape set on fast forward. Then, as suddenly, the blurred images stilled, causing the foursome to bobble slightly, as if it was they who had been on the move.

As Clayman recovered and refocused from the spirit foursome's valley vantage point, he was surprised by what he was seeing up on the tee. *More players! Hadn't the lightning and the siren chased everyone off the course? Wait a minute. They're not golfers!* In fact, they resembled nothing he had ever witnessed . . . except for themselves. Could spirit forms hallucinate? he wondered. "Hey," he shouted to the others of his group who were still reorienting from the carnival ride's spin, "what do you guys see on the tee?"

Randall was the first to react. "Oh, no. This has to be trouble. And just when I was getting accustomed to things."

Danikov was more reassuring. "Well, this should be very interesting. And if we're lucky, enlightening."

Santan sensed potential change of the status quo. "Don't let 'em play through," he said, nervously joking. The others didn't laugh.

After only a moment the new spirit foursome had joined the others on the green. Carefully observing the visitors Clayman realized for the first time since their transformation that the individuals in his own group had no sharp physical definition. They simply "knew" each other. What an unexpected turn of events this unimaginable group's arrival might bring, he thought.

What was equally astonishing to Clayman was their simple greeting. "Hello," one of them said. "I'm called Barnabas. These are friends of mine."

Santan floated toward the newly arrived group and began peppering them with questions. "What is this? Halloween? Who are you? Where are you from? What can you tell us?"

"Tell you?" answered another of the interlopers. "We were hoping you could enlighten us. We don't even know where we are. Personally, I only met Barnabas and the others as we were summoned to this location." Yet another of the unnamed visiting spirits looked around, seemingly only mildly interested about their circumstances and saying, "Why are you delaying us?"

"Delaying you?" asked Santan, incredulous. "From what? Summoned? Summoned by whom?"

The last newcomer to be heard from responded. "Forget him. I find his attitude irritating. As for a summons, it's on my mind to encourage you to think about a collective faith perspective."

"Hmm . . . yes, that's my thought also," said another of the visiting spirits.

"And you are both correct," Barnabas said, smiling.

Danikov addressed the visiting group's apparent leader. "Welcome. My name is Danikov." He turned to the others of his group. "This is Clayman, and next to him is Randall.

You've heard from Santan. Thank you for your comment. Actually, we have been working on the faith perspective. We simply haven't gotten anywhere. I'm beginning to think religion can't be proved true intellectually."

"That's because one's faith comes from the heart," Barnabas said. "I believe even my three newly-arrived co-horts probably think a faith perspective refers to 'what' and 'why.' I suggest that faith is a deeper matter involving 'whom.'"

"O.K.," Randall said, "would you care to be a tad more specific?"

"Certainly," Barnabas said. "First, think about who you were before your transformation and what your relationship was with your maker."

Santan laughed. "Maker?" he said. "What's the difference now? I think *you've* missed the point. We once were! We are no longer, yet we are somewhere. My question is what's next?"

"Have you shared with one another anything of your journeys with the Lord? "

"You mean pour out our guts about our personal doctrines?" Santan asked.

"No," Barnabas said. "Your soul's survival is not about a systematic set of beliefs or doctrines. It's about a relationship with the Lord. The story of Christianity continues to be a dialogue between human beings—with all their strengths and imperfections—and a loving savior."

"With Jesus Christ, of course," Danikov said, who was all but overwhelmed. Not so much by the group's appearance as by Barnabas' affirmations. This was needed verification for him that they weren't in some isolated time warp or something. "Barnabas, for the benefit of all of us, please explain how if trust in the Lord means complete faith, why we can't come to God through our own faith."

"Brother, you cannot come to God merely through your own faith any more than God's old covenant people could come to Him through their own sacrifices. First, you must accept his gracious offer of forgiveness with thanksgiving. Then comes the planting within you for the seed of faith. It is through God's grace that by faith we are saved."

"Those verses in Romans," Danikov said, "have never had as much meaning for me as they do this very moment. God bless you. That also explains why I'm having so much trouble in witnessing to my group."

"You're probably progressing better than you think. Thank you. Well," Barnabas added, "as we have no further reason to be here. We wish you the best on your journey."

"No!" Randall shouted, his face contorted with anxiety. "You can't leave us like this. We have questions. How does our past affect our future, if we have one?"

"He's right," Clayman said. "Can't you offer us something more tangible? Can't we each go our own way from here, as your group appears to be doing?"

"You can do anything you like, just as you did in life. This is not for me to say. I once asked myself questions about my own behavior. I found change not only to my liking, but necessary. Just as my more famous contemporary."

Randall frowned. "Your contemporary? What do we care about your pal? What's he got to do with us?"

"He was further removed from understanding than any of you. If he could turn from violent persecution of Christ's followers to belief and apostle for Christ, then believe there is also hope for you."

Danikov appeared mystified. "Are you an angel?" he asked.

"What do you think angels are?"

"Spiritual beings created by God," Danikov said, recalling some of the answer once given him by a church pastor. "Don't they help carry out His work, bring messages, protect God's people, offer encouragement and fight the forces of evil?"

"Well," Barnabas said, "I've been accused of providing a little guidance here and there, but I can't say I've ever delivered punishment. Why do you ask? Are you lost?"

"Yes," Randall said.

"No, we're not," Santan said adamantly.

"Oh, yes," Danikov countered, "some of us are as lost as a golf ball."

"That's all right," the visiting group's leader said, "Christ came for the sinners and for the lost, not for the righteous."

"You seem to be just like us in appearance," Santan said. "Are you better spirits than we? What makes one righteous? And what has your god done for us that we should heed your advice?"

Clayman was unnerved at Barnabas' reaction. The visitor seemed not only taken aback at what he might easily call blasphemy, but looked to actually be in pain. Was the pain for himself or for them?

Barnabas slowly turned and nodded almost imperceptibly at each of the members of his spirit foursome. One visitor then turned to face Santan, saying in a grave tone, "Jesus could have gone to heaven without you."

The second spirit added with some emotion, "But he willingly and painfully died on the cross for you."

And the third said with broad expression, "And in so doing, erased man's sins, past, present and future."

Barnabas concluded the four-part response by saying, "In other words, Mr. Santan, your Lord chose to go to hell for you." Barnabas gestured in turn to each of the other three of the vicarious golf foursome, saying, "And for you, and you, and you."

Randall appeared fearful at first, but then shrugged them off as if he were dismissing a front-door evangelist. "No, thank you," he said. "Not today." Clayman somberly shook his head as Danikov simply said, "Amen."

After an initial moment of silence, Santan recovered to say, "Now that's really cute, gentle spirits. With a little music you could be a regular barbershop quartet. Before you leave do you have a word of encouragement for the doomed?"

Barnabas put up a hand as if asking Santan to allow him to get in a word. "You're the mathematician, aren't you?"

Surprised by that knowledge Santan cautiously provided confirmation. "Why yes. Why do you ask?"

"Do you know the name Blaise Pascal?"

"The 13th century French mathematician?"

"Yes. As you probably also know he was a philosopher and scientist as well. He said there is enough evidence for the Christian faith to convince anyone who is not set against it. But there is—"

"Santan interrupted him. "Well, I reject Pascal's opinion!"

"Sir," Barnabas said, sternly, "you are a textbook testimonial to Pascal's quotation, which you interrupted: The full quotation continues like this: 'But there is not enough evidence to bring anyone into God's kingdom . . . who will not come.'"

"Barnabas," Danikov said, "I'm not giving up on him. More than a few minds have become converts to Christianity out of their efforts to refute Christianity."

"I have a suggestion," said one of the other visitors, a little tentatively.

"What's that?" Clayman asked.

"You could all try singing."

Santan's response was once again to laugh.

"Singing?" Randall said, shaking his head. "Sing what? And why? You know, I think my partner just might be right. I think the four of you are plain daffy." Randall thought about what he had just said, then added, "Look, I'm sorry for that, but we really could use some help here."

"That's all right," Barnabas said, "but my friend here was offering you practical advice. Do any of you know the words to *Amazing Grace*?"

Clayman and Santan both glanced in Danikov's direction, frowning.

Danikov pointed at Barnabas and said, "Excuse me, but I finally put together what you said about your contemporary. You were referring to the apostle Paul, weren't you?"

The spirit foursome at once realized that their potential 'guiding lights' were suddenly no longer present.

Clayman responded first. "They're gone," he said. "What was with the song question? You think there's a clue for us there?"

"I don't know," Danikov said. "Let's examine it, if you like. Praise and worship songs are, after all, exactly that. 'Amazing Grace's' most famous lyrics are, 'I once was lost, but now am found, Was blind, but now I see.' That speaks directly to me."

"Thanks so much," Santan said sarcastically. "What a sorry bunch they were," he added, facing the direction of the departed spirits and gesturing obscenely with one finger.

"Wait a minute," Randall said. "You know, as it turns out the first half of that first line is pretty descriptive of our situation, but as to the second part . . ."

"Let me tell you something," Danikov said, more emotion to his voice than he had yet displayed as a spirit. "Ever since I learned about the sorry life of the hymn's author, John Newton, I have been moved by this hymn as by no other."

"Are we talking thief, coward or murderer?" asked Randall.

"Yes. And worse: a blasphemer. By his own words grace at once taught him to fear and then relieved his fear. In lyric form he said he was blind, but came to see, and from his first hour of belief grace saved and led a wretch like him home."

"That's purely amazing," said Santan, mocking both Danikov and his message. "And what did old Newton come to in the end?"

"As a matter of fact," Danikov said, "he built that very expectation into the lyrics of the fourth verse, which go like this: 'When we've been there ten thousand years, bright shining as the sun, we've no less days to sing God's praise than when we first begun.'" Danikov had barely recited the last word when for the first time in spirit form he wept.

"O.K.," Randall said after a moment,. "you've made your point, but that brings up another problem I have with a lot of Christians. They get on board with God and everything is fine for awhile, as long as they're prospering and not suffering. But when things go wrong they're the first to question their God."

"Stop right there," Danikov said. "That's Satan's view of suffering. God's view is that suffering causes us to trust God for who he is, not for what he does."

"Will it never end?" Santan asked, waving off both of them. "Let's resume play. The rain, lightning, thunder and visiting spirits are all gone. Only the wind remains, gentlemen, and on yon tee we have new life."

"Let's do it," Randall seconded, feeling the need to escape the troublesome direction of the conversation.

"Tell you what we're gonna do," Santan began his proposal. "We need to liven things up a bit. Let's each pick a number from one to four and match the numbers to the order in which the new foursome tees off. That'll give us our players."

Randall and Clayman, who had contributed nothing whatever to the preceding discussion, each wrinkled their noses out of general protest, but shook their head in assent.

No sooner had the foursome zipped back up the hill after selecting their numbers, than Randall complained. "What's this bit?" he said, referring to his player which was the lead-off hitter.

The player had bent to tee up his ball, but instead of using a standard wooden tee, he produced a short piece of a green tree branch. He then proceeded to force the crooked stick—six or seven inches long—into the ground. Following that he carefully pressed a regular wooden golf tee into the top of the pulpy stick. On top of this arrangement he gingerly placed his golf ball. "Hey," Randall said, "I picked Dopey! Look, you guys. He's going into the tank before he even takes a swing." Seeing what was happening, all four spirits positioned themselves to watch, amusement on their faces.

Santan whispered to Randall, "Don't worry, partner. Unless the guy's a real dunce, anyone trying such a stunt in a serious game—and these guys seem to be in exactly that—has to have the shot in his bag." Santan turned to his and Randall's opponents and said aloud, "Tell you what we'll do. In spite of this entertaining little aberration, and since you boys are sucking from where the milk is a little thin, we'll let you press us. Speak now, bold spirits, and you can double a one-time, one-hole bet."

Clayman, city-bred and raised, liked Santan's farm humor. But still, he couldn't believe the offer. "Welcome to the breeder house, gentlemen," Clayman said. "We accept your doubled offer, and redouble, subject to my partner's O.K." He turned to a wide-eyed Danikov. "Go along with it, Tommy Ray," he said. "This tee-branch player is a clown. We're two down, and with four points on the line we can not only climb out of the well, we can throw the bad guys in head first."

"Greed has cost many a man his stake, partner," cautioned Danikov. "There are lots of holes to come."

"Man," Clayman said, "in both finance and golf you have to recognize opportunity before you can seize it. The big 'O' just jumped up in front of us. Carpe diem!"

Danikov sighed. "If you insist."

Clayman had logic on his side. He first recognized that physical objects did not exist for any of them in this confounding environment. Then he reasoned that their vicarious game was nothing more than an activity taken on to occupy their minds. Therefore, aside from their on again-off again faith argument, banking points *was* the real goal. So why was his partner so annoyed?

Santan and Danikov were on opposing teams, but both of them had correctly sized up the twig-tee player. In the face of Clayman's aggressive stance, however, Danikov let a little of his own greed quiet him. The center stage player stood closer to the ball than normal, playing the ball off his right heel in order to give it a lower trajectory. He was going with a club with two less elevations and a shorter grip than normal for him as he addressed the ball which was sitting nearly eight inches above the ground.

The player rehearsed his starting swing plane with an abbreviated version, then slowly brought the club head to a full stop immediately behind the golf ball. A waggle followed. Two seconds later he initiated a smooth, but shortened take-away followed by an abbreviated follow-through. Club head met ball. At first look, the ball seemed to be have been struck "thin," above the center of the golf ball. The ball barely rose in its flight, but it covered the distance with almost no hang time. The missile unerringly found a runway at front center of the green. The ball hopped once, then rolled and chugged up the minor incline like it was braking for a pit stop. The ball come to rest a mere fifteen feet short of the hole.

The spirit team backing the trick shotster were in a delirium, dancing and whisking about in a mock Highland fling. In contrast, Danikov shrugged and grinned with resignation, as Clayman went to his knees in tragi-comedy imitation, wringing his hands and saying, "Oh, great architect of the universe, where is thy justice?"

The other three players' tee shots were anti-climactic and scattered everywhere except on the green, although close to it and not in the sand. As the spirit foursome whisked themselves into position to watch the second shots, Santan spoke to Randall, "Artie, from this I hope you've learned to trust me. I know golf. Even better, I know people. What just happened wasn't even a gamble."

"What do you mean?" Randall asked.

Santan confided, "I watched the faces of the other three real-life players as soon as the trick shot player began to tee up. I don't know what their own bet was, but one of them— probably his partner—betrayed a look of recognition."

"Really? I'm impressed," Randall said.

"I've also been doing some mental tinkering and I may have figured a special angle worth testing in this curious afterlife of ours. Remember something. No matter what happens, we're a team. I may be the captain, but you're first mate and you'll share fully in our success in both the golf match and in the missionary prosecution."

"O.K. by me," Randall said. "I like your lead. I have to tell you though that I'm a fair-weather player. Read anything you want into that."

Neither of the two players—one from each team— whose tee shots had been well off the green managed to chip anywhere near the hole. The other Danikov-Clayman team player, however, coaxed his second shot close enough for a conceded par three, giving the team newly-found hope. It was short-lived. The other team's trick shot artist confidently stroked his medium distance up hill putt for a dead center drop, a birdie and a huge win. With an unprecedented and devastating eight point surge on a single hole, Santan and Randall were up a staggering ten points in the continuing match. Even better, they could only slip backwards two points at a time, barring other presses.

Clayman tried to wring his hands over his team's steep slide caused by his poor judgment alone. Danikov made an effort to counter his partner's despair saying, "It's a game. It's only a game. And furthermore, we can recover." To himself he softly voiced two rhetorical questions, overheard by no one. "When and how will this match ever end? And why should either answer be important?"

TWELVE

CLAYMAN WAS STILL AGITATED. He sidled up to Danikov to confide his concern, " We're ten down and playing for two points a hole. We need to press again."

Looking up from his momentary reverie, Danikov replied, "No. What we need to do is assess the potential. Let's don't ask for a prescription without a diagnosis." He paused a moment. "You know, I wonder why it is we haven't recognized any of these real-life players? We were all relatively new club members, but surely we should see someone known to at least one of us."

"I dunno," Clayman said. "But since you bring it up, here's something even more weird. The next foursome on the tee are all *women*."

The built-in alarm in Danikov's golf psyche apparently carried over into the new life because it just went off. "What?" he said. "This is Saturday, isn't it? How'd they get a starting time?"

"Well, now, Mr. Righteous," Santan said, happy with the opportunity that had just presented itself. "Why are you so intent on looking at the speck of sawdust in your brother's eye and yet pay no attention to the plank in your own eye?"

Danikov was silent. Clayman watched him, assuming he was meditating on Santan's incisive observation about his male chauvinism. After a long moment Danikov nodded and said, "Guilty as charged. That's discriminatory and I admit it. I've carried that bogey for a long time." He then looked away from both the spirit and the flesh-and-blood groups and said softly, almost singing, "Change my heart, O God, make it ever true. Change my heart, O God, may I be like you."

Only Clayman was close enough to actually hear the words. He said nothing, but Danikov gave him a sharp half-nod as he turned back to the group.

"Confession accepted," Santan said in a mocking tone. "As for recognizing someone, boys, I think you can suspend both that and your notions of time. Who knows 'when' this is for these players, or for us for that matter?"

Santan watched the female foursome as they carted down the short distance from the top of the hill to the lower ladies' tee, then he turned to Clayman. "Your turn to start the pick order."

Clayman whooshed himself up the hill to the ladies' tee. How could he pick up on anything here? The equipment all looked comparable. What about their dress? Would that tell him anything about their relative abilities? He could observe, but what was he looking for?

Further, he thought, none of them were taking practice swings off to one side. But so what? Both Danikov and Santan were skilled when it came to reading something from another player's set-up and swing, but not Clayman.

He had to choose before the lead player teed up her ball. What difference? he wondered. He may as well go with the first person to tee up. Besides, he reasoned, in order to have the tee box honors, her team had to have either won or tied the previous hole. "I go with the lady in red," he said. The others took their prescribed rotation choices and the action was set.

As Clayman's player choice was about to swing, she apparently felt a sudden fresh breeze and stopped in mid-swing. She stepped back and glanced up at the treetops to see a slight bending of the top branches. Clayman followed her gaze and observed the same wind indicator. Top branches in motion usually meant the wind was blowing at about ten miles per hour, or one-club greater or lesser degree of loft than normal, depending upon the wind direction. To check the *actual* wind direction, she glanced at the flag's motion atop the pin on the green.

The flag abruptly changed direction from flying with them to flying against them. "Fickle wind," the player said aloud and quickly returned to her cart and bag to retrieve a one greater-distance club, and then confidently hit her shot. She pushed the iron shot a little, but it was solidly struck. As it angled to the right, she anxiously watched the ball's flight, expecting it to be slowed by the breeze and land just off the green to the right. However, the ball completely flew the right side of the green and bounded towards a house built just beyond the fairway. Out of bounds.

"What happened to the wind?" Clayman asked. "That ball should have finished in good shape."

"Misclubbed," said Santan, shrugging. Clayman shook his head.

The other three players made their own wind assessments and hit, with both Santan's and Randall's players catching the right hand bunker, but with decent lies. Danikov's player ate too much turf with his swing and the ball ended up way short of the cart path at the bottom of the hill.

As the spirit players floated down the hill, Santan beckoned Clayman in his direction. "You know, your problem doesn't lie with your player choices," Santan said. "Your problem is with Danikov. He's a good golfer, but he has you thinking too much instead of obeying the feelings that have always served you well."

"What do you mean?" a wary Clayman responded.

"Well, for example, your sense that your girlfriend is off on a whimsical tangent with her attempt to somehow twist two religions together to make a whole one. Danikov as much as said it's your problem as much as it is hers. I doubt he cares that you're confused."

"I suppose you do," Clayman said.

Santan nodded. "I wouldn't be talking to you about it if I didn't, would I? And I'll take it a step further. You're smart to be a skeptic on this religion thing. If you spend your time thinking there'll be a better tomorrow, you'll miss life's boat entirely. Today is yesterday's tomorrow, so it's important to live for today. Live for the present. Live for your feelings."

"You know," Clayman said, appreciating Santan's empathy even though he suspected his motives, "I've never had an interest in the supernatural, and I don't have a clue as to what's going on with us. I don't like to be pushed in *any* direction, but Sheila used to try being my conscience. For example, she used to get on me about my acts of righteousness."

"Too few?"

"No. Too visible."

"Too visible?"

"Yeah. She used to quote a scripture about being careful not to do your righteous acts merely in order to have them be seen by men."

"Like I say," Santan said, "you were worried about your future when you were alive, and that turned out to be fruitless. As a result you suffered both in the present and in your perception of what the future would bring. Don't let everything get away again. There simply aren't any absolute answers. Besides, you'll never find a more hypocritical group than Christians."

"Well, I guess they're as fallible as the rest of us," Clayman admitted.

"Look," Santan said, "I'm a mathematician and for me to admit to the lack of absolutes isn't easy, but it's the truth. You gotta get the odds on your side. For example, the odds favor my team winning both the match and the argument," Santan said smugly.

"You haven't won anything," Clayman protested. "You're only ahead. And I wouldn't give you an edge yet on the other matter."

Santan's eyes narrowed. "You're wrong on both counts and I'll tell you why. First, we obviously exist in a spirit form and since we're external to the actual play, we're merely observers. Interpreters at best. Yet—and get this—I've learned how to physically impact the match."

Clayman smiled. "Have you now? That sounds to me more like a wish than an absolute. You aren't even likely to win this hole. Your two players are in the sand and my partner's player is in great shape."

"That's my point. Player talent aside, you only have one good chance, while we have two. You originally had two chances also, but I interfered with one of them. Granted, we may not actually win the hole, but I certainly improved our odds."

"Look," Clayman continued his argument, "I picked a player talent by chance. She misclubbed when the wind suddenly shifted. You got lucky."

"The wind shifted, did it?" Santan asked. "If you had been watching the treetops when she actually hit, you would have noticed there was no wind direction change at all. All that changed was the flag's direction."

Clayman blinked once and then frowned, shaking his head in disbelief. "The flag?" he said. "You mean you want me to believe you somehow changed the wind direction of the flag so that she actually hit with the wind instead of against it?"

"What are the odds of that happening coincidentally?" Santan asked.

"Several things come quickly to my mind," Clayman replied. "First of all, I don't believe you can manipulate physical objects. And if you did, that's cheating. And if you could do it and if you don't mind cheating, telling me about it is stupid."

"For something to be a violation there would have to be a rule forbidding that specific thing." Santan measured his words carefully. "None exists. More importantly, understand that I am capable. The others aren't. Forget Randall, he's a loser. Although Danikov has confidence in himself and in his beliefs, by his own admission he doesn't really care what you or I believe. That's his weakness. I, on the other hand, have a conviction to show you that blind trust is not nearly as admirable as talent."

"What are you trying to do, Santan? Get me to go into the tank on the match? I wouldn't consider doing that under any circumstance."

"No, of course not. I enjoy matching wits with good competitors. We wouldn't have anything to occupy us if we didn't have the golf challenge. In the event this match lasts forever, however, I want you to know I have the talent to help you reach other opportunities which may make themselves known to us at some point. Without me you'll need great fortune because you certainly won't have the advantage."

Clayman found himself both irritated and confused by Santan.

"What was that all about?" Danikov asked as he joined Clayman in hovering over their remaining viable player and the approach shot she was about to make.

"Nothing. He was just talking trash to me." Then, almost as an afterthought, Clayman said, "What can you tell me about hypocrisy in the church?"

"Whoa," Danikov said, throwing up his hands in exaggerated surprise. "Where did that come from? Was that part of Santan's trash talk? Look, Paul, people are human. Some people feel that if they can find an excuse for rejecting the church on grounds of hypocrisy, real or imagined, they can feel free to reject Christianity as well. Lots of otherwise good people hide behind that rationale by not attending church or reading the Word."

Clayman himself wondered why he had asked the question.

Randall approached Santan, saying, "Well, partner, what did you learn fraternizing with the enemy?"

"Merely probing. I haven't yet located Clayman's hot button, but I will."

Clayman's player had chosen not to hit a second ball from the tee and had retrieved her wayward ball from the homeowner's yard while Danikov's player barely reached the green's fringe with her shot. "Damn!" Clayman cursed, his confusion turning to anxiety.

Neither of their opponents' shots managed to clear the sand on the first try, however, which elicited two loud cheers from Clayman. The two players each settled for two-putting, making fives on the hole. Danikov and Clayman watched with growing enthusiasm as their remaining player stroked her long putt. The ball crept closer and closer on its slightly downhill roll until it finally stopped close enough to the hole for her own opponents to concede the next one. Clayman exulted in his team's win as he once again attempted unsuccessfully to high-five Danikov.

As Clayman glanced at Santan with a 'take that!' look he was also puzzled on several counts. Firstly, what had his opponent meant by saying he could physically impact their game? How would that be possible? How did he come by such confidence? And why then hadn't Santan won this hole? But he didn't actually claim he would. Could he be setting him up by not showing his claimed trump card? After all, there had been no additional bets on the hole.

Secondly, Clayman was confused by his own demonstrative, out-of-character shot reactions on the last hole. While he didn't know the answers to these questions, he did know his team had whittled the match deficit from ten to eight. Big deal, he thought. He couldn't resist needling his partner. "I told you we should have pressed."

Thirteen

Waiting for the next group to appear on the tee, Santan said to the others, "You all remember that we dropped our 'trash' game when the lightning took us out because it didn't fit our spirit match format. Now, to liven things up—sorry, no pun intended—I propose we put 'trash' back into the game, but in a different form. Suppose on a given hole, if someone opts to invoke it in advance, we allow the team making the first player selection the option of also naming a two point bonus feature for that one hole."

"Give us an example," Clayman said.

"Doesn't matter," Santan answered. "Could be a birdie or even winning with a bogey, or something really wild. Or if someone wants to take an altogether different approach, he could call the point for the team taking two or more shots from the sand, like a player did on the last hole. Call it 'bingo, bango, bongo,' or 'creative trash.'"

"Wait a minute," Danikov said, an old habit causing him to attempt to scratch his nonmaterial hair. "I wonder if we could put 'goofy' golf on hold for a little bit. Let's consider our precarious predicament. I doubt we've been thrust together into this situation merely to enjoy ourselves."

"Spoken like a fool," Santan said.

"If so I'd have to say I'm in pretty good company."

Randall took the remark as an insult and made a tentative hand gesture to object, but then dropped his hand and with it his objection.

Danikov completed making his point. "Solomon," he said, "who may have been the wisest man who ever lived, on his deathbed looked back on his life and arrived at a single profound conclusion. Which of these two statements do you think he made, 'He who dies with the most toys wins?' or 'Fear God and keep His commandments?'"

"We're not on our deathbeds. We're well past that point," Santan said sarcastically as he anxiously looked up hill for the next foursome to approach the tee.

"Hmm," Clayman said, becoming more and more pensive, "You don't suppose our presence here might somehow be a metaphor?"

Randall waved his hand downward and frowned. "Metaphor?" he said. 'Blind accident' maybe, but 'metaphor?'"

"Paul," Danikov said. "You may have something. Barnabas as much as confirmed our earlier notion about our needing to sort things out."

"Now that idea is dead-flawed," Santan said. "Neither Randall nor I believe in your God to begin with—and Clayman is closer to our position than he is to yours. And if you say your God is personally taking a hand in our little group affair, I say that's superstition talking!"

At that Danikov dropped his head into his hands and prayed aloud. "Father God," he said, "forgive these men. They simply don't understand that you love them regardless of what they've done." Danikov appeared overcome and could say no more for the moment.

Randall laughed and said, "I'll bet we could think of a few things that wouldn't qualify."

"Never mind," Santan said to Randall. He turned to Danikov and with an exaggerated motion with his hands, said, "Rise, my son. You are forgiven your sins. Go and sin no more. Now, could I have an 'Amen' for getting on with the game?"

"Praise the game," Randall said, but without a full measure of conviction.

"Let's play," Clayman said, frankly uncomfortable with either side of the argument.

Danikov spoke slowly, resolutely. "I don't know what it is in some men's character that permits them to openly blaspheme, but there are some sins even Jesus will not forgive."

"I'm not surprised to hear that," Randall said.

Clayman wondered if either Randall or Danikov had a back-up to their points, but apparently not. Clayman shrugged it off.

Danikov was studying the beautiful vista the seventeenth tee afforded. For the first time he realized that the season had apparently not changed from their real-life time. Summer's greens still prevailed. How long had they been on their journey, he wondered. Days? Weeks? Longer?

The group was still waiting for Danikov's vote on resuming play. "Look," he said, "if what you all want at this point is to continue the match then I won't be the one to break it up. In fact, we might all be here for that very reason, to play out the match. That's fine with me, but beyond that it's my fervent prayer that each of you come to realize a far more important opportunity."

"And that would be . . . ?" Clayman queried.

"That each of you accept God's grace in choosing to spend eternity *with* your Maker, rather than *without* Him. Personally, I would call the latter being cast into Hell."

"Suspending for a moment the truth or not of that statement," Randall said, "why do you honestly care at all?"

Danikov was surprised by the question, but also appreciated being asked the reason for his hope. "There is no Plan B," he said. "Christ nas no other plan for reaching unsaved people except to use people who are already saved."

"Randall," Santan said sternly, "stop asking open ended questions of the Right Reverend here, unless you don't mind him mounting the pulpit. I have a question of my own. Does anyone have an objection to my game modifications?"

"Not me," Danikov said, "but I'm curious as to why the change. I don't suppose you'd care to share your angle with us?"

"Angle?" Santan asked. "You have a suspicious mind, preacher. But all right, let's analyze 'my angle.' We each pick our players without knowledge of their relative game and we rotate that first player choice among us. Seems to me one team has precisely the same chance of success as the other, unless someone—actually, a team of two—should have a long run of bad luck. Now what's wrong with chance? You're pretty big on unseen forces."

Danikov flinched. His instinct before he had begun to mature in his Christianity would have been to bare his teeth and snarl, perhaps even make a move towards his offender. That was before he grew to become more sensitive to wrongdoing. In fact, even since they had turned their spiritual corner he was finding himself even more moved and grateful when he thought of what Christ had done for him on the cross. "Full-flaps," he said to himself.

Clayman was aware of Santan's increasingly hostile attitude. He could also see that restraint for Danikov, while it didn't seem to come naturally, was now solidly under his control. Both men were changing with the spiritual transformation.

"Gentlemen," Danikov said, "this is hardly an accountability group, but I need to remind myself that some Christians and non-Christians alike believe that faith is a personal matter that should be kept to oneself. While no one wants to be confronted by obnoxious witnessing, it is stated very clearly in First Peter that we should always be prepared to give an answer for the hope Christians have. The last part of that verse is what I'm having the most trouble with lately: 'Doing so with gentleness and respect.'"

Clayman wondered why these two men baited each other so openly. To him it was increasingly clear that both their arguments were reasonably persuasive. Clayman didn't care for Santan, personally, but neither could he entirely dismiss some of his points. Clayman was no less confused than he had ever been. As much for himself as for them he realized they could all use a diversion.

"Time out," he said, making a 'T' with his hands. "Look, speaking of a challenge on the golf course, let me tell you something that happened to me a few years ago."

Randall and Santan groaned in unison. Danikov said, "I yield the floor to the honorable spirit from Georgia."

"Bear with me on this one," Clayman said. "You'll love it. I bought a hole-in-one insurance policy for my grandfather for his birthday. Granddad had only recently taken up golf at age seventy-five. I loved him, but he was obstinate and immediately adopted his own version of the game. A week after his birthday I got a phone call from the pro at the club where I played. The pro said, 'Your grandfather just signed himself up on your ticket and asked for a bucket of practice balls'."

"I said, 'O.K. What's the problem?'"

"'The policy you bought him," the pro said. 'He isn't playing. He's planted himself on the shortest par three on the golf course, with the practice balls. He's trying to make a hole-in-one, for crying out loud. Come and get him.'"

"That's rich," Danikov said, laughing.

Santan also laughed and said, "There's a man who knew what he wanted."

Randall said, "What'd your granddad say when he was hauled away?"

"He didn't see the humor in it. When I explained how the policy actually worked all he could say was, 'That's a hell of a birthday gift!'"

All of them cracked up again. Clayman smiled at their reaction, but then his expression took on a distant look. *I told that story again! Why do I do that?* Clayman had no grandfather that he recalled ever meeting. When he had first entered college he discovered that all his friends liked to tell funny family stories. Clayman hated that he had no good family stories to tell. No warm ones. No funny ones. So he made up both a story and a grandfather.

Santan sobered quickly, saying, "Players on the tee! My partner is in the barrel this hole. Pick your player, Randall, and name your tune."

The spirit foursome had been milling around near the green so they quickly whooshed back up to the tee to inspect the new arrivals. "O.K.," Randall said. "Let's try the bonus deal at least once. I like the birdie-or-better idea, and . . . I'll go with this guy." He pointed to the golfer with a full-sized, but quite worn golf bag filled with a lot of persimmon woods, but very few irons. "Either he doesn't play much," he said, "which makes him an unfortunate choice on my part, or he trusts his swing. I'm banking on the latter." The answer to that question would not be the grand surprise on this hole.

FOURTEEN

Randall's player's shot with an eleven-wood arched beautifully from left-to-right toward the center of the green, but the ball was struck a little too high of dead center and as a result it touched down a bare two feet short of the green. Landing as it did from such elevation into the modestly uphill, medium-soft fairway the ball's advance should have been immediately arrested, never to reach the green. Shouldn't have. As the ball left the player's club head, Randall was calling the shot as if it were a horse race: "He has the green covered, but does he have enough club for the height . . . I don't know, maybe . . . no, has to be a tad short . . . yeah, it is . . . whoa, whoa, look at that crazy bounce . . . must have hit a sprinkler head or something . . . hey, it's gonna make the green . . . no, even better than that . . . it's still rolling . . . rolling . . . still rolling . . . I don't believe it! It's a gimme. A tap-in for a birdie."

Danikov was amused by the one-in-a-thousand shot, but Clayman was incredulous. "That didn't look natural," he said, glancing at Santan, who said nothing, but shook his head and smiled.

"Sometimes you get a break," Danikov said, "and sometimes the other guy gets it."

"Yow," said an excited Randall, "that'll not only stop the hemorrhaging from the last two holes, partner, but it comes on the new 'bonus' hole. Can I call 'em or what?"

The next two players—one selected by each team—both hit wayward shots, one off to the left of the green and into the rough and on the steep down hill. The other apparently out-of-play shot dug itself a miniature crater in the left hand green side bunker. Sitting in the sand as it was the ball looked like a fried egg. Danikov said to Clayman, "We still have our anchor player. For fun, why don't you call the shot like Randall."

"I'm in, coach," said Clayman, responding instantly to Danikov's effort to settle him. In his best Howard Cosell imitation he bent to the task with even more enthusiasm than had Randall. "Laaadieees and gennntlemennn," he said, "on the tee, the Danikov-Clayman match saver. In the brown two-tone soft spike shoes with matching golf shirt, and hailing from Hotlanta, Georgia, we have Frankie Finesse, the player of this spirit's choice."

"Save your creative breath, Clayman," Randall chided. "What are the chances of two guys in a foursome with twenty-plus handicaps both hitting career shots?"

Clayman ignored the logic and glanced at Santan as he answered Randall's question with one of his own. "What are the chances of *anyone* getting the kind of freak break your man got?"

"Listen up, gentlemen," Clayman said as he continued his tee shot commentary. "His take away is fast . . . whoops, his down swing faster . . . he sends the ball forward and low in the general area of the green, but a little right . . . one soft bounce on the fringe parallel to the pin, and . . . what's this? . . . yet another lucky break! The little white ball has struck the giant fan on the first bounce . . . it caroms left onto the green. Now it's rolling, rolling, rolling towards the hole . . . and right on line . . . oh, no, this couldn't happen, could it? . . . maybe. . . just maybe . . . yes! It's *in* the hole! I don't believe it! Folks, you've just witnessed an unbelievable shot culminating in a once-in-a-million hole-in-one!" Clayman clutched his chest and made his best imitation of a backward fall and a mock faint. He quickly rose and again attempted an unsuccessful high-five with Danikov as both laughed uproariously.

Randall was sullen-faced. Santan looked sharply at Danikov, saying, "That was a lot more than a lucky break. We declare outside interference, and the shot void."

Danikov responded by shaking his head and frowning. Then, with a quick glance heavenward he said, "Father, I'm sorry, but it's easier to beg forgiveness than to ask for permission." Turning to Santan he said, "You're not only arrogant and asinine, you're a no-class jerk. Appeal rejected!"

Clayman was more subtle in his response. "As my high school basketball coach used to say, 'suspicious people proceed from experience.' So, in wrapping up, ladies and gentlemen," Clayman said, returning once more to his commentator role, "all points figured, the Danikov-Clayman team is now only four down to Santan-Randall. The 'mighty mo' now belongs to the team with the greatest . . . fans!" He turned to Danikov, saying, "Sorry, partner, it was too tempting."

Danikov covered his ears and in a patronizing tone said, "The only one listening to you is me and I'm getting a little nauseous."

Santan would not yield without rebuttal. "You have some serious payback coming," he said, looking directly at Danikov. "Momentum has positive value only for a body in motion. Stop the body, stop the momentum. 'Dead' don't move," he said in deliberately lapsed grammar.

FIVETEEN

THIS IS REMARKABLE, thought Clayman. We're revisiting the same tee for the umpteenth time and yet I'm as excited this time as I was the first time. *And I'm not even playing!* Of course he wasn't exactly limited to watching either, but he couldn't resist musing about why the game of golf was so innately appealing to most golfers, however poorly they played. Maybe it was the individual nature of the game, or perhaps the continuing opportunity to start over after a mistake, or was it simply the potential for instant gratification for the expenditure of such a small effort? Since taking up the game Clayman had felt that the inherently personal nature of the game in its unrestricted and inspiring outdoor setting made golf the ultimate escape from stress.

He was also aware that he was unusually introspective following the unlikely events of the previous hole. Then another thought struck him. If he represented the spirit form of his own living body, then all humans must have spirits, whether that implied a faith belief or not. The thought also occurred to him that perhaps he could *sense* the spirit of one of the real-life players. After all, Santan claimed to be able to effect minor external influences, which he claimed to have proved with the pin flag flying against the wind. And in spite of Danikov's disclaimer to the contrary, Clayman still suspected his partner of having some sort of influence on that incredible hole-in-one. Well, then, might he also have some special undiscovered ability?

The new group arrived at the hilltop and dismounted from their golf carts. The player picks were made, including the random choice by Clayman. The other three spirits then whisked themselves downhill to watch the incoming shots, but Clayman stayed behind. He checked the name badge on his player's golf bag and tried calling to him aloud. "You, Johnny Simpson, look around if you hear me." Nothing. Clayman repeated the phrase several times with varying loudness and concentration. Still no response.

He tried again to communicate. This time, although as before he focused on his player by name, he used thought rather than voice, and added a slight variation of the message. "Yo, Johnny Simpson, look around if you sense me." Nothing. He tried it again and again. Still nothing.

The players all hit. As the riders mounted their carts for the steep, downhill-braking ride, Clayman had yet another idea. He would also ride, but not entirely passively.

Clayman boarded the cart and entered precisely the same space as his player cart-driver. Not knowing what to expect, he again projected his silent mantra. "Hello, Johnny Simpson's spirit. If you detect my presence, look around." Two things suddenly happened. Clayman first felt a rejecting, almost rebuking, presence. Secondly, the player-driver jerked his head at the exact moment they were making the third and most deceptive of the four turns of the serpentine cart path. As he looked sharply left on the right-turning curve the cart continued straight ahead and off the path, instantly overturning and spilling golf bags, clubs and one player.

The driver only half fell out as his left arm was pinned by the weight of the cart, breaking it. Clayman emerged from the player's space as if under attack, emotionally appalled by what had just happened. All he could do was observe the ensuing commotion. The second rider was unhurt and rushed to the fallen player's aid as he called to the two other players for help. Within minutes they had removed the two golf bags from the second cart and loaded all four players into it. Off to the clubhouse they sped, leaving the scene of the accident with the littered evidence scattered across the hole in the form of golf clubs, four golf balls in play, and one totaled golf cart.

The other three spirit players had quickly and excitedly arrived on the scene and offered mixed reactions. Danikov, looking incredulous, had simply said, "What happened?"

Randall laughed and said, "I've heard of using 'gotchas' when your opponent has an edge, but this is the ultimate. You tried to take out our man?"

Santan tried to gauge a hidden meaning and asked, accusingly, "Just how were you involved in this?"

"I'm innocent," Clayman protested. He then tried to explain the accident. "For laughs I got into the cart with them." The need for rationalism then set in for Clayman and he put some spin on his revelation. "The driver was looking around instead of paying attention to his driving and he overshot the curve. I hope he'll be all right."

"Well," Santan said, "here are the facts as I see them: the two wrecked players effectively withdrew, your uninvolved player was trapped on the left with no green to work with, and our free man was on the green and would have easily two-putted for par. We claim the win."

"Glad you're so concerned about the accident victims," Danikov said, derisively. "As for your usual claims agent tactic, forget it. The hole's a carryover. We're still four down with four points riding on the next hole. Paul, don't worry about it. Broken bones heal."

As the foursome lazily floated off Santan approached Clayman and motioned for him to hang back for a moment, saying, "Look, I know you were a party to what happened. I watched you merge sprits. I'm impressed. The real facts are you and I can do things the others can't. Or if they can, they either haven't the imagination or the will to try. That's what sets us apart. That's why we get what we want. We're aggressive because we believe in ourselves. We worship Lombardi: 'Winning is everything.' What you just did proves you're a lot closer to my philosophies of life than Danikov's."

Feeling guilt from his effort, Clayman shrugged and said, "Maybe so."

Sixteen

Another live foursome was on the tee and Clayman could see from the seventeenth green that Santan and Danikov were animatedly discussing something. The increasingly reluctant intermediary turned to Randall and said, "Artie, I don't know which we have here, a match being constantly distracted by opposing spiritual perspectives or a spiritual discussion being continuously interrupted by a golf match."

"I hadn't thought about it that way," Randall said. "Either way, though, you really are a classic fence sitter. You ought to fall one way or the other. Frankly, I think Luke is less of a bigot than Tommy Ray. Personally though, I'd rather get back to virtual golf."

"Surprising as it may seem to you," Clayman said, "I admit the need to get off of dead center. And I think the only way to get there is with greater input. You might benefit as well. Since we have no resources at our disposal other than ourselves, we need to dig deeper with what we have. Come on, I've been thinking about this for a while. Back me up."

Clayman and Randall whisked themselves to the back of the seventeenth green where Santan and Danikov were still talking, their hands and arms carrying much of the burden for communication.

"Gentlemen," Clayman said, "we've been going at both this golf match and the wherefores of our spiritual limbo without rest since the lightning dispatched us. I propose a serious break. For starters I suggest we let the next few groups play through without being harangued by the spirits of RiverTree."

"I agree," Randall-the-shill said. "In fact, the best place to do it is on the terraced flat at the left side of the fairway, under a shade tree."

"Good idea," Danikov said, moving in the direction of the tree Randall had pointed to.

Santan reluctantly drifted in the same direction, commenting as he went, "Yeah, we wouldn't want to get sunburned."

Randall joined them, beaming at the others' acceptance of his suggested site. "Now," Clayman said, as he shuffled around unnecessarily in making himself symbolically comfortable, "since we don't really need rest, here's what I propose we do for a change of pace. Artie and I have come to the conclusion that serving two masters is not particularly productive."

Randall raised one palm, saying, "That's because I serve no master, mate, but sail on."

"Thank you for your forbearance, Mister Randall," Clayman said, appreciating the lightness of the moment. "While we have virtual golf on hold, I would like to examine our different spiritual perspectives in greater detail. I suggest we each try to explain how we have come to our particular belief, or lack of it. Go as far back in life as we care to. This might actually be the first time in our lives we've done this. Who'd like to go first?"

"I'll sing," Randall wisecracked. "But I'm not a lead."

"You all go ahead with your sob stories," Santan said. "I'm not interested."

"Well," Danikov said, "in spite of your notions to the contrary, Paul, I'm a pretty private guy to be hanging out my soul on a clothesline. This is your idea to champion, so you solo first."

Seventeen

"Well, I asked for it, so I might as well get it on," Clayman began. "Frankly, I don't know how a shrink would see it, but I think I became a sometime seeker of truth out of my parents' and stepfather's confusion. My mother divorced once and she should have a second time. With all their problems I had to distance myself too early in life. That made me cynical and as a result I worshiped activity. With those sort of opposing forces pulling me I ended up on the fence—a skeptic in search of fulfillment. My favorite color was gray."

The other three settled in as much as their personalities and spirit forms would allow. Santan floated upright with folded arms while Danikov stretched out horizontally with hands clasped behind his head. Randall simulated propping himself up against the tree as Clayman continued his oral self-examination. "I read a lot as a young man, biographies mostly. Everything from Red Adair to Warren Buffet. Of course you know I'm Jewish, but that isn't all that defines me. In contrast to Danikov I've never had a desire to seek spiritual answers through reading, including the Torah or the first five books of what Christians refer to as the Old Testament. College was the last time I read anything on comparative religions."

Danikov pulled one arm from behind his head and gestured, saying, "Don't most religious Jews substitute the word 'only' for the 'old' testament, and in fact replace 'testament' with 'covenant?'"

"I can't honestly say," Clayman answered. "But I've certainly never contemplated reading your New Testament." He paused. "Actually, if I analyze that statement, it's rather curious. Since we're in sort of a confessional mode here I recognize that I'm a self-declared Renaissance Man who professes no interest in reading any of what is supposedly the greatest collection of biographies in the history of man: the Bible."

"Tell me, Did your friends feel the same way as you when you were growing up together?" asked a suddenly brightened Danikov.

"Good question. My friends were a mix of mostly secular Jews and non-religious Gentiles. Only one really had faith and he called it Reformed Judaism. He liked to make general distinctions among what he referred to as Conservative, Hasidic, Orthodox, Reconstructionist, in addition to his family's Reformed version."

"I take it," Randall said, "that the Reformers are the most liberal and assimilated group."

"I think so. Most of our little group seldom or never attended either synagogue or church. My faith friend referred to the rest of us as pagans. Several of my friends called themselves Christians, but none of them actually claimed to read the Bible. I recall one particular Christian friend who attended a lot of activities at his church, but didn't accept Christ as his savior. I asked him about it once, but he had no explanation."

"Your friend," Danikov said, "entirely missed the point of Christianity. If one does not believe in Christ, it will do him no good to wait for the Messiah for salvation. Salvation will not go looking for your friend. He has to go looking for the Way."

"You mean," Santan said very deliberately, "*a* way."

"No," Danikov said, rising to face his perpetual challenger. "The *only* way. Scripture repeatedly says of God, through his prophets and through Jesus himself, 'No one comes to the Father except through the Son.'"

"Sorry," Santan said, "that's no sale for me. I'm Popeye. I am what I am. And that means belief in *no* God. You want my credo in a nut shell, here it is: Success in defending my belief in a lip-service, God-fearing world consists of knowing that blind faith and a supposed hereafter are fanciful substitutes for reality and belief in self."

Clayman laughed and said, "That's all well and good, but the four of us now at least believe there is life after death."

"These times are transient at worst, dreams at best," Santan rebutted.

Randall, who had given up on an esthetic attachment to the tree and had been lazily floating about was becoming uneasy with what Clayman's self-revelation might portend for his own case. "You want to wrap things up so the others can have a shot?" he said.

"You'll get your turn, Artie," Clayman said. "I always knew I'd land right side up if I persisted, so I got myself through college by way of geology. Surely, I thought, that would lead to some immutable answers. Turned out that studying rock and mineral deposits, sprinkled with the remains of prehistoric sea life, is no place to ponder the meaning of intelligent life."

Clayman was riffling through memory files of his many field trips to rocky places. "I recall being tremendously impressed by the awesomeness of the time line in the Grand Canyon. Some of those Canyon cuts are so deep that there are exposed fragments of Precambrian rock as old as two billion years."

"A trip to the Grand Canyon messed up your life?" Santan asked.

"No. It's only that the record of new life form appearances, cataclysms and mass extinctions are so vivid in those rocks that it suggests something of our own fate."

"Well," Santan said, "I see we have at least two votes for evolution. Randall, you in?"

Before Randall could respond, Danikov said, "Let's don't manufacture yet another subject for divisiveness. This might surprise you, but I don't think science and faith are mutually exclusive. Nowhere in the Bible does it say that God prohibited any of his living creatures—including His people—from any sort of physical change with the progression of time."

"Heresy!" shouted Santan in mock surprise.

"No," Danikov said. "But maybe the perception of it. Neither I nor the church can stomach macro-evolution, which is what you're advocating. For the same reason I think your hero, Sagan, should have recognized that the very intricacies of subatomic particles and the incredible vastness of his 'billions and billions' of stars make a statement for awe of the God who caused everything to be. How could order possibly be the result of randomness? So too should

Christians believe some micro-evolution of life can't diminish the awesome power of the Creator." Danikov paused. "Sorry, Paul," he said. "This is supposed to be your time."

Clayman took a deep symbolic breath. "All that geological stuff was only the beginning of critical mass for me. Then came the volcano . . ."

Randall interrupted. "Volcano?"

"One Sheila Levin. Volcanic. Lava meets seawater. Gray meets black or white. But you know, I think I messed her up, too, with what I told you earlier. One man's lack of faith tangles with a strong faith, hybrid or no, and whadd'ya get? Desperation. I'm still a guy in search of his soul, if I have one. I missed not having family I could turn to. If my Mother hadn't aborted my only sibling, I might have had *someone*."

Clayman wanted to weep. He had neither anticipated the fullness of such a confession nor the depth of his hidden feelings on the subject. He had buttoned things up for so much of his life that the emotional gate holding everything back suddenly collapsed. Softly, he cried out in despair, "Oh, God."

No one said a word at first, then Danikov rushed to him and offered symbolic comfort by placing an arm around his shoulders, "God has not forsaken you, even now. He simply doesn't do things on our timetable. He won't be late, however, and that I can promise you, Paul."

Danikov turned to the others and said, "Clayman has been very candid. I don't know what's more precious than sharing personal insights. As I said earlier, witnessing is a big part of Christianity, although until I met this group I admit I was reluctant."

To the extent that their spirit forms allowed it, Santan wrinkled his face as he said, "Danikov, when your turn comes you'll no doubt burden us with your own convictions, but in defense of poor Clayman's—or anyone else's—beliefs, let me ask you a question."

Danikov nodded.

"You believe that your God, Jesus Christ, and the Holy Spirit are three persons in one. Yet the Jewish version of the 'one truth' acknowledges the same God, but rejects your Holy Spirit altogether and simply recognizes Jesus as one of many teachers or prophets. So, can one belief in an aspect of the world be more correct than another, without scientific proof by either?"

Danikov was surprised that Santan would actually care to participate in an open ended spiritual discussion. Jumping eagerly into the subject matter Danikov said, "Let me ask you this question in response. Does stacking one false assumption on top of another build a foundation any stronger than its base block?"

"My point precisely," Santan replied. "Let me illustrate the underlying false premise of your one faith argument. Suppose you were a totally objective visitor arriving on Earth from another planet. You're intent on learning some truths. We can safely say your civilization is far more advanced than ours or you wouldn't be arriving on the scene at all. You're studious, and one of the first things you learn is that there are about as many different religious beliefs on Earth as there are different races and populations. Would you expect only one of those beliefs to be absolute? Or would you have to conclude that most, if not all of them, served some beneficial, however subjective, purpose?"

"That's a good point," Clayman said.

"Thank you," Santan said. "Now before you answer, let's take the analogy further. Suppose you were simply an objective new world visitor to America when the Pilgrims first landed. The different American Indian tribes all had very different gods and beliefs. Were some better or less than others? Or is a personal, spiritual belief, however it's formed, a natural condition for man? And to logically extend that argument, why would the *lack* of owning any one particular set of spiritual values be much different than having any one of them?"

"I know," Danikov said, "that you think anything I say can and will be used against me in a court of worldly men, but there is only one way given to us by God to be forgiven of sins—through believing in Jesus Christ as our savior. No other person, method or ritual can give eternal life."

"Such tolerance!" Santan's tone was sarcastic.

"Truth is more important than tolerance," Danikov said. "Opinions don't count, only truth does, otherwise you're dwelling in ignorance. Some people believe that all religions are equally valid paths to God. In a free society, people have the right to their religious opinions, but this doesn't guarantee that their ideas are right."

"But there *are* many other opinions and perhaps one or more of them is truth, " Randall said. "There's Buddha, there's Muhammad, and there are another half-dozen or more religion founders of the last hundred or so years."

"Of course, Artie," Danikov said, patiently, "in addition to those you have named there are Joseph Smith, Jr., Charles Taze Russell, Sun Myung Moon, Mary Baker Eddy, L. Ron Hubbard and others, but God simply doesn't accept man-made religion as a substitute for faith in Jesus Christ. He has provided just one way—his only begotten Son, Christ Jesus."

"You want to distill that a little?" Randall asked.

"All right," Danikov said. "Suppose your same visitor in either instance observed good people acting beneficially for others, and that they claimed redemption as a result of their acts. The problem here is that if this is the only reference for the individual's redemptive qualification the potential for also covering up sin is obvious. In other words—in the book of Ephesians—we're taught that Christianity is unique in teaching that the good deeds we do will not make us right with God. Good deeds are important, but they won't earn us eternal life. We are saved only by trusting in what God has done for us."

"And why do you think that would be?" Randall asked. "Because I don't think we can know the answer to that one."

"Artie," Danikov said, persisting as gently and respectfully as he could, "your ancestors and mine took it on faith that the sun would rise each day even though they didn't know why. Faith in the Lord is of a different—much more profound—nature."

"But what if truth is relative?" Randall responded with a searching expression.

"I think you know right from wrong just as Pontius Pilate did when he asked Jesus essentially the same question. Jesus had revealed Himself as 'the Way, the *Truth*, and the Life,' but the Roman governor failed to recognize that *the* Truth stood before him at that very moment."

"Thanks for putting me in the same boat with old Pontius," Randall said.

Clayman was fascinated not only by everyone's contributions, but by the fact itself. There wasn't much agreement, but there was dialogue. He had been guilty of subverting dialogue in many of his relationships over the years, fearing compromise of what little he had been able to hold on to that defined him as an individual.

I need to keep this group therapy rolling, Clayman thought. "Artie, why don't you take the next turn at bat?"

"O.K.," Randall said, "but if I'm steppin' into the batter's box—" he looked toward Santan and Danikov, pointing at them as he finished his comment, "then one of you two guys is on deck."

EIGHTEEN

Randall hesitated, fidgeted, then began slowly. "My story is short, but ironic. You're right about one thing, Tommy Ray. I don't much go for Clayman's grays. I like reds and yellows. A little color in life, like my skin. I never saw my greatest handicap in life as color, though. Heck, this missing right index fingertip caused me as much flak as being half black and half brown."

"You mean half black and half white," Santan said, simply intended as supposed factual correction.

"No. I mean half coal black and half sweet potato brown! My brown Jamaican daddy and my black New York mama taught me that everything has a purpose and nothing is without it. They could rationalize anything. So where'd I end up? As a reporter. Hah! Someone who finds objectivity in everything. First with a newspaper, then with a bigger newspaper, then it was a TV station, and finally I found home to be with a large ad agency.

"I wanted long titles and big money and I got both of 'em." Randall fully extended his arms and then snapped imaginary suspenders against his sprit's chest in symbolic punctuation. "The car I drove to this golf course has a bumper sticker on it that reads 'Greed Is Good.' I was happy with that. I might still be. What my employers got from me was a lot of talent and a bit of loyalty. All they had to do was point me in the direction of the enemy and say 'sic 'em.' I rolled back my lip and bit down hard. Too hard. Sometimes I broke a tooth."

"Sounds a lot like me at your age," said Danikov, nodding.

"Really? I wouldn't have guessed," Randall said. "Well, since I don't owe you guys anything, I'll be candid. I think maybe my positive public posture . . . well . . . my, my . . . aren't I alliterative in confession?"

"Don't take this personally," Santan said, "but some say alliteration is a subconscious way of compensating for insecurities."

"You mean you say so. What a charmer you are, partner. O.K., enough. That leads me to the big question, which is: Who am I now that I'm dead? Well, I'm still R. T. Randall, a believer in life being too complex to be defined by any one simple value, spiritual or otherwise."

"Artie," Danikov said, "you would deny the truth of a life after death when you yourself are speaking through a spirit form?"

"But we exist in isolation," Randall said. "This is no afterlife. It's neither heaven nor hell. We didn't even get to pick it."

"Salvation isn't so much a matter of choosing," Danikov said. "You either believe or you don't. You need only accept the salvation offered you by God's grace and you'll be by Jesus' side in the life hereafter."

"And woe to you who does not conform to that notion," Santan said.

Clayman couldn't let that pass. "And woe to anyone who accepts faith of *any* kind. Is that your gospel, Lucas?"

Randall eyed Danikov before asking him what he wanted throw onto the fire which had just been lit. "I'm ready to yield the floor, Padre, but I want to know what happened on your watch that qualifies you for Sanctimonious Witness."

"Thank you," Danikov said. "This very moment I was thinking that I've spent too much energy sharing *the* faith and not enough time sharing *my* faith. I couldn't possibly qualify for salvation on the basis of merit because Christ himself told us that not one is without sin."

Randall was startled by that comment. "Then exactly how has your supposed salvation come about?" he asked.

"Simply through the repenting of my sins and asking for forgiveness. God's store of Grace is always available. He's 24/7. You and Clayman and Santan could gain salvation in the same way as I did."

As Randall was about to pursue the point Santan preempted him by holding up an index finger and then using it to cock an ear. "I don't see or hear anyone coming down the aisle, preacher," he said.

Clayman leaned forward and pointed at Danikov. "I guess the floor is still temporarily yours," he said.

"We can only hope he sticks to his own story instead of minding ours," Santan said.

NINETEEN

CLAYMAN KNEW Danikov wanted to tell his story if only for the opportunity to 'witness' on behalf of the message in which he so strongly believed. At the same time, he sensed an odd reluctance on Danikov's part.

After several moments, Danikov spoke. "I appreciate that both Paul and Artie shared some very personal thoughts with us. That took guts. I've been thinking and praying to God a great deal since we made our unexpected, collective 'passing' yesterday . . . or last week . . . or last year . . . or whenever it was. Since we haven't yet seen either a sunrise or a sunset, I don't really know if time exists for us. Well . . ." He paused for another moment. "Sorry. I'm not used to talking about myself. When I first knew that Marilee was the one for me . . ." This time he paused involuntarily, blinked twice, then lowered his head. After another moment he raised his head and took a deep sigh.

Clayman was intently watching him, thinking. This man could not bear the thought of having lost his wife, which is obviously how he viewed the event of their dispatched foursome. Now that it had been discovered that this spirit group possessed the surprising ability to shed physical tears—if that's what they were—the ground beneath Danikov might well turn to mud. Clayman wished he felt such closeness with Sheila. Actually, he did, but then not being able to resolve their greatest difference also left Clayman confused and uncertain about his feelings for Sheila.

Danikov regained his composure. "Well," he said, laughing lightly, "I once had a naked lady tattooed onto my upper arm. Later in life I became embarrassed enough by it that I had it covered with a second tattoo. I lied about that for a long time."

"A naked lady with a cross, no doubt," Santan said.

"Actually, no. I'm a fourth generation Russian-American. My great grandparents emigrated here and brought with them their Russian Orthodox religion. I'm not absolutely certain they weren't Jewish, however. Over the years my family came to know Christ and even embraced Protestantism. At the time I arrived for this golf match I liked to think of myself as a disciple."

"You mean an evangelist," Santan said.

"I never thought of myself as possessing that particular gift, but since my maturity during our group journey, maybe evangelism is one of my God-given gifts."

"Don't be so bashful," Santan said. "If you aren't a bald-faced witness I sure as hell don't want to meet one."

"If I tell you a little more of my background maybe you'll better understand how that happened."

"Capsulize it," Santan said. We've got a golf match here."

"Patience, Luke," said Danikov. "Time is on holiday, remember? Besides, you'll get your turn in the witness chair." Santan propped his hand and arm under his chin in mock interest.

"If I had to name each of my parents with a single word," Danikov continued, "I'd use Pilgrim Progress-type names and call my father 'Instructive,' and my mother 'Encouraging.' I was self-confident, however, and thought I didn't need the approval of others." Clayman winced in appreciation for the characteristic most opposite his.

Danikov continued, saying, "I only started reading something other than the sports and business sections of the newspaper after I dropped out of the university before I finished my Freshman year. Too confining, college. One day, after a fight with my parents over my lack of taking an interest in anything I was loudly challenged by my father, but softly encouraged by my mother. Practically overnight I began reading anything and everything, from Louis L'amour to bricklaying-made-easy. I admit I wasn't reading the Bible, however."

Randall said, "'Evangelist Without A Message,' can be the title of your first book."

Danikov paused and shook his head. "If you'll be good for a bit longer, Artie, I'll promise to let you out to relieve yourself." The other two laughed. Randall looked annoyed.

Danikov continued. "It's a funny thing about how time can change a person so gradually you hardly know it's happened. Then one day you look back and see how far you've come. I served a little time in the early part of the Vietnam insanity. After having witnessed my share of death and destruction I had gradually came to fear my own death. Not the pain that might accompany it, but the result. I took that fear home with me." For all their wisecracking Clayman was aware that both Santan and Randall were interested in what Danikov then had to say.

"After a long time," Danikov said, "I finally began to both read and study, asking questions about my quasi-faith. The more questions I had, the hungrier I was for answers. My wife and I started going to church and we—well—I started praying for the first time in my adult life. Marilee had been there for a long time, but for her own reasons hadn't pushed me.

"I calculated that if I read sixty pages a week of my three-thousand page Bible I could finish in a year, which I did. To simplify a process that was much more than what I'm suggesting, I both found Christ and lost my fear of death." With that, Danikov nodded, tight-lipped.

Santan was about to say something, but decided to submerge the interest. Danikov was aware of Santan's hesitancy and paused before continuing. "Before the year's end we joined a church. For the next few months whenever I traveled on business I talked to people about their faith or the lack of it. Some people didn't want to talk about it at all. Others did. I met a messianic Jewish rabbi who had recently returned from Russia who told me how difficult, but rewarding it was to establish a messianic congregation in that post-Cold War country."

"Thanks to state-decreed atheism," said Clayman.

"Yeah," Danikov said, "used to be. Now it's even worse. The government, the Jewish community and the Russian orthodoxy are all hard-liners against establishment of *any* new church. That would likely mean more order in a basically chaotic and corrupt land. Add to this mix the Russian mafia which is fighting the messianic Jewish beachhead for the same reason. But my point is that this rabbi and his wife found a great hunger for the Lord by Russian Jews."

"That sounds paradoxical," said Clayman.

"I know. But simply declaring a nation atheistic doesn't chase God away. It only hides him and makes him more precious. My friend told me people begged for Bibles wherever they went."

"Interesting," said Clayman. "I need to understand something very basic. Let's move that same notion way back in time. What do you think first caused man to turn to religion in any form?" He gestured to the others as if needing a seconding interest in the subject..

"That's easy," said Santan, dismissively. "Lack of self-confidence."

"Actually," Danikov said, "I don't think you're far off. Only I'd call it human frailty. Man may not have been able to control disease or tragedy, but he could pray to the God who could. I've done some research into religion's impact in today's American society. I was shocked at what I discovered simply by 'clicking' on a broad variety of crusaders' and evangelists' efforts."

"There you go," Randall said. "Pornography and salvation; only a web site apart."

Danikov nodded in agreement. "I have to admit that it's easy to find religious guises geared to generating merchandise sales. But the thing that scared me a lot more than that was a Billy Graham message about the 'unrelenting aggressive secularization' in this country."

"Discriminating against unbelief again, are we?" Santan said.

"I'm simply calling a secularist a secularist. At the root of this challenge to Christianity is exclusion of God from the world and from daily human life. I've even heard the refrain from you, Luke, that you essentially live for the present with no reference whatever to God or divine morality."

Santan turned sharply to face Danikov. "Just who the hell do you think you are, John the Baptist?"

Danikov blinked twice as if regrouping. "Look, Luke, I'm not attacking you personally, only what you've been spouting. I still have plenty of live-and-let-live attitude in me. If you really want to go to hell, that's O.K. with me. I further confess that such attitude is still one of my own shortcomings."

"I rest on my position and you know what that is," Santan said.

"Let me jump into this kettle with you guys," Randall said. "There are those who would grant that a supreme be-ing exists, but surely not as a human son who lived as flesh and blood, let alone as the savior of the world."

"Artie, let me end this response to your comment with one of the most powerful statements ever uttered by Jesus. It was recorded in the gospel of John and has to do with the time of Abraham, Isaac and Jacob, about 2,000 years before the birth of Christ. The relevance is in the six words Jesus used to proclaim his divinity: 'Before Abraham was born, I am!'"

Clayman thought about that for a moment before speak-ing up, sensing that as interesting as Danikov's narrative had been it had come to an unorchestrated end. Turning to Santan he said, "This looks like a perfect segue for you, Luke. We're as interested in your story as everyone else's."

Randall echoed encouragement. "Yeah, that's right. Tell 'em what you told me. How can three-fourths of the world's population be either totally ignorant of the Way, or dead wrong?"

Smarting from some of Danikov's poignant remarks Santan quipped, "O.K., wise guys, but hang on to your wings. I'm not cuttin' you any slack!"

TWENTY

"DANIKOV," Santan said as he began his enthusiastic, personal eulogy over Christianity and all other religions, "you're a blind man being led by blind men. You forsake reason for sentiment. Clayman here at least puts his beliefs where he sees hard evidence. And he allows an indeterminate period of time for that evidence to develop. I think he's coming to the realization, however, that fence-sitting is hard work. Randall was the least misguided of the three of you in that he was convinced that absolute evidence of your God simply can't exist. It's a simple transition from that position to the growing and clear-headed movement of world atheism."

Clayman coolly observed the voiceless reaction of the group's members to Santan's opening argument. This would not be revelation so much as exposition, Clayman thought, but he would personally suspend belief in any direction until all the evidence was in. He could see Danikov recoiling, and noticed a deep sadness in his eyes. Randall nodded approval at Santan's generous recognition of him.

Then Santan softened his initial accusatory tone. "You men aren't entirely to blame for your convictions or the lack of them, however. There is a small, but disproportionately powerful and growing body of people in this country who believe that our choices in life are much more predictable than anyone would have imagined. By this I mean that man's free will is not nearly as independent as we have always thought."

"Your honor," Danikov said, apparently as perturbed as Clayman had observed, "the *persecution* has absolutely no case. I move for dismissal."

"Motion denied!" Santan said, eyes flashing as he glared at Danikov. "I'm about to present the first of the two parts of my case. A highly creditable outside group I once worked with labored for years in developing a software program that analyzed personal test data.

"What emerged was what we called a 'thought profile.' This profile gauged an individual's thought processes and placed a percentage on each of four thinking categories: rational, ordered, imaginative and empathetic. The higher the imaginative and empathetic percentages the greater the tendency for illogical belief systems. The higher the rational and ordered profile, the greater the likelihood for a more realistic set of beliefs. In other words, for the most part we are products of what we think about, and conversely we think about what we are."

Danikov was shaking his head. "Santan, if ever anyone has ever been found to be absolutely full of sh— . . . sand . . . it's you. You're one of those liberal, pseudo-academics who labor over words or numbers to 'prove' your theories and then advertise them as uniquely discovered universal truths. That's how cults develop that brainwash young people willing to buy the first mystical answer to wash up against their floating souls."

Santan looked angrily at Danikov before carefully measuring his words in response. "Thank you for the 'open-mindedness' you've brought to this little exchange. I suggest that you don't know the difference between what's real and what's vividly imagined. But you can't be blamed for that. We're all bound by some set of circumstances. If you merely trusted yourself to peer over the fence of spiritual imagination, however, reality would appear blinding.

"But this is all rhetoric," Santan continued. "Let me continue with the simpler second part. Basically, I don't believe in a deity simply because I don't believe in anything that isn't supported by scientific evidence."

"You do a great job as devil's advocate on things religious," Clayman said, "but if I may hop up onto the fence once again before you continue, I don't think yours is actually a majority position among scientists. According to surveys I've recently read, sixty percent of scientists believe in a deity."

"I don't believe that for a moment," Santan said, "but I'm glad you brought it up," He had an anticipatory gleam in his eye. "However many their actual number, they suffer from a common malady these days which is the attempt to rationalize incompatible belief systems. They would link logic with faith by wrapping them together with spaghetti. It's a quantum leap from possibility to probability."

"Santan," Danikov said, jumping in to take advantage of Clayman's interruption, "I've read a lot of books by scientists looking at religion. A good many of them make the case for life evolving by mere random chance as being smaller than the odds of hitting a golf ball around the world by caroming it off of satellites."

"I've read them also," Santan said, "and I heard your earlier argument refuting evolution at best and tweaking it at worst. The fact is you won't find more than a few of those same scientists who buy the Bible's creation story any more than skeptics like Clayman. At best they see it as a metaphor for evolution."

Randall finally felt compelled to weigh in on the subject. "I'm not so certain of that. MENSAS wanting to make their case that universe-spawned life could not be the product of mere chance are no less guilty of tweaking numbers than commercial marketers. We held to the theory at my agency that numbers tortured hard enough will confess to anything."

Clayman, sensing that they had not only gotten far off the track, but weren't allowing Santan his say said, "Gentlemen, we divert Santan from his turn here at Spirits Anonymous. I suggest we yield the floor to a serious devil's advocate." Clayman couldn't help himself. But there wasn't so much as a snort or a whuf from anyone. Where was this group's sense of humor?

Santan continued speaking without so much as thanking Clayman although he nodded as he spoke, looking directly at him. "I used to lament having no close friends until I learned that few people actually do have a same gender, non-sexual relationship friend close enough to regularly share their problems, feelings and struggles.

"That lesson not only reconfirmed my own loner tendencies, but explained my parents' materialistic and hedonistic values. Of course, those notions might have had something to do with my two failed marriages, but that's about average in this country, regardless of personal beliefs."

"Yeah," Randall said. "Marriage is a lot like Spam in a can. It's a tight fit, but it also comes with an opener." Only he and Santan laughed.

"Exactly," Santan said. "There's a lot of stuff out there without having to resort to pleasure-for-pay. In fact, I've found that the superficial nature of man can actually serve him well. By listening to your instincts you can avoid pain and hurt. For me there's no funnier sight than man's failures and ineptitude. They're not only predictable, they're confirming in themselves. I choose to rely on self because I see the math in it."

Clayman was surprised. He hadn't expected Santan to offer anything of a candid, much less sad, nature. He wondered how Danikov was taking all this. He glanced at him, but all he could read in the believer's face was restraint.

Santan continued with his litany. "Human life possesses five basic senses: sight, hearing, touch, smell and taste. Ever since the universe's Big Bang and then Darwin's evolutionary run some billions of years later, man has tried to wish a sixth sense into the matrix, more often than not involving spiritual mush. I can't blame early man simply because he knew so little and was afraid of the unknown. I find that attitude in this day and age extremely curious, when the fact is you live, then you die. It's that simple. We all live. We all die. Finis."

"You're only half right," Danikov said. "Everyone has to die, but not everyone has to stay dead. That's Jesus' promise."

"Spare me," Santan pleaded. As for us, I doubt this 'state' we're in is anything more than a phasing out. Then we'll be dead and done. Haven't you noticed we're all a little more wispy than we once were?"

Randall laughed uneasily, glancing down at himself.

"As hard as it is too believe," said an uncharacteristically agitated Danikov, "in spite of your words, you still have as good a chance as any of us to make it to the next leg, providing you rethink your position before it's too late. As for me, I ask the Lord for help in fighting the devil himself in not caring if you go straight to hell."

"Wow, that was close," Santan said, feigning wiping his brow. "At least you stopped short of actually wishing it. Now I ask the rest of you, is that any way for a born-again Christian to behave?" Randall raised both his hands, his eyes widened, but said nothing.

Clayman was also surprised. As he watched Danikov more closely he noticed that he twice wiped his face, unnecessarily of course.

Under pressure from the others Danikov replied, "None of us are sin free. I freely confess that I come up way short. And for that I genuinely ask the Lord's forgiveness. And you know what? I'm forgiven . . . though I may suffer the consequences of my sin."

"Fine with me," Santan said. "Stake out any position you like. That's exactly what I've done."

Randall couldn't resist the impulse to mime the monkey trio cliche by quickly and successively putting his hands over his eyes, ears and mouth.

"Good sense of timing, Artie," Clayman said. "A little 'comic relief' is in order. This is like a tennis match, with our heads snapping back and forth from one player to the other."

"O.K.," Danikov said. "then let me spank that ball again from this side of the net. Some of the Big Bang and other scientific notions Santan puts so much stock in are changing. In fact, in some ways they've actually undergone a reverse evolution. I recently read an article entitled 'God, the Evidence,' in which - -"

Santan interrupted, shrugging as he said, "By which evangelical Christian author would that be?"

"Christian, yes," Danikov said, "but also a scientist, a mathematician *and* a lifelong atheist until eight years before I read the article. His argument went that there has to have been a Creator, for all signs in every field point to intelligent design. He wrote of the overwhelming scientific body of truth that infinitely detailed purpose had to have been woven together or there couldn't be life anywhere in the universe."

Santan glared at Danikov. "I don't suppose you can put a name with your champion?"

"Patrick Gwyn."

"Big deal. You tweaked Randall's 'tortured numbers' to find your mathematician quote."

"Care for a biochemist?" Danikov asked. "Michael Behe, in 'Darwin's Black Box' proved through biophysiology that evolutionary chance is impossible under the laws of probability and common sense. To him, and to an increasing number of other scientists, that leads to the inescapable conclusion that there had to have been intelligent design, hence a Creator."

No one commented.

After a few moments Randall broke the silence, but looked a little nervous. "Enough chit-chat, men, what do you say we move the match along?"

"O.K. by me," Clayman said. He sensed that Randall might be uneasy over the toll Danikov's arguments seemed to be taking on Santan's position.

"Good idea," Santan said. "Let's go top side."

"You all go ahead," Danikov said. "I'll be along."

"Uh, oh, boys, that means he's going to break out in prayer again," Santan said, a smirk on his lips. "What is yours, or anyone's, purpose in praying?" Santan motioned for the other two to join him as he turned to depart, con-

sidering the question more rhetorical than otherwise. Before they could leave, however, Danikov answered. "When
I pray I believe my prayers will be answered."

Santan turned to respond. "Then expectation is your
motivation," he said.

"No, faith is my motivation. But if your question is
prompted by the mathematician in you, consider this:
There's more evidence to show measurable health benefits
from prayer and faith than scientists have supporting the
benefits of vitamin C as a treatment for the common cold."

Santan shook his head, glanced uphill and again motioned for the other two. He gathered them on either side
of him, placing one arm on a shoulder of each. They
whooshed up to the 17th tee. Clayman looked back at
Danikov, who had kneeled, but he couldn't hear the prayer.

TWENTY-ONE

"DEAR LORD," Danikov said, softly, "I need to say this. Not only have I put my complete trust in Jesus' death and resurrection for my salvation, knowing I've received forgiveness of sin based on His provision, and not on my behavior, but I now come to you to guide me through this unsettling experience with these unbelieving men. Affirmation was everywhere in life, but now I'm alone except for you, Father. I think endlessly about my beloved wife, Marilee, and my family's challenges in the face of my abrupt departure. I ask that you strengthen them. I praise you and ask these things in Jesus' Holy name. Amen." Danikov arose, turned and swished up the hill and back to the game.

"You're late," Santan said. "We've made our picks and everyone but your guy has already hit. You get the ninety-year old fart with the one-quarter swing."

Welcome back! Danikov thought. "Whatever happened to the concept of handicapping players in order to even the game?" he said, glancing downhill to see only one of the three balls in decent play. Santan did not address his complaint. Danikov watched his player take a practice swing from off the tee and well behind all the players and spirits. As he continued with his peripheral observation he pursued his point. "We did away with handicaps when the match shifted from live action to virtual reality, but my player is at a pretty obvious disadvantage."

Randall decided he could handle that objection. "By lot, you had the last choice. Would you have given me a stroke if I had been saddled with your guy?"

"I see what you mean," Danikov said.

"We'll make the most of it, partner," offered an encouraging Clayman. "Come on, let's try to psyche Santan and Randall while your guy is trying to find a club to use."

"Psyche?" Danikov said, turning the word over in his mind. "That gives me an idea."

Clayman briefly wondered what that could possibly mean, but both he and the other two spirit players were more intent on staring down the hill at the lead player's shot result, which was plainly showcased in good shape on the green's surface. After an initial hesitation Danikov made a decision. Unseen by the other spirits he quickly darted into and then slowly backed out of the super-senior's body as the older player took a practice swing with a well-lofted wood.

Simultaneous with Danikov's action, the player looked up sharply, swiveling his head to the left and then to the right, as if someone had spoken and disappeared. After several moments, the nonagenarian's eyes began to take on a steely look. His back straightened with determination. He aligned himself from well behind the teeing area to take a single, unobserved practice swing. He first took his routine club wag, but then he made a longer and much crisper back swing than normal. His down swing was equally fluid, with the follow through ending higher than normal. A surprised, can-do smile registered on his face.

Satisfied with his team's tee shot position Randall provided the initial kibitzing of Danikov's player. "I hope this guy has a fast down swing," he said. "because I don't think he has long to live."

"With little expectation Santan said to his opponents, "Tell you what, boys. Given that we have a player on the green with no more than an eight foot uphill putt for birdie, and given that Danikov's Methuselah has a five-metal in his hands on a short par three . . ."

Randall quickly jumped in, saying, "Partner! You aren't gonna do anything foolish are you?"

"Trust me," Santan said, continuing, "And seeing as how the 'B' team is crying over their misfortune in the player-draw this hole, suppose we give your guy a half-stroke and then accept a press on the bet?"

In other words," Danikov translated, "if our ninety year-old player suddenly finds his long lost swing *and* game and manages to *tie* your player already on the green . . ."

"Which player, by the way," Clayman said, interrupting Danikov, "is not only *on* the dance floor and directly in front of the judge's box, but is the *only* dancer on the floor."

"Yeah, yeah, I know all that," Danikov said, appearing to want to muzzle his partner. "You've had your turn calling the shots. Let me call this one." Looking at Santan, Danikov spoke to him. "Now let me get this right. Given your big advantage you're generously offering us the win if our man ties the score, providing we double the bet? Is that correct?"

"Keerect." Santan said, facetiously adding, "Although now that I've made the offer, I halfway regret it. Your man seems to have picked up a step in his stride." Santan glanced at Randall and winked.

Clayman didn't like it. Hadn't it been only a few holes since Danikov had cautioned him about letting emotion call his shots under negative circumstances? After having made such a fine comeback, they would now quite likely find themselves six down. He was about to object again, but Danikov caught his eye and nodded almost imperceptibly, lips closed and eyes intense. The message was clear: "Shut up!"

"You're on," said a nevertheless hesitant Clayman.

Randall's man was bunkered on the right while Clayman's was trapped in the sand on the left. Danikov's revitalized golfer strode briskly from the back of the tee to the markers and unfalteringly teed up his ball. As he straightened up he said aloud, "Boys, it must be all the sex I had last night, because I suddenly have the confidence of a senior on the Tour. I'm ninety-two and in search of my first par of the week."

Randall knitted a painful-looking frown onto his spirit face and glanced at his partner. Santan waved him off. "It's false bravado. It'll be a career shot if he keeps his ball in play. I overheard one of our guys saying the reason the forty-handicap geezer was playing with them is that their fourth had canceled at the last minute and the pro had to put this paid up limp-stick with *some* group."

Bristling with confidence after his practice swing, the geezer had swapped his five-wood for a seven-wood. He stepped forward and effortlessly stabbed his tee and ball into the ground between the white/senior tees, from which his stubborn pride reluctantly allowed him to play. Santan was instantly alerted by the oldster's sudden vigor and began hovering close to the player as if he were an airport security agent inspecting a suspicious acting passenger.

In an almost perfect imitation of his practice swing the elderly player's smooth take-away stretched from his usual quarter length to a nearly three-quarter turn. His hands paused ever so slightly at the top and then he brought the club back to life in the downswing as authoritatively as if he were mimicking the graceful unhinging of a Sam Snead swing.

Club head met ball on the upswing and the oldest member of the club finished his swing higher than he had in over twenty years. The golfer had an expression frozen on his face that Mona Lisa would have envied. The ball flew high and far, but not too far. It gained altitude on an unerring straight line just right of the green before drawing slightly.

Now seriously sensing bad news, Santan sprang into a frenzied flight towards the ball. As he did so he hurled a curse back to the tee: "Damn you, Danikov!"

The golf ball was being furiously, but ineffectively swatted at by Santan as it began its free fall. He grabbed at the ball, trying to capture and hold it. As the ball's leftward-drawing action was overtaken by gravity at a height of two-hundred feet, the little white missile plummeted to earth. Gouging the green as it landed, the slight forward tilt of the green and the ball's great height combined to negate the lack of much backspin by the metal 'wood'. Santan had continued his mad, but ineffectual piggy-back ride on the golf ball, disappearing for a moment below ground. After a short bounce the ball began rolling from the back toward the middle of the green. It slowed on the upper plateau made faster by the huge whirring, green-side fan's drying effect. The ball finally came to a stop only twenty-five feet away, uphill to and left of the pin.

The other three of the spirit foursome had instantly followed Santan and then quickly assembled in the center of the green in order to greet with silly grins his return from the momentary disappearance below ground. Santan came up snarling and saying, "I don't know how you pulled off that shot, Danikov, but the hole's not over. I still like the odds on either my boy making his birdie putt or your fluke-hitter three-putting. Or both."

"Since you're so confident," Clayman said, knowing at least where his match allegiance lay in the fierce golf competition, I have a suggestion. Do you want to press the press?"

"You mean double an already doubled bet?" Santan turned and hesitated long enough to observe a slight smile on Danikov's lips. "No," he said.

The two bunkered players each remained beached following their second shots. Neither would make bogey on the hole, let alone par.

It was the old man's turn to putt. Standing over the putt he was still savoring his remarkable swing and delicious tee shot. He tried to recapture the thoughts that had preceded the grand swing. From where had they come? The words hadn't been natural for him, but he had them firmly in his memory and repeated them aloud in very deliberate fashion. "Look alive, Alvin. On this shot, whether you think you can or can't, you're right!"

Distracted by the analysis, not to mention the adrenalin build-up, Alvin struck his putt much too hard. To the chagrin of Danikov/Clayman and to the delight of Santan/Randall the ball overshot the hole by a full nine feet. He not only had a significant length putt remaining, but it was both fast and downhill. The most dreaded words in putting rang out sing-song style from his team's two live opponents: "You're still away!"

Clayman turned to Danikov. "What can we do?"

"Nothing, except watch."

"Yeah, watch him two-putt from there as we go down six while Santan's guy putts bindfolded to hole a tap-in."

"Paul, if your short game had as much 'up and down' to it as your emotions, you could have made your living on the golf course. Don't judge the ability of others by your own."

As the ball waited to be struck its master crouched over it, possessively. First, he repeated his new-found mantra: "Whether I think I can or can't, I'm right." To that he added even newer words that expanded on his new-found measure of confidence. "Well, I sure as doggone can! O.K., now. Softly downhill with a little right-to-left roll. Soft. Don't stutter. Do it. Just do it."

He did it, making par three. The geezer danced, light as a spirit, leaving no spike marks on the green with his soft-spike shoes. Clayman danced with him. Danikov smiled broadly. For the spirit foursome, however, the first putter was only one-half the equation. Santan's man had yet to counter with his much shorter, yet challenging four-footer. The ball's line was close to that of the geezer's, so his player had already learned something about the roll. Santan was poised over him like a mother about to instruct her six-year old for his first day on the school bus.

Santan couldn't think of what to do. At first he tried darting in and out of the golfer's body, remonstrating the need for him to make the putt. The golfer, about to putt, looked around several times as if a gnat were bothering him. As the player then drew back the putter head, Santan tried, to no avail, to guide it on line. The ball was hit hard and straight toward the hole. Velocity took a little break out of the roll, but the ball homed in like a bat to its cave. The ball struck the hole dead center, but it was accelerating rather than decelerating. Santan dove toward the hole, trying to cap it.

The ball's speed caused it to hit the back lip and jump up before landing no more than a grass blade's width directly behind the hole. Santan began instantly and futilely stomping at the ground near where the ball lie. When his player quickly moved forward in disgust to tap it the rest of the way in, Santan unsuccessfully tried to restrain him, shouting, "It'll go. It'll go. Wait. Wait!" But it was too late.

Clayman initiated a symbolic soft-fist knuckle-touch with Danikov and then danced away, saying, "Great call, partner! Great call! I never doubted you. Only two down with infinity to go."

But was there?

TWENTY-TWO

CLAYMAN was only marginally aware that he had become hyper-active over the match. The competition had taken on entirely new meaning for him. In fact, the match itself was becoming his purpose for being. His thinking was staccato. *This is life. But for how long? Yet, what's the difference? It's the only one I have. Our existence is neither life nor death. It isn't even personal. So only the win counts. But win what? I'm confused. I'm a gray. Santan and Danikov demand black or white. What's my instinct? Yeah, that's it. Do what you've always done . . . follow your instincts. O.K., what are they?*

The new foursome showed up on the 17th tee and the spirits again picked their players according to the random formula. Clayman found himself either agonizing or exulting aloud with each succeeding player's tee shot.

Danikov was aware of Clayman's change of demeanor. "Did you tromp through some spirit weed back there in the rough, partner?" he asked, as they whizzed down the hill to position themselves for the second shots.

"What do you mean?" Clayman answered with a question. "We have a chance to cut our deficit to one. We don't want to go backwards when we have all the momentum. In fact, I got so excited on the tee I forgot to press. We could have squared the match right here! Why didn't you say something?"

"Whoa, Sea Biscuit," cautioned Danikov. "You're running hard on a slippery track. This new group could be tricky. High-handicappers again. Hard to tell what any one of them might do. No one's near the green and Santan's player is lost, deep left. We have the better position. A four could be big time."

"Then let's get that bogey," said Clayman, eyes blazing. Clayman turned his attention to Santan as he and Randall briefly exchanged comments about Randall's player, who was the furthest away and in the left hand bunker. As Randall's live player advanced to the bunker's edge with three clubs and a rake in hand he complained aloud about the sand having been left unraked from someone's previous shot. Then suddenly the player began laughing. "Get a load of this, guys," he said. "The jerk who last played from here apparently left a message for the next schmuck. He scratched out a tip in the sand. It reads, 'PUTT!'"

Clayman was beside himself over such an obvious ploy by their opponents. He glared at Randall who feigned innocence. Clayman suddenly lost it and raced toward him, yelling, "You're cheating! You and Santan are both cheating!" he yelled, shaking his fists in unison.

Randall tried to calm him. "Relax, man. It's no big deal. Just a little gag. The guy's probably too proud of his macho sand wedge to use his putter, anyway, even if there's no lip and he has a level lie."

Clayman's mind began racing. He saw the hole being lost, and if the hole was lost, wasn't the match doomed? He glimpsed the irrationality of that thought and tried to put it aside, but desperation returned. "If he *putts* that ball," Clayman said to Randall, fanning one arm out in front of his body, "I'll have to retaliate!"

The live player could see that the lip of the bunker was not severe enough to be a deterrent, but instead of choosing either the high percentage putter shot or the standard wedge blast, he opted to try 'picking' it clean with an eight-iron. Instead, however, thinking he might actually top the ball, the player unintentionally submarined the club and the ball advanced no more than a foot. "See?" Randall said, feeling vindicated.

Clayman was not mollified. He turned to Danikov and whipped his head back and forth several times, still certain they had been victimized. Danikov dismissed his protests, saying, "Forget it." To add fuel to Clayman's fire, however, the inept sand player reacted to his own shot with a stream of curses. He followed that by throwing the eight-iron he was still gripping towards the golf cart.

As the bunkered player looked around to assess his situation he very deliberately picked up the putter he had brought with him to the shot and readdressed the ball. He swung much too hard, but this time the club caught the top half of the ball and it skittered through the trap like a tender-footed lizard on hot sand. So wound with over-spin was the ball that it ran up the slight bank and onto the green, coming to rest not more than five feet from the cup. With that shot Clayman found renewal for his illogical cause. He shouted in fury at Randall, "Blatant cheating! You can't have this hole!"

Danikov rushed to pacify him. "Paul, what's the matter with you? Settle down. Just calm down. O.K.? Lots of golf left on this hole, and it's only one hole at that. You're spooked."

"I don't need counseling! I need action!"

"No you don't. You need to catch a symbolic breath."

Clayman was still highly agitated. "If he sinks that putt," he said, "his four will win the hole and we'll be running backwards! It mustn't happen!"

"But it may not happen," Danikov said, trying anything to calm his partner. "Look, our guys are both still in there. This sort of reaction is dangerous. 'In your anger don't sin. Don't give the devil a foothold.'"

The message was lost on Clayman. He reasoned that they simply could not afford to lose the hole. That would surely mean the match itself. Then their souls would be lost, too, wouldn't they? Now where was his own player? There, short of the green and chipping. "Hit it on! Hit it on!" he said. "Oh, my God he caught it flush. He's over the back of the green and into the deep rough. He'll be lucky to make five from there. We're dead. Where's our other player? Oh, yeah. Near the green. He'll save us." *He has to!*

Santan and Randall exchanged surprised glances with each other over Clayman's antics. They looked at Danikov, who merely shrugged in response. Clayman had been whooshing from one place to another and now he stopped, huddling over Danikov's player, who was preparing to chip his third shot. His second shot had lit on the treacherous left side slope of the green and had rolled through the green, finishing on a rocky patch of soil.

The player's own live partner was encouraging him to move the ball so as not to damage his golf club in the process of the swing. Clayman wildly supported the notion.

"Take a drop! Take a drop!" he exhorted. One of the live players' opponents, however, qualified the call saying, "That's not marked 'ground under repair.' Drop it if you want, but it'll be an 'unplayable lie' penalty if you do."

Clayman charged the critic as if he were a bull after a matador. The matador didn't flinch. The live player, whose ball and rocky lie were the focus of the moment, swung lamely at the ball with his nine-iron. The blade predictably bounced off the rocks and into the ball sending it careening across the green to the opposite side and down the right hand bank.

The golf ball came to rest with almost no green to work with in a comeback shot. Both this live player and his partner managed to hit their shots back onto the green, each making five on the hole. A four from either Santan's or Randall's player would win the hole for them. Santan's man had squibbed his third shot out from the nearby woods, but then saw his fourth from the green's fringe run up to within a club's leather grip-distance of the pin. A gimme, but yet another five. The spotlight once again came to rest on Randall's player.

At that point Clayman's mind was in total turmoil. His thoughts weren't being processed at all. Instead, they were running at maximum speed, like a software search engine trying to find a file under incomplete identity. It was only a five foot uphill putt and Clayman darted towards Danikov, raving, "He can't miss it. He's gonna make it. And when he makes it, I lose. I lose everything. Therefore, he simply cannot make the putt. He can't. I can't *allow* him to!"

Danikov and Randall were wide-eyed at Clayman's display. Santan looked away.

Clayman shifted his energy from demonstration to introspection, continuing to mumble out loud, "If I can't let him putt, what can I do? How can I stop him? . . . What if he's hurt? Then he couldn't putt." *That's it! How do I hurt him?*

Again, Clayman went flying around, even alternately charging the player who he saw as threatening him with unacceptable failure. He stopped his motion only long enough to actually and erratically, but totally ineffectively, dart into and through the player before returning to his circling frenzy.

Danikov rushed forward and tried to intervene, but he could no better grasp and restrain his partner than Clayman could touch the live player. Finally, after several moments of coming up with no success with that tack, Clayman saw that the player was about to stroke his putt. Clayman froze and then curiously raced to the hole and crouched over it like an animal defending his kill. He was on all fours, his face wrinkled into a comedic, if snarling and menacing countenance.

As the ball rolled swiftly towards him on a dead straight track to the hole he cried out in pitiful supplication, one hand raised as if he could deny the ball's progress, "Please! No! No! No!" The ball fell into the hole and Clayman collapsed over it.

Santan and Randall suddenly found the entire bit hysterical and began laughing uncontrollably, stopping only long enough to congratulate themselves. Randall declared himself the hero. "Did I carry us on this one, or what?"

"Your certainly did, my man," Santan said. "Nice sand work."

"Well," Randall said, "I have to give you credit for the idea itself. But what set Clayman off on his weird track? Is he sick? No. We're spirits . . . how could he be sick?"

Santan was smiling at Danikov as Danikov looked up from comforting Clayman at the hole. Santan answered loudly enough for Danikov to hear, "I don't know. I guess we just got lucky."

Danikov returned Santan's look and spoke softly but deliberately, "You've become the devil's tool."

Santan smiled again, this time shrugging. He held up two fingers, jabbing the air with them several times. That was followed by a brief pause before he popped up a third finger and then made a sharp downward motion with all three of the fingers. In the process of indicating that his opponents had just gone from two down to three down Santan's patronizing smile also turned upside down. He and Randall then exited the area of the green in favor of the tee box.

Clayman had finally risen from where he had collapsed on the green and was vigorously shaking his head as if trying to rid himself of something. "I think I'm O.K. now," he said. "What happened?"

"I don't know," Danikov said, "but I'm working on a perturbing theory."

"Thanks for the help. Hmm . . . hmm," he said, recalling his actions and trying to shake off whatever had happened. "I appreciate your support, but I have to ask this question. If Santan was actually responsible for this, wouldn't you have to call that sort of power awesome?"

Twenty-Three

Clayman had left the green's area to join Santan and Randall on the tee as the next foursome was making their appearance. That left Danikov kneeling just off the seventeenth green. This time he prayed aloud. "Father, I am besieged. Satan is living among us in this hellish paradise. At first I didn't seek to help the others, content in my own salvation. Then I realized their needs. I've tried to turn their hearts, and failed. I now realize all I can do is deliver your message. Count on me for that, Lord. Amen." He arose and whooshed enthusiastically back up to the tee.

"So, what have you been up to?" Santan said almost immediately upon his arrival as he was flanked by Randall and Clayman. "From here it looked like repentance. Or," he said, smiling in condescension, "were you cursing your God for what has happened?"

Danikov did not immediately respond. He looked up to the heavens, then back down and finally around at each of the other two before facing Santan. "Why is it you have no empathy for either us or man's plight in general?"

Randall and Clayman looked defensively to Santan for his answer. He paused a moment before replying, symbolically stretching his neck first one way and then the other, as if he were about to engage in physical exercise of some sort. "My atheism is not without empathy," he said. "I have a profound love for the universe and its wonders. My protest is merely with the gods man has fashioned to explain what he doesn't understand. If I could take myself back in time as easily as we unwillingly arrived here, I'd go to a time just before the religious torment began in earnest, in thirty A.D."

Danikov was incredulous, his jaw, mouth and eyes giving him away. "I can't imagine what could have rotted your soul to speak so venomously," he said. "But as for placing the blame for your lack of faith precisely with Christ's beginning discipleship on Earth, you're a tad off center. God is not 'in time.' The human concept of time is that it amounts to moments following one another. For God, time isn't linear. His purpose in sending us his only Son—"

Santan interrupted in a sudden rage. Pointing to Danikov, he said, "I curse your Christ! And I cite Nietzsche: 'Christianity is the one great curse, the one enormous and innermost perversion, the one great instinct of revenge for which no means are too—your word Danikov— 'venomous,' too underhanded, too underground and too petty.' He called your belief 'the one immortal blemish of mankind.' And that's where I camp."

Clayman and Randall had moved to one side of Santan amid the surprising vitriol being spewed by their champion. They were simply following the alternating verbiage of the duo's exchange, as if at a tennis match. It seemed to Clayman that Randall was embarrassed, but for whom he wondered? As for himself, he was becoming anxious again, not knowing what to make of yet another start in an apparently new direction.

Clayman tried to settle himself by focusing on a more familiar picture. Throughout his life, he had rarely been anything but confused as to answers about religion and faith. Finally, in defense of his confusion he had come to think of his Jewishness as simply cultural. He pondered that thought. Did it then follow that Christianity and Islam and all other religious beliefs had a cultural base also, rather than one of faith? That was ridiculous. Was one's religion or faith such a complex concept that rather than choose incorrectly, one should not choose at all? That seemed to smack of Santan's logic.

Danikov was initially upset with Santan's provocation, but then he calmed. In a sympathetic, but authoritative tone he said, "Luke, I can't adequately express my profound sorrow at your obvious anger with God. When you interrupted me a moment ago I was about to explain what's wrong with regarding Christ's life as a particular period in the history of God. God has no history. Think of the existence of our marvelous universe for a moment as not being contradictory with a belief in God. He was there before it all and is responsible for all of it. He doesn't have to micro manage the laws of physics."

Santan was back in control of himself. "Words," he said, "are like Randall's numbers. They can be used to prove anything for the speaker. I, too, am good at it, but if I'm among the damned merely for that, then you're its leader."

"Listen, my friend," Danikov said, "you're in grave danger. While Jesus said that whoever acknowledges Him before men He will also acknowledge before His father in heaven, he also said that whoever disowns Him before men He will disown before His father in heaven."

"So you say."

"No. So Christ said. But I am genuinely concerned with what you say. Frankly, I think you're possessed. Man's natural condition is to live, love and reason. It's also natural for him to have a spiritual life. I pray to God the Holy Spirit somehow comes into you before it's too late. All the sins and blasphemies of men can be forgiven them, but blasphemy against the Holy Spirit will never be forgiven."

"Not interested!" said Santan. He turned to the others. "Let's get back to the game. Team Danikov is three down and falling."

"Team Danikov?" Clayman said in exaggerated indignity, but nevertheless feeling slighted. "Mind you it's O.K. to give my partner top billing, but I refuse to ride the bench."

At that Randall snorted. Danikov closed his eyes and said aloud, "Father, guide and support us in this challenge to your will."

Santan laughed in insult. Randall and Clayman did not. Both sensed things were getting out of hand and preferred to withdraw.

After an awkward moment of silence, Danikov said with a certain sadness, "You laugh at prayer, but prayer is the helpless and needy child crying to the Father's heart. As the Father's heart is touched so can His hand be moved."

"Yeah, well I'm not moved."

"That's because your heart has been remarkably hardened."

"Call me Pharaoh."

"I'd much rather call you a seeker."

"Spare me your pity. I'm the ultimate independent. Safe. Secure. And I might add, non-divisive."

"Those are three big strikes."

"So," Santan concluded, "am I out?"

"Fortunately for man, God doesn't call us out, only unrighteous. Look," Danikov said, carefully choosing his words, "I think all of you would agree that we need a total change of pace. Something has just occurred to me to try."

Suspicious, but not wanting to outright reject whatever Danikov had in mind in the way of doing something new, they each signaled a tentative willingness. He then reached out with one hand and encouraged another to place a hand on top of his. Curiosity compelled them to do likewise until eight ghostly hands completed the stack. "Hang on to your golf hats," he said. "We're going to visit another golf course, but not like any you've ever seen."

Twenty-Four

"Hey," exclaimed Randall, "we *are* on a different golf course! It's rinky-dink, though."

"I know," said a semi-apologetic Danikov, "This par three set-up may be the only golf course in the entire country. But I didn't bring us here to play vicarious golf."

"We're in another country?" Clayman said, startled at the revelation. "How are you getting away with coloring outside the lines?"

"Call it 'intention.'"

"Yeah, well if you can do it," Santan said, "we can duplicate it. We'll be looking for a way out."

"Don't be in such a rush, Luke," Danikov said. "You can handle this. Besides, if I were you, I'd keep a low profile in these particular parts." He laughed before qualifying his remark. "Satan's recruiting scouts already have your letter-of-intent on file. Now draw yourselves up and look down and beyond the physical bounds of this little golf course. Our eyesight is considerable. What do you see? We could be in Eastern Europe, the Middle East, or even the Far East."

"People," Clayman said. "Thousands and thousands of people, all milling about."

"They aren't actually milling," Randall said, squinting for better focus. "Look more closely. Some are laboring, some are begging, some are being beaten. What are we supposed to be looking for?"

"You've found it," Danikov said. "This is a microcosm of the onslaught of secularization in many former Christian strongholds. You can't begin to see the emotional beatings taking place, only the physical ones. The political and commercial managers of these systems have developed many different attitudes toward religion, from indifference and biases to threats and violence. In whatever form, the secularist lives only for the present and always excludes God from daily human life. There is very little spiritual diet here."

"So what?" Santan said. "Your own Bible begins with the basic tenet that man has been granted free will. Life isn't perfect and you can't make it that way. Let it go its own way. And you didn't have to drag our butts to wherever we are to help me make that point. The US of A guarantees that right and backs up the law with penalties for those who would impose their own brand of 'free will' on others, at least in public, tax-financed institutions. "

"That's right," Clayman jumped in on a note of personal conviction. "Even though I don't practice my Jewish religion I think it's absolutely undemocratic for a majority religious belief to trample minority view points."

"Nothing like taking a basic people's rights principle and making it into an idol, is there?" Danikov said. "The answer isn't to delete structured exposure to all beliefs in the mistaken notion that that very action will somehow preserve fairness. All that does is encourage greater secularization."

"Man wasn't made to glorify your God. Man is secular, by nature," Santan said."

Danikov squinted in taking an odd, long look at Santan. "That statement is nothing more than the devil at work through you," he said. "I've noticed a distinct and continuing change in you since we passed. I'm afraid you've become demon-possessed. You were vulnerable and ready for it and it happened. You've read scripture and you know scripture, but you've chosen to deny it. That's far worse than ignorance."

"I laugh at that."

"No. Listen to me. If man who has had any exposure to God and scripture remains secular, it's because he chooses to. A lazy man doesn't attempt to find answers to the questions he surely has about his God. In fact, God had imprinted Himself in His universe in so many ways that God has proclaimed through His prophets that any man's lack of recognition of Him—with or without scripture—is simply without excuse."

"O.K., Mr. Interlocutor," said an increasingly challenging Santan, "I suppose you think some capitalistic success in Russia or China will ultimately solve not only their economic, but their so-called spiritual woes?"

"I really don't. In fact the writer, Alexander Solzhneitzen, addressed that very subject, although I think he may have been referring to the United States, or maybe even Israel for that matter. I think his words were, 'The disease of rampant prosperity is the declining dependence upon God's will.'"

At that, Randall weighed in, saying, "I think your complaints are too general, Danikov." Even though he let his voice drop, he quickly took another symbolic breath and then noisily managed to release it as if to indicate he wasn't yet relinquishing the stage.

"You know," he said, "the crowd I run with . . . *ran* with . . . not only doesn't give a moment's thought to religion as a meaningful subject, but if you asked any of them about it a typical answer would categorize adherents of organized religion as weak-minded people dependent on others telling them what to think."

"Then think about this," Danikov said. "Is it possible that you and your friends are yourselves a bit weak-minded when it comes to doing a little serious study simply to understand why so many put so much credence in faith?"

Randall took exception to the accusation. "What do you mean by 'study'?" he asked.

"Have any of your friends read the Bible through? Or even read one or the other of the two Testaments? Or read even a *few* of the books of the Bible? Have you? Many people will quote scripture to make an out-of-context point, but they've never actually read scripture. Whether it's high school homework, graduate study or Bible study, study is still study."

"Big deal, study," Randall said. "I was so busy in life 'studying' to survive my job that everything not connected to that was on indefinite hold."

"Where did compassion for others live?"

"It had no home with me."

"That's a very unhealthy state," Danikov said.

Randall appeared a little uneasy. "Let me ask you this: can you tell me exactly what it is you believe? I mean without mouthing some ditty?"

Clayman followed Randall's lead, saying in nearly as challenging a tone, "I'd be interested in that, too." Santan simply shook his head.

"Thank you, gentlemen. I'd be happy to oblige. I believe in God the Father who made heaven and earth. I believe in Jesus Christ, his only Son and our Lord. I believe he was conceived by the Holy Spirit and that he was born of the Virgin Mary. I also believe and know that Christ was crucified, that he died and was buried, and that . . . "

"O.K. O.K.," Randall said, interrupting, "I get all that, but what *makes* you believe what you believe?"

"As I was about to conclude, I believe because Christ rose from the dead. If He hadn't risen from the dead, as He said He would and as was prophesied in the Old Testament, then Christianity would never have been born."

"Arise? You mean spiritually," Randall said.

"No, Artie. Physically. Before Mary could return to the tomb to prepare Jesus for proper burial on the third day after his crucifixion and death He arose. And that resurrection was witnessed by more than five hundred people."

"Yeah, maybe," Randall said. "What about his second death, after his supposed crucifixion and resurrection?"

"There was no second death," Danikov said softly. "Christ did not die a second time. After forty days he ascended into heaven to sit at the right hand of God. The ascension, too, was witnessed. From there he will come to judge the living and the dead. Lastly, and thank you for asking, I believe that true believers will see resurrection of the body and everlasting life in the Lord's Kingdom."

"O.K., so you got in the whole commercial," Randall said, pursuing a different tack, "but now let's play devil's advocate. Pun intended. How does all this square with Judaism? I mean, if Clayman here followed his Jewish faith, he'd probably make an argument questioning why the same God would create two different religions."

"Thank you, Mr. Randall," Clayman said, bowing slightly and then turning to face Danikov. "How about that?"

"Hebrews," Danikov said.

"Hebrews?" Randall asked, turning to the others with his palms raised.

"The Book of Hebrews. It was written in answer to questions such as yours. Judaism *was* divinely inspired with the commandments and rituals, and the Old Testament prophets described God's promises and revealed the way to forgiveness and salvation."

"So, was that second-rate or something?" Clayman said.

"Of course not, but Christ *did* come, fulfilling Jewish law and prophesy about the Messiah. Christ conquered sin and shattered all of Judaism's barriers to God. In the process, he freely provided direct access to eternal life and not through priestly intermediaries."

"If I had been a Jew at the time," Randall said, "that message would have been difficult to accept."

"It *was* difficult for most Jews to accept. In fact, they didn't. Though the Jews had sought the Messiah for centuries, they were entrenched in thinking and worshiping in traditional forms. Following Jesus seemed to repudiate both their heritage and their scriptures. Many labeled the message *and* the 'messenger' heretical. And many of those who did accept Jesus tried to live a hybrid faith. The Book of Hebrews was directed to Hebrew or Jewish Christians evaluating Jesus and struggling with the new covenant He brought to the world. The New Covenant," he said gently. "I've been praying I may be allowed to read it once again."

"We had to ask . . ." Randall said.

"Santan asked why I dragged you here," Danikov said. "My objective is for the three of you to appreciate that man needs a vital and living faith in life. It would be so easy for man to lose sight of the Biblical message and God's promise of everlasting life if we weren't so tenacious by nature. It seems that every age must torment Jesus anew, as if the lesson can never be learned except through each generation's renewal. The lesson is so simple to understand, but so difficult to maintain without constant repetition. Randall, as an advertising man you can surely appreciate this point."

Randall begrudgingly nodded. "And what's the lesson?" Clayman asked.

"Christ died to atone for our sins. Christ's resurrection was the unmistakable sign that he is the Messiah. And Christ will one day return in the 'second coming'. In the meantime, our job is to prepare the way for Him."

"I've said it before and I'll be saying it 'till the day I die . . . or . . . expire," Santan said. "Free will belongs to man. Even your God makes that clear." Inflection was rising in his tone as he spoke. "Believe what you will, but don't try to plant your narrow views on us. We're allowed our opinions. After all, how stiff-necked a people were your God's own 'chosen' predecessors?"

"Can't refute that," Danikov said, obviously encouraged to have an interested lead of any kind.

"Of course you can't," Santan said. "Take the Old Testament's King David, for example. Your God supposedly refused David's expressed desire to physically build the mighty temple simply because David was a warrior and had shed blood. Now, shouldn't that biblical 'fact' have alerted the Jews to an obvious assumption? Namely, that their Messiah would not be either a military or political leader. Seems to me your God's choice of a people came up woefully short. But if they couldn't cut it, why should anyone else? "

Clayman was surprised that Santan had obviously studied enough of the Bible to use it in defense of his anti-Biblical positions. He idly wondered if Danikov could—at some point—find a way to use that to his own advantage.

"The Jewish priests didn't want to lose their jobs," Danikov said, "so they sabotaged Jesus. Aside from that unfortunate fact, however, you would blame the Jews as a culture for your own warped perspectives about faith?"

"No. I blame everyone who can't see the foolishness in relying on an invisible and unrevealing God," Santan said, insisting.

Danikov appeared thoughtful and then spoke slowly. "With King David's help his son, King Solomon, ultimately built the temple you so easily disparage, and Solomon may as well have had you in mind when he wrote the Proverbial verse: 'Better to meet a bear robbed of her cubs than a fool in his folly.'"

Santan reacted to direct challenge the same as he had on his college debate team. Rebuttal is everything. "All things are permissible," he said, "but most men have a conscience which serves to protect both the individual and others. I think your God waived yours."

"'Please come in, said the spider to the fly,'" Danikov said, smiling. "As for man's conscience, even collectively it's nowhere nearly good enough to protect us from ourselves. And from somewhere in this very land—if we are in Russia—one of her countrymen, Dostoyevsky, essentially said, 'Only if there is no God are *all* things permissible.'"

"Then I give you permission to worship what you like," Santan said. "Personally, I prefer to bank my beliefs along with my self-sufficiency."

"Does history never stop repeating itself ?" Danikov asked, rhetorically. "We've committed the same error the Israelites made. We act as if we're the authors of our own prosperity, rather than the recipients of God's bounty."

Santan turned away. "This visit has been a monumental waste of time," he said. "Now I, too, fully understand the meaning of 'intention.' I hereby return us to the game."

TWENTY-FIVE

THREE OF THE GROUP instantly found themselves back on RiverTree's seventeenth tee. Santan was missing, but he shortly joined them. Clayman was restless. He was further confused by the event which had just taken place and the discussion preceding their return. He had provided very little input. He whisked himself back and forth on the tee as if waiting for news from a hospital emergency room. He began talking to no one in particular. "This is no good. The match is no good. The game—we have to change the game."

Danikov took on a pensive look as he pondered what might be causing Clayman's continued mood swings. Danikov raised his head and nodded, as if in agreement. "O.K., Paul," he said. "I've been thinking about that very thing. I have a proposition you won't be able to refuse, especially since you see me as the spiritual thorn in your side."

"Could I get an 'Amen?'" Santan said, derisively.

Danikov ignored him. "Before I state my proposition, hear me out on something."

"Annnd nowww . . . " Santan said, employing the same boxing match announcer style that Randall and Clayman had used earlier, "from the Department of Spiritual Apologetics . . . with his continuing irrational defense of Christianity . . . Doctor. . . Damn . . . i . . . kov."

Danikov ignored the remark, the multiple insults and Santan himself. "Fellow spirits," he said, "if you think this state in which we find ourselves at the moment is a sad one, I can tell you things are likely to worsen for you."

"You mean," Santan said, "that your insurance is paid up, but because atheism, agnosticism, skepticism and any actual faith other than what lobotomized Christians believe have had their applications denied and thus are going to hell?" He tittered, barely able to contain himself.

"You're not too far off on that account," Danikov said. "According to Jesus, not believing in him is sin. But you're not necessarily damned to hell, because all sin is forgivable. The catch is that you must ask for that forgiveness."

Clayman was on the verge of breakdown. If he could have sweated, perspiration would have been rolling off of him. "But how can we know what you say is true?" Clayman asked.

"It's in the Bible and it's stated precisely: There is no other name under heaven that has been given among men, by which we must be saved."

"Behold," Randall said, "the preacher of doom. You seem fond of biblical cliches. Here's a cliche right up your alley, from St. Francis of Assisi, no less. 'Preach, preach, preach the gospel. And if necessary, use words.' Not exactly your mantra, is it?"

"Artie, whatever your sins, they're neither too small nor too great for you to accept that Christ died to atone for them. If you're simply willing to transfer your trust to him, he'll receive you."

"And exactly how would that benefit me?"

"The two greatest benefits ever devised for man," Danikov said. "Firstly, you'll find yourself in a wonderful, loving eternity with no sorrow, crying or pain. Secondly, you'll be so surrounded by friends and family without hunger or thirst that you'll wish with all your heart that those you left behind would know how important it is to be faithful to Christ."

Clayman was suddenly calmed. As he measured Danikov's words he looked around at each of the others, trying to assess their takes about Danikov's accumulative input. Randall apparently continued to shrug it off. Clayman supposed that Randall thought Danikov had become something of the shrill John the Baptist Santan had earlier accused him of being.

With respect to Santan, Clayman saw Danikov's effort to refute his position as valiant, but ineffective. Santan seemed more convicted of his atheism now than before they had been thrown into this mess. Randall would remain tied to Santan if for no other reason than being stroked. As for himself, he had now come to the conclusion that the argument for Christianity seemed to be no less a stretch than before, in spite of his first-hand exposure to someone as convicted as Danikov. It wasn't that Clayman was so swayed by the self-secure Santan, or that Danikov's message wasn't heartfelt, but rather that Santan's arguments were less troubling. That latter fact recalled for him a message he had taken to heart from a college professor in his senior year.

Clayman clearly remembered the course. It was an elective in philosophy and the instructor was a young, new faculty member heady with the opportunity to influence thousands merely by opening his mouth. The instructor's words had been, "If you find it difficult to swallow your parents' religion remember that choking is allowed."

As if on cue Santan responded to Danikov's comment on Christ's promises, looking alternately at Clayman and Randall, "I don't know about you guys, but I wouldn't want to be in heaven with a God who sends people to hell and then punishes them forever. Personally, I would rather go to hell and defy such an unreconcilable deity."

Clayman and Randall nodded solemnly in agreement.

"You're one foolish man, Luke." said Danikov. "How can you not see that it takes more faith to deny Christianity than it does to actually embrace it? Listen carefully. I want to share with you the single most important promise ever given to man."

Both Randall and Clayman unwittingly leaned forward.

Danikov paused a moment, then said simply and slowly, "Christ said, 'I am the resurrection and the life; he who believes in Me shall live even if he dies, and everyone who lives and believes in Me shall never die.'"

For a moment no one said anything, then Santan responded, saying, "Well, we died. I doubt we're in heaven, but we still *are*."

Clayman didn't understand it, but he was again becoming more nervous by the minute. After all, he had finally taken a position in all this, even if unstated to the others. He shouldn't be unsettled. "You said you had a proposition for us, Tommy Ray," he blurted. "What is it?"

"O.K.," Danikov said with a sigh, "here it is. As you can see, we've somewhat overcome our earlier seventeenth hole geographic limitations. In view of that I propose we take an even bolder action in order to find closure. Here's my proposition. We'll play three more holes to resolve the match, but with a lot more than that riding on the outcome. And I'm going to spot you a big advantage."

"Watch it, boys," Santan said. "Never play the other man's game."

"It's time to either put up or shut up," said Danikov. "I repeat, we vicariously play a maximum of three more holes—except for possible ties— to determine the winner of the match. It's my player's ball against the best ball of all three of your players. You not only get to pick your own players and the holes we play . . . but you can pick *my* player on each hole. No handicap strokes."

"Partner," said Clayman, surprised by the offer, but also a little offended in suddenly remembering that he and Danikov had been enjoyably teamed, "you're dumping me."

"Yes, but I'm also increasing your odds for winning."

"Randall weighed in to try lessening the appearance of the too-good offer, saying, "A hole's a hole, whether you or we pick it, and I don't know that we can move to any other holes on RiverTree. We couldn't before."

"Of course you can," Danikov said. "We established that with our little travel incentive trip to Russia. I have only two conditions. No one can sneak a peek at any live foursome's scorecard. If you win *any* one hole, you win the match. In addition, if you win I'll cease my witnessing efforts."

"Why this sudden generosity?" said a suspicious Santan..

"Because if I lose, I'll be content to go to heaven and leave you to make your way to hades to wait for the call from our Lord that will never come."

"Interesting," Santan said, looking around at the other two, "but we do have to ask about one teensy, weensy little proviso that 'Suddenly Tolerant Tommy' has yet to share with us." He turned back to Danikov to continue, "The second condition is obviously what's in it for you. Spit it out."

"Gladly. It springs from the kind of bargain which literature usually reserves for the devil, with his inevitable loss. Each time you lose a hole, if you do, you must designate one of the group to take a short walk with the Lord, with me as your guide. That's all."

The group's response was not instantaneous. Clayman and Randall looked at each other and then at Santan who had a self-assured grin on his face. By their looks the lead was Santan's.

"I figured you for being more savvy than that," Santan said. "Apparently you aren't. As captain of this team I accept your proposition. To recap: No handicaps. We pick our players. We pick the holes. We pick your player. It's the best ball of our three players against your player. Any time you win a hole one of us has to sit still for a sermon. We kick your tail and you let go of ours. Let's get it on." The other two nodded enthusiastic assent.

Santan pulled his new three-man team to one side as the next live foursome wheeled up to the cart path area adjacent to the seventeenth tee. "Look," he said, "which holes we play now don't really make a difference since no strokes will be given or taken. Our big advantage obviously lies with having three players to his one, but we need to choose the best players for ourselves and the poorest for Danikov."

"Wait a minute," Clayman said, "the holes might make a difference if Danikov's player is the poorest of the lot and gets the most strokes from his fellow players. We wouldn't want one of our guys to bag it if he thought he was beaten by the stroke."

"Well, now," Santan said, "who made you the chief strategist here?"

"But he has a good point, Luke," Randall said.

"Hmm, maybe so. We've been playing the number seventeen hole forever and it's only the sixteenth handicap hole. What's it gotten us? Nothing. So let's play the number one hole. It's much more difficult as the seventh handicap hole."

The other two agreed, both eager to shut Danikov down and out.

"But first," Santan said, hoisting his hand for emphasis, "strategy meeting. Danikov, we'll meet you at the first tee."

As Danikov whisked cross-fairway towards the appointed tee, Santan said, "Boys, we got ourselves an inside edge. While y'all were catching your breath on the return from the Russian front, I got a good look at all of the swings in this group coming up on the sixteenth hole."

"Is that fair?" Randall asked. "Tommy Ray said the deal was we couldn't look at any scorecards."

"I didn't."

"Still," Clayman said, "it's a little unethical."

"No it isn't. My reconnaissance was done before he put his proposition on the table. Would you rule out *all* experiences prior to his offer?"

"I see your point," Clayman said. Randall quickly nodded in agreement.

Santan continued with his assessment. "Of the foursome I mentioned, three appear to be in the ten-to-fifteen handicap range, but none of them are long off the tee. They're really pretty evenly matched, except for one. I saw him hit a couple of shots. His swat would make a seventy-year old's swing look like a touring pro's. That's Danikov's man."

"But that group will be finished after they play the eighteenth hole," Randall said. "How do we get them to the first hole?"

"They'll do it for us. I overheard one of them say they should skip going to the halfway house at the turn. They obviously started the round on number ten instead of number one and are anxious to finish."

"Captain," Clayman said, irreverently. "remember the hole where Tommy Ray was saddled with an old fart who was nearly on oxygen? How'd that turn out?"

"Don't worry," Santan said. "I learned something from that Sunday school lesson. You two see to your own players. I'll see to mine and Danikov's."

Clayman was nervous. His thoughts were churning. This was sudden death in a potential match for their souls. Once again he was anxious. *What is my problem?*

"This isn't the Ryder Cup, men," Santan said. "it's a lot bigger. It's all the matches that have ever been played rolled into one, and our starting time has been called." With that the threesome whooshed to the same tee the group had started out on when they were flesh-and-blood.

That they were actually successful in actually advancing to a different hole at all awed both Randall and Clayman. "Well, look at us," Randall said. "This is what I call a promotion."

The three of them touched milky fists in salute to themselves as they approached a waiting Danikov. All four waited for what seemed like only seconds as the live foursome finished hole numbers seventeen and eighteen and swung their carts onto the path behind the eighteenth green which led to the first tee. Both carts continued past both the blue tees *and* the surprised spirits, however, until they reached the senior teeing area.

Clayman commented to Santan, "Did you figure on this? They all have a twenty-five yard advantage from the forward tees. How will that play?"

"No differently. Let's see whose tee shot goes where."

All three of Santan's team's players got off the tee in good shape. It was Danikov's player's turn. He appeared to be the youngest of the group of senior players, whose life's interests apparently included regular time on the golf course. The odd-swinger took a mighty swing, but came around on the shot so sharply from right to left that the club hit only paint and the ball barely fell off the tee. Santan instantly jumped up and symbolically high-fived both Clayman and Randall. "He just cooked himself," Santan yelled in jubilation. The two younger spirits both pumped their fists and beamed confidently at Danikov who merely blinked and waited.

The flesh-and-blood group laughed out loud. They weren't laughing at the unfortunate player, however, merely with him, since the shot was more comical than pathetic. The duffer was also laughing. The would-be hitter collected himself, then bent over and swept up his ball, re-teeing it. None of his playing partners objected, even though doing so was an apparent infraction. In addressing his ball he said, "Come on Mulligan, sing to me."

At this point Santan roared in protest. "He can't take a freebie, it's his tenth hole!"

"Relax, champ," said Danikov. "it's their game. They probably always take a second tee shot on the first and tenth tees. A lot of seniors do that when they aren't playing in tournaments. We're playing the players, remember? We don't control their game. Would you have objected if your players hadn't hit good shots and elected to take their Mulligans?"

Santan seemed at a loss with the stroke advantage instantly wiped out. "O.K.," he said in disgust, "I don't give a crap. This guy is an egg-sucker anyway. I can see all we need here is a five and you'll be choking before you can land another sermon. Come on, boys, let's move on down the fairway and play forecaddy for this jerk-off's next wayward shot."

In the few seconds it took for the spirit threesome to move out of earshot of the live group, they missed a classic proposition from the player who had all but fanned his first tee shot of the group's second nine. "You guys beat up on me pretty good that first nine," the hacker complained. I appreciate your letting me play with you as a first-time visitor and all, but I must be down a hundred dollars, counting all the bets, skins and 'trash.' What do you say we double up on everything and leave presses open?" There was no immediate response. The whiner sweetened the pot. "All right," he said, "we're just out here for fun so I'll challenge myself. You guys continue playing from the 'white' tees and I'll back up to the 'blues.' Whadd'ya say, sports?"

This time his opponents couldn't oblige him fast enough, not even giving the loudmouth's own partner a chance to object.

The innovator moved back to the blue tees and promptly whistled his drive to the right center of the fairway and fifty yards past the other three, leaving himself only a hundred yards from the center of the green. As the tee shot came screaming past the spirit threesome on an arrow-true course, Clayman and Randall instantly panicked and began assessing the supposed hacker's dramatic shot and what that might mean. Santan raced back to Danikov, certain he had been instrumental.

"What have you done?" he said, practically in Danikov's ghostly face.

"Do?" Danikov said. "I told my man that if he couldn't play better than that, he'll be worrying about where his next moon pie is coming from. What do you *think* I could do to affect that kind of shot? Nothing. The man reached back. Looks to me like you might have drafted poorly."

Santan glared at him out of ironic self-righteousness. Then he whisked back to his own team's live players who had arrived at their tee shot positions while Santan and Danikov were conversing. Both Santan's and Randall's players laid up short of the creek as expected, while Clayman's player tried to hit over the narrow waterway from 180 yards out and caught the ball well below its equator. The ball failed to clear the creek. Santan cursed in their turn the player, the creek, Clayman and himself.

At the instant Danikov's player drew back his club to hit, both Santan and Randall were trying to hang onto the sand wedge to somehow disrupt the swing. Clayman found the sight so comical he overcame his previously building anxiety and bent over with laughter. Desperation, he thought, thy name is us. The Santan/Randall effort, however, had no impact whatsoever and the shot found the green, though nowhere close to the pin.

Both Randall's and Santan's players could only manage two putts each for bogey fives while Clayman's creek-diverted player limped in for a seven. Danikov's player was totally oblivious to Team Santan's continued hi-jinks and converted his own two-putter for an easy par four. Santan was indignant and again claimed foul, refusing to immediately concede the loss.

Clayman said, "Luke, we lost the hole. You gave Santan the 'hustler' and we all took the hit. O.K., so Danikov wins a shot at one of us. Let him work on Randall. He's up to holding his own. And even if he isn't, it's not our problem. That's a big deal to Danikov, but we still have two holes in which to win one. Advantage ours."

"Yeah," said Santan, who was preoccupied with straining to hear the live players' own animated discussion over the events of the hole. Then he turned his attention to Clayman and said, "Well, the news isn't all that good, Boy Scout. Danikov is now your problem, not Randall's. You let your player take himself out of the hole by dumping into the creek so it's only fair I throw you into the Christian's den."

Twenty-Six

"What's the scenario here, Tommy Ray?" Clayman asked, once he came to grips with his situation. If he had been flesh-and-blood he would have been hyperventilating. "Are you going to exorcize me or something?"

"Don't worry," Danikov said. "No one can be argued into the Kingdom of Heaven. "

"That's for sure," Clayman said, trying to scratch a non-existent itch on the back of his neck. "Your message hasn't exactly caught on like sauce at a barbecue."

Danikov smiled and said, "That's because no one has tasted it."

Clayman stared at him for a moment. Then he blinked. "OK, talk to me."

"Look, I've talked more about God on this golf course with the three of you than I have in my entire life. I probably should have done more witnessing before this, but I wasn't called to it. What I simply want to share with you is that biblical teachings are essential for man to accept if he's to find salvation. Being lukewarm as you are is even worse than falling on the wrong side of faith. During the Civil War a man once put on a blue coat and grey trousers. What do you think happened to him?"

"No one knew what he stood for?"

"Worse. Both sides shot at him."

Clayman was feeling anxiety overtake him again. "You know full well that I was raised a Jew," he said. "Why do you want to take my Jewishness away from me?" *There, he had finally laid it out.*

Danikov seemed surprised at Clayman's question. "What?" he said. "I'm sorry if that's what you really think, Paul. I'm not trying to make a Gentile out of a Jew. Messianic Jews are not leaving the God of their fathers to follow a foreign deity. They're merely affirming their faith in God's eternal covenant with Abraham, Isaac and Jacob. You've been worried sick hiding behind a defenseless argument for lack of a better one."

"What do you mean?"

"Well, you told all of us you don't actually practice Judaism. Tell me, do you know what the word Israel means in Hebrew?

"No idea whatever."

"'One who struggles with God.' Israel might just as well be *your* name. Remember our earlier conversation about Jacob's Ladder?"

"I do. Actually, that was very real for me. How'd old Jacob manage in his wrestling match?"

"He didn't manage at all. God did. The story is recorded in Genesis. I mentioned earlier about Jacob's dream, the ladder to heaven, and his having come to a sorry state of affairs. Then, many, many years after having been cruelly tricked out of his cherished birthright by his brother Jacob, Esau was coming to meet him. With four hundred men."

"Doesn't sound like Esau was in a very good humor," Clayman said.

"Jacob feared the worst, so first he tried prayer. Then he panicked and sent lavish gifts, trying to pacify his brother, but he was still worried. One night, as he was still traveling on the road to meet Esau behind his own sizeable group of men, Jacob, his two wives, two maidservants and his eleven sons crossed a stream. After they had all safely crossed, he sent over all his possessions, leaving him alone. Before he could cross the stream himself he encountered a 'Man,' who wasn't an ordinary man at all, but divine." As Danikov was telling his story he could tell Clayman was keenly interested.

Danikov continued. "The Man 'wrestled' with Jacob through the night until daybreak. The divine wrestling match was agonizing and arduous and when it was over Jacob was not only wounded and weary, but as a result he walked with a limp for the rest of his life. Every step he took from that day forward, he was reminded of his life-changing encounter with God, which since has been called Jacob's Ladder."

"Sounds like Jacob could have used a good chiropractor," said Clayman, laughing to mask his latent interest.

"The bottom line," Danikov said, "is that Jacob had struggled with God and had overcome, so the angel changed Jacob's name to Israel. How long have *you* been struggling with God?"

Clayman was silent for a long moment as he placed his head in his hands. "Since I was sixteen," he said.

"That's a good start, admission. Let's fast forward. Let me reiterate what I think your estranged girl friend was trying to communicate to you. Sheila is a Jew who simply came to accept Jesus as the promised Messiah of Israel and Savior of the world, but she is maintaining both her Jewish identity and her style of worship. Understand this, that as a Messianic Jew she believes in the same Christian tenets I do."

"That's a difficult concept to grasp," Clayman said. "What would you say to my religious Jewish friends who say they can't accept Jesus as the messiah simply because he is regarded by Christians as divine? They say the Jewish God is but one God, and has no sons or daughters. And they say they are taught that the messiah will not be divine, but mortal."

"You've studied more than you let on," observed Danikov. "I don't want to belittle your friends' position, but as I said earlier that sort of thinking is purely defensive. The Old Covenant prophets foretold the messiah's crucifixion and resurrection. Now that in itself prophesies someone fully human *and* fully divine. Look, Paul, God created the universe and everything in it. Do you think that kind of a God couldn't cleave off a part of himself to be delivered as a newborn from the womb of a virgin?"

Clayman tried to sit, but he merely floated with his legs folded. He didn't care for the effect so he again "stood," but this time he raised open hands and held them out in front, moving them first away and then toward one another before attempting to wring them. "I don't understand you," he said. "Why are you so insistent on preaching your gospel to me and to others?"

"Two reasons. First of all, it isn't my gospel. It's God's gospel. I want my family and friends to find salvation, to gain eternal life. The Bible offers people no hope apart from personal faith in Christ."

"And the second reason?" Clayman asked.

"Because Jesus commanded us to do so," said Danikov, placing his right hand on Clayman's left shoulder. "The Gospel isn't mine to keep secret. Our Lord didn't say to 'make friends,' he said to 'make disciples.'"

Clayman again tried to wring his hands. "I simply don't understand it," he said. "Where does your all-consuming faith come from? Why do you really care, aside from that trite 'love your neighbor as yourself' phrase?"

"I'll put it as simply as I can," Danikov said. "No earthly enterprise is as important as helping an individual come into a saving, liberating relationship with the God of the universe." Danikov pondered for a moment and then added, "A close friend of mine puts it even simpler: 'When God saved me he gave me such a jerk toward wanting to be like Christ that I've been out of step with the world ever since.'"

Clayman tried to shuffle his feet in delaying his response, but gained no respite. "I think I'm beginning to at least understand where you're coming from," he said, "but how can you be so certain in what you believe that you're willing to put those beliefs out there for everyone to see and challenge?"

"O.K.," Danikov said, relishing the conversation. "This may be confusing, but think about it: Faith is both being sure of what we hope for and certain of what we don't see. For example, in Genesis we understand that the universe was formed at God's command. Christians believe that. Faith begins by accepting that what is seen was not made out of what was visible."

"Think you could simplify that?"

Danikov laughed again and then grew thoughtful before responding. "Let me put it in Jewish context. A messianic leader once wrote that Mark Twain was asked why he believed in God. His immediate reply was: 'The Jew, my friend. The Jew!' Remove the Jewish contribution from Christianity and there would be no Christianity.'"

"Exactly why is that?" Clayman asked. "Wait! Could it be because the Jewish people gave the Gentiles both the word of God and the prophets?"

"Bingo!" Danikov said, "Not to mention Jesus and the apostles."

Clayman found himself plunged deep into thoughts of Sheila. He realized that the questions he hadn't been able to ask of himself and the answers he had been unwilling to accept from her, were now being addressed by Danikov. "Tell me again," he said, " so that I can be clear about the things you think Sheila would have me believe."

"Well, never having met Sheila, but based on what you say about her," Danikov said as he symbolically caught his breath before continuing. "She and I believe in one God who is eternally existent in three persons: God, the Father, God the Son, and God, the Holy Spirit. We believe in the Messiah's virgin birth, His sinless life, His atoning death, His bodily resurrection, His ascension into heaven, and His future return in power and glory. That's it."

"Are you telling me that I'm going to Hell if I'm not saved through Christ?"

"No. Jesus said that. Look, you're obviously distraught over your relationship with Sheila. I don't know what the future holds for you, Paul, but I've been praying for you in that regard, as well as for your salvation."

"Thank you, but frankly, I don't even know that God could forgive me. My sins are many." Clayman's eyes suddenly grew moist, but with a saddened expression.

Danikov's eyes, too, were wet with joy, but he realized he hadn't concluded his work and held himself in check. "God's offer of salvation is to all people, regardless of past sins," he replied. "Christ's resurrection proved not only that He had power over sin, but also over death, and could offer each of us this power as well. God's offer of salvation, however, is still hidden to unbelievers."

"What do you mean?"

"I mean that unbelievers either refuse to accept the offer or choose to ignore it."

Still in denial, Paul said, "But if one simply hasn't heard about it—"

"But that doesn't apply to you, does it?" Danikov said gently.

"No. I admit my sins, but on the other hand I've done my share of good works over the years. That must count for something."

"With all due respect, they count for nothing. You aren't the only one who thinks trying to be moral or even religious means he is automatically made right with God. The problem is you never know when you've done enough. We're warned us of that in the book of Matthew."

"Warned?"

"By the scripture. 'Not everyone who asks will enter the kingdom of heaven, but only those who do the will of the Father. They will testify on that day, 'Did I not do many good things in your name?' Then Jesus will tell them plainly, 'I never knew you.'"

Once again defensive, Clayman said, "Tell me how Christians should dare tell Jews—even me, who has never admitted to being religious—to believe in Jesus?"

"Humbly, Paul," Danikov said softly. "But as to why, simply because the gospel is truth itself. Without the true messiah the Jewish people are destined for eternal destruction, just as the Gentiles. You dreamed Sheila said that *not* to witness to Jews that Yeshua of Nazareth was the fulfillment of God's promise to send the Messiah is the worst anti-Semitic act of all. I believe God sent her that dream for your benefit. Because it is their . . . our . . . and your . . . only hope."

All of Clayman's repressed denial and all his desperate longing for the truth now evaporated as tears overwhelmed him. Danikov was crying too, with joy and thanksgiving. Former skeptic and about-to-be born-again Christian—Jew and Gentile—hugged as best they could, given their spiritual form.

After a moment the tears dried themselves and Clayman looked at Danikov. "I have one remaining question," he said.

"Ask it."

"What about eternal life? How does a man qualify?"

"You know, Paul," Danikov said, tenderly, "I believe we all were put on this earth to ask that one question. The answer is to love the Lord your God with all your heart, with all your soul, with all your strength, and with all your mind. And your neighbor as yourself."

"Well then, glory be to Jesus, because I think I'm ready to walk the walk."

"The walk is long and you're merely beginning. But that is what counts most. If you pick up the Lord's bag in full trust, you'll be rewarded in great measure. As your namesake wrote in Romans, 'Everyone who calls on the Lord will be saved.'"

"Then help me if I falter in prayer," Clayman said, preparing to earnestly pray for the very first time in his life. "Yeshua God," he began haltingly, "I confess my sin . . . I accept that you died on the cross to erase my sins . . . and I hereby invite you to come into my heart. . . . I . . . ." Clayman again wept.

"Father God," Danikov continued, his arms around Clayman, "thank you for your free gift of forgiveness for this newly-found brother in Christ. And thank you for your blessings during this group's confusing journey. I ask for your help in Paul's awakening to your holy presence in life and in the ever after. Please allow him to fully understand and desire to be brought home to you. I ask this in Jesus' holy name. Amen."

Eyes opened, Danikov concluded by saying, "The Lord is counting on you, Paul. He wants to encourage your faith as you embark on your walk."

"I hope it's a wide road."

"I can promise you it's not. Matthew tells us to the contrary. We must enter through the narrow gate. Only the road leading to destruction has a wide gate and a broad road, and many enter through it. This means being a Christian is a way of life, not occasional acts. Being born again isn't enough. You'll now have to transform yourself by renewing your mind."

"I think I'm beginning to understand. I don't exactly know how to go about that, but it will cost me what life remains to me, won't it?"

"It will, brother."

Then, in an effort to lighten things Clayman said, "In the meantime, my friend, you have some serious vicarious golf to see to. Danikov versus Santan and Randall, with—hopefully—two holes remaining. Let me tote your bag."

TWENTY-SEVEN

A PRACTICAL LUKE SANTAN acknowledged Danikov near the tee of the second hole as the real life foursome the spirits were standing near dropped their putters and wedges into their golf bags to retrieve their driving clubs for the 507-yard dogleg par five. "You won the last hole on a fluke," said Santan, "but that's history. We'll go ahead and play the number two hole with the same golfers. Randall will stick with his same player, but you and I will switch players. The hot shot's mine and you inherit Clayman's sorry player. The leftover is Clayman's dead soldier. Your luck can't hold."

"I don't know about luck," said Danikov, "but I know that surviving your morality's manipulative efforts is hard work. I don't suppose you'd be interested in a conversation about your need for repentance would you? Don't take the request too personally, however. You sin. I sin. We all sin. Therefore we all need to repent."

"I can't repent and you know why."

"Of course I do, but I'll be surprised if you have a clue. C. S. Lewis said it best: 'The worse you are, the more you need repentance and the less you can do it.'"

"I find that a stupid misinterpretation of my intention," said Santan. "I can't repent because there is no reason for it. You Christians and all others of your ilk have made one colossal mistake."

"How's that?"

"You put your faith in a redemptive God."

"Where would you have us put it?"

"Nowhere. Faith is not necessarily a virtue."

"Such ill-directed conviction," Danikov said, shaking his head. "Christ redeemed us by paying the price to buy us out of our sorry state and sad condition."

"I hate to ask just what that price was," Randall said, pre-empting Santan's response.

"His blood, shed on the cross," Danikov said. "Santan doesn't agree with that, Artie, but how about you? Don't you really think it's important for a man to believe in something other than mere self?"

"I used to think so, but when I wasn't able to discover what that 'something' ought to be, I defaulted. As my partner has pointed out, my taking a positive stance in defense of that notion is a position in itself. So, ironically, I really do have a 'faith' of sorts."

"Player's up!" interjected Santan.

The three tee shots that counted—Danikov's, Randall's and Santan's players—were all in modest play after their tee shots, in spite of hitting into a suddenly-developing breeze.

Santan's new horse—no longer able to hide either his previous deception or his talent—unashamedly rode a big drive way out front of the others, even though he was hitting from further back. Clayman was trying to assess the situation. The number two hole, he thought, is not necessarily a driver's hole because even most lower handicappers at RiverTree can't reach the green in two from the blue tees. Danikov and Santan both knew that, Clayman realized, but it was difficult not to feel you have an advantage when your ball or player is much longer off any given tee, and in the fairway. And both the hustler and Santan had that distinct advantage.

Both Randall's and Danikov's players hit excellent second shots, each leaving himself to the right with approximately 150 yards to the center of the green. Both shots, however would bring a treacherous green side bunker into play.

Clayman observed Santan's player's hesitation prior to his second shot. He realized the player had to be new to the course. Perhaps this was even his first round at RiverTree. Otherwise, Clayman reasoned, he couldn't have gotten away with his up-to-now sandbagging ruse with three veteran club members. "Watch this," Clayman said to Danikov in amusement—armed with local knowledge of the hole. The long-knocker pulled his three-wood from his bag before looking around for a fairway yardage marker in the vicinity of his golf ball. He walked nearly twenty yards in search of the embedded fairway yardage plate, but all it yielded was the inscription: "Forget it." The hustler was not amused.

Clayman and Danikov smiled at the club pro's sense of humor, whereas Santan immediately sensed an attitude change on the part of his winning ticket. Clayman also picked up on the subtlety and turned to Danikov, asking, "What do you make of this?"

"I don't know, but Santan will do his level best to plant the seed of caution in his player's subconscious and . . . well, looky here," Danikov said. Santan's player had stuffed the three-wood back into his bag and withdrew another, larger headed-club. "That's it, laddie," Danikov said softly to Clayman. "Pull out the cannon! Tear off that 'Biggest-ever Bertha' head cover and give the ball a ride!"

Santan cringed at the sight of the seemingly vertically-faced, eight-degree driver being selected for a fairway lie. Clayman looked at Randall who had taken Santan's cue and was grimacing. The player gritted his teeth and took a smooth practice swing with his small-angle elevation club, then addressed his ball. It was lying well enough on the Bermuda grass fairway, but he was still minus a wooden tee that usually accompanied the club's use.

As the player finished his routine pre-swing waggle and had moved up to address his shot, the usually well-controlled back swing yielded to a glimpse of ego waving from the mind's corner. The result wasn't disastrous, only a slight left-to-right push. 'Slight' was magnified, however, through 250 yards and the result came up ten yards short, right, and in the deep bunker over which the other two players would have to negotiate their third shots.

Santan's player drove his club once into the ground in reaction to the missed shot while Santan instantly raced to where the shot finished in order to inspect the damage. Clayman uncrossed his fingers and Danikov breathed a temporary sigh of relief, saying "We're still in trouble. This guy has to be a good up-and-downer from anywhere. We need a shot to the center of the green to give us a good chance at five and maybe even a crack at birdie."

"You mean," Clayman said, "assuming Randall's guy doesn't do the same."

"Yes, that."

Randall's player hit first, aided and abetted by every positive effort the player's spirit mentor could bring to bear. Randall's mantra focused on his player's taking one more club than normal in allowing for the head wind, as suggested by Santan. The player had taken two clubs out of his bag and now dropped the six-iron in favor of the seven-iron. Then, as if in response to a sudden inspiration, he switched clubs. Randall had a triumphant look.

Unfortunately for Randall and Santan, however, the shot was pulled well left of the green and into long grass. He would ultimately make six and be no factor in the hole.

Danikov's man also allowed for the wind in his club selection and did exactly what both Danikov and Clayman had tried to put into their player's mind. The result was a fine center-green approach leaving himself no more than a fourteen foot putt from slightly below the hole. The swing had been more solid than any of his previous shots on the two holes. Danikov wondered if the hustler wasn't the only one who had been holding back.

The hole itself was situated on the top plateau of a broad-breaking green. Clayman was so elated over their player's last shot that he idly wondered if it was possible for a spirit form to actually be beside himself. He was amused by his own thought. He had already won salvation. If they could win the match, and in the bargain see either Randall or Santan—or both—come to faith . . . well, he didn't want to count his blessings until they had come to be.

Santan's player strode confidently toward the bunker, apparently having shaken off his disappointment at the failed fairway driver attempt. Santan could be seen entreating his player with calming gestures as he repeatedly entered and exited his player's physical space. The player appeared ready to deliver. With his feet planted firmly in the sand he executed a full swing with a slightly open-faced pitching wedge— rather than the sand wedge—and gave it a good follow-through. The result was a shot that sailed softly over the pin where the hole was perched on the upper level. Biting into the green on the second bounce the ball rolled backwards before stopping a mere nine feet above the pin.

The player instantly ran from the deep trap to see the result of a shot he knew he had hit almost perfectly. Seeing the results he nevertheless lightly cursed the fact that the ball hadn't drawn well enough to end up below the hole rather than above it. Without comment Santan nevertheless enthusiastically moved to where the ball lie in order to assess the roll of his man's remaining putt. Randall remained behind and attempted to hug the player.

Clayman and Danikov were about to witness a strange happening. Poised near their opponent player's ball Randall had been exhorting Santan about something. As Clayman and Danikov moved unobtrusively nearer the twosome they managed to pick up the ending conversation: "I know. I know," Randal was saying, "I guarantee I've got it covered."

This was followed by a warning from Santan. "Understand something," he said. "If you can't deliver it will not only cost us the hole, it will cost you even more dearly."

"Don't worry," Randall said. "I told you, this one comes with a lifetime warranty. You agree that the putt's a soft roll, but a full cup's break from left-to-right. I have it. Now stand back. We're in."

"To be perfectly clear," Santan said, "if he misses, you'll find yourself sacrificed to Danikov's personal purgatory."

Randall shrugged off his partner's broken-record message.

Danikov's player was away and while Clayman watched Danikov repeating his 'straightaway-firm' mantra for the unreceiving player, the golfer was very nervous over his surprising opportunity to tie or beat the hustler. As a result he quick-hit his putt, but with enough authority for the ball to arrive at the hole's front door. It lacked the energy to enter, however. A par five. Clayman slapped at his forehead and sagged to his knees in distress. The match was at death's door and he was once more close to being on 'tilt.'

Danikov, however, was intent on their opponent's remaining putt. The putt was obviously no 'gimme', but Santan's player had only to sink it in order to place a lead damper on Danikov's faithful witnessing effort.

Reluctant to trust Randall with anything in spite of the threats, Santan said to his co-conspirator, "That's no easy putt for four, but if he leads it like I told you and he just gets it moving, it'll drop right in and you and I can bury Danikov up to his head in one of these bunkers and cover him with honey."

"Not to worry," Randall said, nervous, but positive. "This is fail-safe." The hustler-player was taking his measure of the putt from every angle. Randall was right with him, at first repetitively planting the notion of the roll: "Unfamiliar greens. Forget your instincts. Borrow a full cup, right-to-left. But softly. Right-to-left, one cup. Softly, one cup, right-to-left. Soft hands."

The player momentarily cocked his head and furrowed his brow. Then he swatted the air as if something was buzzing about. He checked the putt from another angle. Randall eased in again with his thoughts, this time more aggressively. "Softly. One cup out. Right-to-left. Soft, soft, soft."

The player addressed the putt, involuntarily twitching his head twice. As he drew back for his stroke Randall left him with one last thought. "One cup. Stroke it." The result might have been due to nothing Randall was attempting. Perhaps, however, Randall's persistent efforts might have somehow been sensed, with the hard sound of the new word 'stroke' vaguely distracting; a breach of consistency in Randall's repetitive use of the word 'soft.' In any event, the player flinched almost imperceptibly as he putted.

He had correctly borrowed exactly one cup from the right. The ball arched tantalizingly toward the hole, but moved ever fractionally faster than it should. Robbed of a mere one-tenth of its necessary break it nevertheless caught the right side of the hole. It dived downward as well as forward and gravity lost to velocity. Just as if a satellite to Mars were slung out of an Earth orbit, the ball shot left and sharply downhill on the two-tiered green.

Santan let fly a raging string of epithets cursing everything and everyone, including the player's and Randall's mothers. Simultaneously the hustler raised his putter with both hands and brought it down hard over his right knee, muttering to himself and cursing what he believed to be his invisible tormentor. "This is for you, whoever or whatever you are. May your God damn you and cause you to rot in hell for all of eternity." The putter suffered, but did not snap.

Randall was still hovering directly behind the exercised player and had watched the ball as it finally come to rest a full six feet away. This was also the precise moment of a blistering verbal attack on Randall by Santan. Randall was caught off guard to the point of actually staggering. He looked back in Santan's direction with a pleading face, retreating from his position near the player.

In spite of his outburst, Santan quickly recovered, fully realizing all was not necessarily lost. In fact his player had only a shorter putt than before—an uphill one at that—for a tie to set up another hole. This would be no problem. He rushed to support his player, trying to calm him for the relatively simple, straight-up-the-hill putt with the definitely useable, if bent-shafted putter. Or if he chose he could easily putt with the blade of a wedge. Then the unimaginable happened.

The player was so distraught over his failure that he strode angrily to the ball from the hole-side instead of a more typical circuitous and examining angle from the opposite side. He then reached out with the putter and, in disgust, gave the ball a quick flick, knocking the ball away and off the green. Randall's mouth and eyes flew wide in horror, not fully realizing the implications, but suspecting the worst. Had one of the player's opponents possibly conceded the putt? A quick look from both Randall and Santan in the direction of their player's opponents telegraphed the opposite scenario. The hole was lost. Santan exploded with fury.

Danikov and Clayman watched, aghast, as Santan whooshed about in vehement protest, repeatedly shouting "Foul!" and "Void!" After several moments, however, the object of their attention calmed down. Santan closed his eyes and for several moments considered his position before turning to Randall. "You failed. Miserably," he said through pseudo-clenched teeth.. "You should be so fortunate as to go to hell. Instead, Danikov gets a shot at you. Go to meet your punisher."

Randall quivered as he floated away from the green, not certain whether to move up the hill in the direction of the third tee or what. He looked in no one's direction.

Danikov came up to him with Clayman at his side. "Artie," Danikov said, "don't give up on yourself. Santan offered you refuge in your time of need and you took it. I blame myself for that. You followed in the path of a dedicated sinner and, of all people, your partner has rejected you. Before Christ came to let His sins atone for us, you couldn't have been saved for your former actions. But that's no longer the case."

"Why do you bother?" Randall asked. "I'm nothing to you. Neither is Santan. At best he only mocks your witness."

"Believers have a special responsibility to warn unbelievers of the consequences of rejecting God," Danikov responded. "The Lord tells us that if our enemy is hungry, feed him. If he's thirsty, give him something to drink. You're not my enemy, but the biblical phrase to end my point is: 'In doing this you will heap burning coals on your enemy's head.' You don't have a headache, do you, Artie?"

"Leave me alone," Randall said. "All my life I've been trapped between an ill wind and a dead calm. I don't believe in tail winds because I've never known one. It's now apparent to me I don't deserve one."

"Self-pity will not fill your sails any more than good works alone, my friend. All your life you've sought happiness rather than joy. St. Paul perfectly illustrated that point."

"The apostle Paul?"

"Precisely. He obviously wasn't happy with being in prison when he wrote his letter to the people in the church in Philippi in Greece, but he rejoiced."

"He rejoiced over being in prison?"

"No. He simply learned to be content whatever the circumstances. As an illustration I gather that you were an unhappy man long before you came out for this Saturday golf match?"

"Yes."

"And now?"

"Well, we could all be dead, buried and dumb, but we aren't, so let's say I'm tolerant of the current state of affairs. But yes, I'm certainly not happy."

"Get this," Danikov said, "I'm not happy at the moment either, but I *do* have joy. And lots of it."

"Joy in what?"

"Joy in knowing Christ," Danikov said. "You might well ask what that means. If happiness depends upon spending money, accumulating things, searching for new experiences and anticipating the next party, what remains when the money is exhausted, the toys rust, the health flees and people fail us? For most, bitter memories of happy times."

"Are you saying you can be unhappy and joyful at the same time?"

"Yep. Now you could also be happy and have joy as well, but the point is that joy runs deeper and stronger because it depends upon the confident assurance of God's love and work in our lives."

Paul had been drawn to the conversation and unabashedly jumped in, saying, "I wish I had known where to find joy when I was young. I had neither happiness nor joy. Fortunately, I found some happiness in adult life, but joy is so much better. I think it's humility that I have more trouble understanding in today's—or make it 'yesterday's'—competitive life."

"Listen carefully, both of you," Danikov said, catching their eyes, "If you take nothing else from my arguments, this is the crux of it all. I mean this is the Cliff's Notes version from the book of Philippians: 'Christ Jesus, who was in the very nature of God, didn't consider equality with God something to be grasped. So he made himself nothing by taking the very nature of a servant. He was made in human likeness. Then, being found in appearance as a man, he humbled himself and became obedient to death. Crucified on a cross.'"

"That's a mouthful," said Randall, nodding his head in thought. "I think Pauli asked you this question shortly after we arrived, but do you now see this vicarious golf match we're caught up in as any kind of metaphor?"

"Not really," Danikov said as he symbolically rubbed his chin, "well, maybe as the ebb and flow of life. I don't know why we were collectively singled out for our experience, but I do know that with Christ's coming two thousand years ago the opportunity to take your sins—no matter how small, great or repetitive—directly to him instead of through intermediaries became a New Testament reality. All that's required for you to be saved is for you to accept God's grace."

"That's hard to believe," said Randall."

"But that's what true saving faith is all about. Three elements have to be present for it to work. Knowledge, assent and trust."

"I don't understand"

"I don't either," said Clayman.

"Look, it's this simple," Danikov said as he held up three fingers and tugged at the first one. "You have information as to Christ's sacrificial atonement for our sins." He pushed one finger down and pulled at the second, quickly followed by the third, saying, "You accept that knowledge and you place your confidence in Jesus as your Lord and Savior."

Danikov knew they both understood what he had just explained, but he wanted to put it in the clearest and most relevant perspective possible for Randall. "You have heard experts say that Bobby Jones was the greatest amateur golfer who ever lived (knowledge), and you personally believe it (assent), but you don't have any confidence (trust) that he can do anything for you because he's dead and gone. That's the difference in saving faith through Christ."

"It's hard to turn," Randall said, " even if I wanted to."

"I understand, but that's precisely what you must do. We have time. We can talk as long as you like. Santan will wait at our discretion to play the final hole. This is like calling a time-out just before the other guy has to shoot a couple of free throws. We'll 'ice' him a little. What are you thinking?"

Randall managed a slight smile. "By simply saying I buy into this or that my odds for a better end are suddenly assured? I can't accept that."

"You're right, Artie. You haven't accepted it. I doubt if there's ever been a Christian who fully knew what was in store for him when he decided to accept Jesus as his savior. The Walk is a long one with many, many steps. And each step opens the path ahead a little for the next step."

"That sounds biblical enough," said Randall, "but I don't even know what the path looks like, let alone being on it. I have nothing on my petition to speak for me."

"You need nothing that you don't already have. Listen, knowing and serving God is what we were all created to do. I've chosen to commit my life to Him, long before we were placed where we are now. Millions of others have done the same and this is something you need to do, too."

"I'm too proud to turn around, Tommy Ray. I've taken my position with too many others over my lifetime to change, even now."

"Artie. You still aren't listening. Good deeds don't win one's salvation. Accepting God's grace *then* inclines one to commit acts of good for others. By the same token, the lack of having done good deeds doesn't preclude anyone from winning salvation. Consider one of the two thieves who were crucified with Jesus. The robber admitted that he was being justly punished for his deeds, but asked Christ to remember him "

"But did he?"

"On the spot. While on the cross Jesus promised him salvation."

"Tell me," said Randall, looking straight into Danikov's eyes, "do you really know Jesus?"

"Now *that* is a wonderful question. Thank you. Of course I do. I wouldn't dare to claim a personal relationship with Him if I didn't have one. More importantly do you think I do?"

"I don't know, but you seem to honestly care about others. I guess what I really want to know is will he recognize you on the Judgment Day you speak of? All that comes to my mind when I hear the word 'faith' are platitudes and exhortations, rather than salvation itself." Randall said.

"What do you make of Jesus coming to comfort the afflicted and to afflict the comfortable?" Danikov said, rising to the bait.

"Exactly!" Randall proclaimed. "I can quote, too. 'Women, children and unsaved into the life boats!' What am I supposed to make of people glibly quoting scripture?"

"I understand your attitude, Artie. It's born of too much bitterness in life. But that remains your problem, not the Lord's. Look, being a professor of Christianity isn't what counts so much as being a possessor of faith."

"Tell me about that, a 'possessor of faith,'" Randall said, raising his head.

"Thank you for asking another wonderful question." Danikov paused. "Give me a minute," he said, bowing his head in silent prayer.

TWENTY-EIGHT

CLAYMAN WONDERED what Danikov was thinking. He certainly didn't know, but it occurred to him that Danikov had once remarked that before meeting this group and the foursome's transformation he had never once talked about his spiritual convictions with anyone outside a few small church groups.

During that same, earlier conversation Clayman had been further surprised to hear Danikov add that he had once thought a person's religion was an intensely personal thing. He added that he had read that usually meant the individual really had nothing to share. Danikov had also shared with him that even when he became a believer—though his own faith was strong—he found it difficult to witness. Clayman could only assume that Danikov's faith wasn't as strong as he had thought it was and that it had grown much stronger.

Danikov's pause was significantly long enough to cause Randall to look questioningly at Clayman and then back to Danikov. Clayman gently held up one hand and shook his head in Randall's direction.

Clayman didn't suspect anything was amiss. He felt Danikov must be temporarily lost in thoughtful surrender, perhaps weighing something critical. Clayman was increasingly aware of a profound change in Danikov since their first few holes together. He had confided in him that he had previously believed it was actually divisive to try to voluntarily share his faith with unbeliever's—much less to actually try to lead others to consider Christ's Way.

What had changed for him? Clayman wondered. Perhaps the answer was the same as for him. They had both changed. Had *God* changed them? How else? With Danikov admitting that he had come to realize he was better off speaking from a perspective of personal conviction than from absolute faith, maybe that was the 'turning corner.' How might all this ultimately apply to Clayman?

"Thanks, Artie," Danikov said, now fully regrouped. "I have just this moment realized that my former role in life was destined to become afflicted by this group. Thank you for your part. If it's of any comfort to you I can tell you that I was lost for a lot more of my adult life than you've been. You, at least, sampled the meaning of faith. I was as self-confident as Santan, though I didn't possess the curious disdain he has for people. I worked hard, tinkered with cars, read a lot on a lot of subjects other than religion. As I may have mentioned earlier I loved to listen to the music of my father, the big bands of the Forties."

Randall smiled. "I heard that. The ever-broken bridge between the generations: Unwillingness to listen to the next—or previous—generation's music. I'm as guilty for shutting out Artie Shaw and Willie Nelson as you probably are for not liking Jimmy Buffet."

"That's interesting," Clayman said, feeling vindicated by some of what Danikov had just said. "I didn't use to listen to more than a few words of any song. I rarely picked up on the lyrics long enough to remember them. Then, suddenly, one day shortly after college the words to music began to mean everything and for a while the music itself was irrelevant to me."

Danikov smiled. "Hmm," he said. "That strikes a familiar chord. No pun intended. Bear with me, I need to be reminded of something at this moment. One day, in my office during my early fifties, I was playing a tape of a Benny Goodman song. I suppose I had heard it many times before, but never really listened to it. This time the music itself seemed to haunt me. Then, as I played it again to listen more closely to the words, they made me cry. I played it three more times and than called Marilee downstairs to listen to it with me, holding her in my arms and silently weeping. I know she must have thought it strange. I was just so moved by the song's words. And she was the object of that emotion."

"What was the song?" Randall asked.

"Symphony. Symphony of Love."

"Did that incident have a connection with your journey?"

"I don't know, maybe it was coincidental, but within a few weeks, I went to a church for the first time in twenty years, by myself. I didn't even ask Marilee. I didn't go to say I went. I went to experience being in the presence of God."

"And how did you feel?" Clayman asked.

"Like I had found a home. I went back again the next week and then asked Marilee to go with me. She felt the same way and, like I mentioned earlier, before long we both felt called to join the church."

"Did that do it for you? I mean were you, in the church vernacular, 'born again?'" asked Randall, not comfortable with the words he had just used for the first time, but willing to risk the effort.

"Was I saved at that time? No, but I was excited about where I was heading. When you become involved in something that interests you, that's exciting. And when that interest has to do with your soul, 'passion' is an understatement. That's when I started praying on a regular basis. Prior to that, although I had considered myself a Christian since childhood, I don't think I had prayed to God, that is, outside of a rote prayer."

"So how did you begin praying?" Randall asked.

"It wasn't for things. I prayed thanksgiving for being able to accept Jesus as my savior, then I prayed for guidance in continuing my walk with the Lord."

"You didn't pray for yourself or others?"

"As time went on when I was sick or injured I prayed for help in getting well, and I prayed for my family and friends who were sick or injured. My main concern was to grow in a relationship with the Lord. I tried to stay open to possibilities without leaping at superficialities."

"What were your thoughts of yourself as you did this?" Randall asked, intrigued by Danikov's story of hope.

"Only that as long as I was active in making an effort to grow I was making progress. When I sloughed off—didn't attend church services due to an illness or business trip or something, then I felt like a backslider."

"Is that all a part of what you mean by this 'walk with the Lord' business?" Randall asked.

"Precisely. I signed up for a long weekend at a spiritual teaching and reflection retreat, called Walk to Emmaus. It's named literally after Jesus' own walk to Emmaus, immediately following his resurrection."

"What was that all about?" Randall asked, a man suddenly thirsting for the water of life.

"He joined two believers on the road outside Jerusalem, but they didn't recognize him until Jesus allowed them to. In my own early journey I joined a small men's group whose weekly-meeting purpose, aside from studying the Bible, was accountability and sharing of spiritual, personal and family concerns."

"What's the thread here?"

"That's exactly the word to use. I was—and still am—weaving a tapestry of growing faith. Each step up in participation not only provides me with a meaningful new thread, but as I weave it into the mix I also move forward with my grand design."

"Your grand design? What's that?"

"I haven't a clue, except that I'm certain I'll see more of it as my walk progresses."

"But you're dead now. You died. Remember? You're no more in heaven than I am. What does God yet demand of you?"

"If 'demands' were a part of faith, then we wouldn't be able to come to Christ with free will and a desire for salvation, Artie. And as for our 'death,' I don't really know that. What I do know is that I'm to remain faithful."

"That's another problem," Randall said, shaking his head, perhaps realizing some of the long held reasons for his agnosticism. "Exactly which way is that? How do you know what your God wants?"

"Let's get something straight, Artie. My God is the same as your God. There's only one true God and His Word is the Way. In the Bible we're told how to live rightly for ourselves and for our neighbors."

"The Ten Commandments," said Randall.

"There are many more than ten commandments by which God asks us to live. It just so happens that those Old Testament commandments are the 'trailer' for the Bible's Word."

"Trailer? Now you're speaking my language," Randall said, brightening. A 'trailer' usually includes the most exciting parts of the film production itself. Tell you what, teacher. I'll give you a shot at a commercial. What're the real lessons of the Ten Commandments?" Randall asked.

Danikov smiled. "O.K. Since I know you're an unfortunate product of advertising's tendency to capsulize, I'll abbreviate. First, you might appreciate the drama surrounding their original presentation."

"Drama?" Randall asked. "I don't associate that word with the Bible."

"Have you ever read from the Bible, Artie?" Danikov asked.

"No," he said, and then added only partly facetiously, " but the wrath of God surely excuses ignorance."

"No, it doesn't," Danikov rejoined him. "As a matter of fact scripture addressed this very plainly in Romans. The apostle Paul points out that since the creation of the world God's invisible qualities have been clearly seen such that rejection of this truth renders a person 'without excuse.'"

"That's a pretty damning statement."

"But no less true. The Bible is much more than verses, however. It's the single most important, detailed and dramatic account of man's history. The Ten Commandments represent an agreement between God and his chosen people, the Israelites. The Old Testament tells us that the finger of God wrote the commandments on two stone tablets given to Moses on Mt. Sinai. As Moses came down from the mountain, he saw the Israelites worshiping a golden calf. Enraged at the idol worship, which broke the first commandment, Moses smashed the tablets, but at God's command replaced them."

"Wait a minute. If Moses had yet to present the Ten Commandments to his people, how were they to know they were doing wrong?"

"Early Christian teachers believed that God had stamped the commandments on the conscience of every human being, even before the laws were engraved in stone. Beginning in about 400 A.D. everyone who became a Christian memorized the commandments. I think, even more importantly, that within another 800 to 1,000 years Christian scholars began to regard them as principles of a universal law that governed human conduct."

"And they are, professor—?"

"The first and most important Commandment of all: You shall have no other gods before me."

"That makes sense. There can only be one big Kahunna."

"Danikov smiled at Randall's interested irreverence. "Number two: You shall not make for yourself an idol."

"No servant can serve two masters. Sounds like economics 101."

"Well said," Danikov remarked, not disguising his enthusiasm for Randall's continued interest. "Number three: You shall not misuse the name of the Lord, your God."

"Seriously, now," Randall said, "a lot of good people swear. I can't believe this one made the Top Ten." A lot of people take the Lord's name in vain in everyday conversation."

"True, a lot of people take the Lord's name in vain in everyday conversation, but it's just as wrong. I had to work at overcoming it myself. A born-again Christian who swears knows he is wrong the moment he utters profanity. Never act as though God doesn't exist. Number four: Remember the Sabbath by keeping it holy."

"Now if that means no work, that baby is broken by just about everyone. How about you?"

"I make no claim for sainthood. I freely admit that I haven't been able to stand the light from the Lord on this count, even though we're not to be judged by what we eat or drink, or with regard to a Sabbath day."

"That sounds contradictory," Randall said.

"Christians are not necessarily free from struggle," Danikov said, "and certainly not from sorrow or suffering. The Ten Commandments can't be changed to suit individual or cultural needs, yet even Mark said in his gospel, 'The Sabbath was made for man, not man for the Sabbath.'

"I didn't know all—really any—of that," Randall said. And the fifth?"

"Honor your father and your mother."

"That's simple enough."

"So's number six: Don't commit murder."

"What about plain old unpleasantness?"

"Matthew says in scripture that anyone who is angry with his brother will be subject to God's ultimate judgment."

"I can't deny the appeal of being your brother's keeper, but the human condition does make it difficult. Gimme number seven."

"Adultery. Forget it."

"That's a sticky one. Wasn't Jimmy Carter once quoted in *Playboy* as saying he was guilty of committing adultery in his heart? The media had a field day with that."

"I don't know why Jimmy Carter comes to so many people's minds when adultery and the Bible are mentioned in the same sentence. He was probably the most steadfast Christian to ever hold the office of President. More importantly, it's obvious he was simply acknowledging the truth of another of Matthew's quotations from Jesus: 'Anyone who looks at a woman lustfully has already committed adultery with her in his heart.' Christianity can be painful and the President was quick to admit it."

"Well," a suddenly more thoughtful Randall said, "if advertising can be honestly stated to be harmful to your free will, then I guess you shouldn't expect any less candor about your religious faith."

"An Emmy for you, my friend. How do you feel about stealing?"

"Not. Number eight, eh? I'll bet old Matt had a comment about that, too, didn't he?"

"He did. 'If someone wants to sue you and take your tunic, let him have your cloak as well.'"

"Challenge!" Randall held up his first finger to punctuate the point he wanted to make. "If Christians actually followed the Ten Commandments, we'd be living in a much less litigious society. How do you account for that?"

"I can't account for others' decisions and lives, Artie. Only my own. The same for you.

"Now, of all the Ten Commandments, the most person-ally meaningful to me is number nine, the one about not giving false testimony."

"What's so special about that?"

"Since each of us will have to give account on the day of judgment for every careless word we've spoken, I think this commandment, more than any other, reminds us to think before we act or speak, and to take accountability for everything we say or do. It isn't easy."

"Aha!" Randall said, "That's where the crap first hit the fan between you and Santan." Danikov didn't seem to want to revisit that scene, so Randall moved on. "And lastly?" he said.

"Covetousness."

"Greed, huh? I may have to get out of advertising." Randall looked around and smiled as if to acknowledge the shortcoming of his statement. "But that's what we're taught that life is all about," he added. "Commerce is the great teacher. Covet that which my client presenteth as desir-able."

"Almost anything for sale is thus advertised," Danikov said. "But don't mistake me. If you took too literal an atti-tude about advertising you could wrongly condemn lots of things. Each person's reality is still mostly choice based on attitudes and responses."

"So these are God's rules?" Randall asked.

"Yes," Danikov said, "but just as the Ten Command-ments were given as God's law, circumcision and many other requirements were also part of the law of the Old Testa-ment, Christ—who knew no sin—took on our sin in order to save us. When Jesus was nailed to the cross the written code was canceled."

"Canceled?" Randall asked. "Then what was the purpose of the commandments and the other regulations?"

"The law of Moses and the writings of the prophets were put in charge to lead us to Jesus. Christ came to fulfill the laws and justify us by faith. "

"But what was so bad about the law?" Randall asked. He clasped his hands behind him and floated in a small circle in front of Danikov, apparently feeling more enlightened as the conversation wore on.

"Legalism makes believers feel guilty rather than loved," Danikov said. "Because we can never live up to all the rules and regulations, the law produces self-hatred rather than humility."

"What's the bottom line here?"

"Christ, not the law, is all that matters. But believers *want* to serve God, to do the things that are right and good. Doesn't that make sense?"

"Yes and no." Randall said, halting his pacing. "I understand what you're saying, but it's a lot to digest. I think my attitudes have been on trial since our transformation to spiritual form. I've heard it said that trials will refine your faith. For most of my life only my impatience has been enhanced."

"Artie," Danikov said tenderly, "you had no faith to be refined. Your trials will come again, but with faith you'll be able to endure suffering for doing good. That's commendable before God."

Randall was quiet for a moment, then he said, "I've been enduring suffering, but it hasn't been for doing good. I once killed an 'innocent.'"

"What do you mean?" Danikov asked.

Clayman suddenly realized that his vague sense of Randall having a demon to exorcize, or at least to share, was about to come to fruition. Danikov had been masterful in coaxing whatever it was to the surface.

"A baby died in an auto accident," Randall said in painful confession, "and it was my fault."

"How did it happen?" Danikov asked with deep felt empathy.

"I don't remember. The fact is that the baby was riding in another car in an accident in which I was guilty, but not charged. The baby died and I lived. If I can't forgive myself, how could God?"

"Artie," Danikov said tenderly, "God *will* forgive you. You have only to ask. Then you'll be able to forgive yourself."

"But it's too late," Randall said, tears glistening against his wispy face. "We died. God is no longer here." With that he collapsed. Danikov comforted him.

Clayman had been quiet for most of Danikov's and Randall's conversation. He had been thinking of all that was being discussed and was moved to comment as Randall raised himself up. "Artie, in my own religious confusion over the years my head was turned many times. I now suspect this has been true for you. Let me share with you something my girlfriend, Sheila, said to me."

Twenty-Nine

Randall looked up at Clayman in self-pity, saying nothing. Still, he would hear what Clayman had to say.

Danikov nodded at Clayman to proceed. "Actually," he said, "until that particular moment, I had always insisted I knew that *no* one truly knew about God's wishes. At the time we were having an argument comparing the authority of all other religions versus that of her Messiah. Then she hit me right between the eyes. She asked me why anyone would follow the beliefs of a religious founder who was dead. She said that was like going to a marriage counselor who is about to be divorced. I didn't know what she meant until she pointed out that the founder of only one major religion has ever been resurrected from the dead and is actually alive today as our living God. At the time I didn't fully understand her point. I do now. *Living* God, Artie. God is with us, even now."

Randall blinked. "Does that mean it's not too late for me?"

"Not only are you not too late, but your timing is perfect," Danikov said. "And now we need to pray."

"Please," Clayman said. "Let me." All three kneeled as best they could. "Father God, I still don't know my exact position on a lot of things, but one thing I now know is that by Your Grace and with Tommy Ray's help I've been led to your path. I don't know how steadily I can follow it, but I have the will to accept Jesus as my Lord and personal savior." He paused. "And Father, forgive my lack of understanding for my girlfriend, Sheila. I am truly sorry for the misery I have caused her."

Clayman was weeping, but managed to continue. "No less importantly, Lord, come into my friend Artie's life. Be as patient with him as you have with me. I believe he is ready to receive your forgiveness for the mistake for which he has long suffered. As he is ready to submit to your leadership in his life, help him to live in ways that will honor you. I pray in Yeshua's name. Amen."

"Amen," Danikov said. He was deeply moved by Clayman's words. Knowing he could not physically embrace him, he nevertheless attempted it as each had tried before. He simply added, "Welcome, brother."

Randall was moved as he had never been and offered a sincere 'Amen' for the first time in his life. "Thank you both," he managed to say, then hastened to lighten the mood, "Like you said, I'm good to go, but I don't know that I can deliver."

"We don't need promises, Artie. Neither does the Lord. It does you no good to accept God's presence if you don't care about God's will. If you'll accept the promise God makes to all men, that he is the Lord and the Way, then you're saved and you'll make the journey to salvation. You need to say the words yourself, however, but if you have trouble saying them, you can simply affirm what Paul and I have already said on your behalf."

Randall went to his knees, the first significant tears of his adult life falling from his spiritual form. "Lord, I'm a simple man who would be more. I have sinned. I confess. I thirst. I believe. Amen."

Danikov and Clayman moved to flank Randall, each ready to embrace him, but through his tears he still preferred to settle for a symbolic handshake and shoulder clasp. Danikov said, "Thank you Lord for this wonderful blessing and for softening the hearts of these two men. Amen."

"Whew," Randall said. "That's enough. I'm on overload, but hopefully for eternity. Now, don't we have some unfinished business with one Luke Santan? How in the world are we going to deal with him?"

"United." Danikov said. "For where two or three are gathered in His name, He is there."

THIRTY

As they looked around for Santan the three each had an independent notion of an impending presence. For a moment they saw nothing, but looked at one another quizzically. Then their senses were rewarded with the sudden appearance of a friend. "Barnabas!" exclaimed Danikov. The others gathered around. This time he was alone.

"Grace and peace, brothers," Barnabas said. "Do you mind if I play through?" The visiting spirit playfully swung an imaginary golf club.

"Man, did you ever come at the right time," Randall said. "Several of us have just had an epiphany, but we could really use your help with our collective bogey, and—" Randall interrupted himself, seeing that something was wrong with the picture.

"What is it, Barnabas?" Danikov asked, sensing as did Randall that something was amiss.

"I bring you news," he said. "Remember, however, that I am only a messenger."

The radiance on the faces of Randall and Clayman was instantly replaced with fleeting sadness, then worry, quickly followed by fear. "What do you mean?" Clayman asked. "Don't we warrant help?"

"Of course you do, but your needs are not necessarily those of the Lord," said a sympathetic Barnabas. "I know of your concern for one of God's most estranged souls, your friend Santan. Try as you will, the Lord will harden his heart and Satan will cheer. But you must persist."

At that point Santan rejoined them saying, "I see you've unfairly replaced me in the foursome with our occasional visitor. That would mean forfeiture of the match. I accept."

"No such luck," Randall said. "By the way, I don't know who's writing your material, but you need a new writer." Clayman was stunned by Randall's new boldness and flipped him a thumbs up.

"We were just having a conversation with Barnabas," Danikov said. "You're welcome to join us."

"Carry on," Santan said.

"During your discussions of your purpose for being here," Barnabas said, "how many of you have been moved to weep in the presence of the Lord?"

Before Danikov, Clayman and Randall could even nod at the surprising question, Santan quickly moved back from the loose circle, saying, "Damn you! Have you, too, come to judge me?"

Barnabas looked saddened as he directed his comments to Santan, "Who am I to judge the Lord's servants? To his own master each of us stands or falls."

Santan raised both of his hands to chest level, palms outward as he took another step backward saying, "I bow to no one."

Barnabas replied without rebuke, but with confident authority, "'As surely as I live,' says the Lord, 'every knee will bow down before me; every tongue will confess to God.'"

Santan apparently did not hear the meaning of Barnabas' words, only that they were in opposition to his predetermined course. "I now understand that I'm under fire by some sort of unholy alliance," he retorted, "but I use as protection your own defense against the non-Christian claims that your cursed religion perpetually rains down upon man's inequities."

"And what is your protection?" said Barnabas, neither anger nor indignation evident in his voice or demeanor.

"Free will!"

"Luke," Barnabas said evenly, "you are fortunate to have Christian friends here who have not given up on you, but they will not find their task easy. I will leave you with a question to ponder. Your free will aside, what do you do with your guilt? When you are left to your own thoughts, you surely recognize the presence of guilt in some of its many different forms. You can neither deny your guilt nor escape it. And even if you rationalize it, you still have it. Sin is not exclusive to you, however, but is owned by every man and woman who has ever lived, save one."

"I know this is a set-up," Santan said, trying to maintain an offensive position, "but exactly what would you like me to do with this 'guilt' you're so certain I carry around?"

"Christians know of only one solution." Barnabas said, pausing. No one spoke or moved and he continued. "That solution is to ask for your guilt—for your sins—to be forgiven. If you repent of your sins, you will receive remission of your guilt."

Before Santan or anyone else could respond, however, Barnabas was gone. Danikov suddenly found himself stricken with sorrow at the group's growing collective plight. He looked at Clayman and then Randall and saw his reaction mirrored in each of them.

Turning to Santan Danikov said, "In a few moments we'll probably be back at our spiritual golf post, with the vicarious game resumed, but in the meantime I want to set the Lord's table. Luke, if you can do so with purity of heart I invite you to join us in a sprit of confession and acceptance of the Lord. If not, since this is only symbolic, you're welcome to join us anyway. Such communion is the new and different memorial meal of simple bread and wine that Jesus instituted to remind us of the wonderful gift of salvation."

"For that very reason I cannot, will not," Santan said defiantly, and immediately left their presence. The others were eager to participate. Danikov collected himself and said, "Although I have never before performed this ceremony for others, I do so humbly in the sight of the Lord. Partaking of communion's bread is symbolic of the Lord's body which was broken for us. Likewise, partaking of juice or wine is symbolic of his blood shed for us. This was first done by Christ with his twelve disciples—the night before Jesus died—in establishing his new covenant with man. So too, Paul and Artie, may our symbolic gesture of dispensing the bread and wine be appropriate as a blessing in His name. This is our 'Passover,' that saves us from the slavery of sin." He then symbolically offered Christ's body and blood to each of the them, which they each received and symbolically swallowed.

Randall spontaneously—if nervously— returned the gesture saying, "Tommy Ray, this is the body of Christ broken for you. And this is the blood of Christ shed for you."

THIRTY-ONE

SANTAN WAS WAITING ON THE THIRD TEE, fuming as much as a physically disembodied form could manage. "What's been keeping you, Danikov?" he asked.

"You mean 'us' don't you?" Danikov said, glancing at the others.

"The other two are excess baggage and you know it. It's you and me for all the chips."

"Did your mama find you as disagreeable as I do?" Danikov asked.

"Until you and I met I had done fine, thank you very much. Since then my goal has been to rid myself of you. Let's play."

"Is the number three hole your choice?" Danikov asked.

"No, it isn't. We're going to eighteen. See you there."

Clayman and Randall joined Danikov as they whisked over the treetops back toward the eighteenth tee, the one hole they hadn't actually played during the real life match.

Clayman thought that while such a high flying excursion should be awesome, he experienced no friction in the course of the flight, thus no exhilaration.

"This is a curious choice," Clayman said as they arrived on the eighteenth tee. "It's a middle-handicap hole, number eight I believe. No particular advantage I can think of accrues to him on this hole and there's less than a 50% chance of it being a stroke hole for any given player."

Randall added, "You're dead right. But I know Santan best and I can tell you he wouldn't select a particular hole on which the match could turn if he didn't have a plan. I'm worried."

"Well then, boys," said an apparently unconcerned Danikov, "we'll just have to see how his plan develops. Besides," he said with a smile, "worry is the devil's grass seed."

Clayman looked around. Where was Santan? At nearly the same moment Danikov glanced backwards. Suddenly he understood the plan. Santan was well behind them . . . on the gold tee box. This changed the entire complexion of the hole. Number eighteen went from being a short par four 358-yard hole from the blue tees to a 415-yard serious challenge for high-to-mid handicappers.

Danikov quickly surveyed the hole to remind himself of its layout. A narrow lateral water hazard paralleled the fairway on the right and protected an out-of-bounds area immediately adjacent. Zero margin for error in that direction. Two fairway bunkers also came into play on the right with only a few yards separating them from front to back and a full 225 yards from the closest one to the center of the green. The approach from the right to the large, tiered green was also guarded by a thicket of tall pine trees.

On the left was another fairway-bordering creek which emptied into a large pond and occupied all space left and short of the fairway for a hundred and fifty yards out from the green. The left side of the fairway, however, did allow ample landing space for a drive, providing a shot wasn't hooked. Under the seasonally-dried condition of the course, however, even a solidly hit draw from the most forward tee to left of center would guarantee a thirsty ball an opportunity for a lake drink. A short tee shot well left would leave too much water to negotiate in carrying a second shot to the green.

A real-life foursome was on the tee. Clayman wondered which sacrificial player Santan would hand to Danikov. Santan looked each of the group over carefully and then passed altogether before the first player could hit. Another foursome lurched through with no action by Santan. Then another. And another. It appeared to Clayman that Santan was now automatically waving off interest in each group before they could even reach the tee and take a practice swing.

"You think he's waiting for a known quantity?" Danikov said.

"I do," Clayman said. "Even though the hustler has cost him both previous holes, plus Randall and me, I think he still wants him."

Danikov frowned. "That means he'll saddle me with one of the other three. They're a toss-up, but a full notch below Santan's man."

"But you still won't get the benefit of any handicap," Clayman said as he shook his head in frustration.

"He's right," Randall said, nodding, "I don't think this dog'll hunt."

"Ye of little faith," Danikov said.

"I know. I know," Randall said. "But you know you got lucky on the last hole."

"No, I didn't. God doesn't make mistakes."

An anxious Randall turned to Clayman. "As much as I've come to believe, I'm worried, too. Is this where you say all that remains is to trust the Lord?"

"I think you just identified the plan," Clayman said." He looked at Danikov and smiled, who nodded in agreement.

With some anxiety nevertheless heaping itself onto the two spirits-in-waiting, the foursome they had abandoned on the third hole made their way to the eighteenth tee. Time seemed not to be a part of the spirit foursome's dimension, only activity.

In the meantime Santan had again whisked away. Simultaneous with the foursome's arrival Santan also returned, apparently from a scouting trip at the seventeenth green. "The big knocker is mine again," he said, matter-of-factly. "Danikov, welcome to your new guy, the one who nearly shanked a putt in three-putting for double-bogey five on seventeen. Oh, yeah, almost forgot to mention that they'll all be playing from the golds."

Danikov mildly objected, but was actually impressed. "Back on holes number one and two they were all playing from the white tees. How'd you get them herded all the way back to the championship tee?"

"I put a ring in their noses," snorted Santan.

"Luke," Danikov said, "wait a minute. Before we begin this finishing hole I want to ask you a question. If I accept your incredible earlier statement that you aren't interested in your own salvation, let's at least consider for a moment the truth about right and wrong."

Santan was impatient, watching the live group mount their carts near the seventeenth green. "The sheep approach," he said, expectantly. Irritated by Danikov's implication, however, he added, "So you know right from wrong, and I don't?"

"Not at all. My point is that we're all sinners, but each of us makes hundreds of choices every day. Most choices have no right or wrong attached to them at all—like which stories to read in the newspaper or which golf club to select for a particular shot."

"Aha," Randall interjected. "Now, that's *my* problem. I'm guilty of making wrong decisions with both club *and* course management." He laughed, a little nervously.

"Right, Artie, and those are simply choices of incorrect or poor judgment," Danikov said. "But we also face decisions of more critical impact. If we prefer doing right to wrong, what are the criteria for making such decisions?"

"Please share with us your criteria," Santan said sarcastically.

"I'll tell you what the Bible offers as a guide," Danikov said, "which doesn't mean we can always be successful in following it, but awareness helps in making choices on sensitive issues. For example, if we choose one course of action, am I thinking only of myself, or do I truly care about the other person?"

"Now that's ridiculous," Santan said.

"Why?"

"Be practical for once. If weighing every minor decision beforehand on your grand scales of righteousness, the world would grind to a halt. Nothing would be accomplished."

"All right, then," Danikov said, "what's your basis for a decision for not deciding to wave a driver ahead of you in heavy traffic, or in selecting one set of players over another in this final hole?"

"Defending your place in line! Competition! The NASDAQ!" Santan said, practically screaming in objection. "Ever hear of those things? Hey, I live by a code, all right. Mine! Who else will take care of me?"

"Precisely my point," Danikov said. "If each of us develop more of an attitude for considering the good of others, we all benefit."

"You're not only an idealist, you're a hypocrite!" Santan answered. "Are you telling me you don't care whether or not you win this match?"

"Of course, I want to win. But at what expense? If the objective is merely to win or to be first in line at any cost, then the desire is obviously that of service to self rather than serving others."

"Class dismissed," Santan said. "The flock is at the gate."

Danikov sighed. As the two golf carts whizzed down the lower part of the path toward the eighteenth tees, Clayman was suddenly animated. "Look," he said, enjoying the unfolding contradiction, "Only Santan's Bubba is still on the gold tee. Could be a revolution at hand. The others have stopped and are waiting in their carts for him to hit! Crunch time."

Santan raced to pull up short of both the real life and the spirit threesomes on the middle tee box and shouted defiantly at all of them, "*Everyone* has to play from the golds!"

"Santan," said Danikov, "you're not only paranoid, you must be the first spirit to suffer from Alzheimer's. Just because you somehow inserted ego into the hustler to influence him to move to the back tees, I doubt he could over-come the others' desire to service their own need to win the hole. Ironic, eh? I think you've miscalculated."

Clayman joined the fun. "Luke," he said, "the flames have been licking at your brains for too long. "

Randall liked the remark and said so. Then, as Randall appeared to Clayman to be struggling to come up with a clever follow-up comment, Santan suddenly cursed and took a healthy, if ineffective, hand-swipe at the spirit pair before whooshing on up to the gold tees where his player stood, surveying his challenge.

Santan's player teed up and walloped a shot with the same huge-headed titanium driver he had tried to play from the fairway on the second hole. Practically as a part of the ball's paint, Santan flew alongside the missile, still in a fit. His efforts to cajole the ball to perform for him were wasted. The ball flew like a bullet drawn to a huge magnet, arcing from left to right and growing in altitude with each ten yards covered until it peaked safely to the right of the lake. It dropped just inside the fairway marker which indicated the distance to the middle of the green was one hundred and twenty yards. The ball barely hopped forward in the low-lying, thus always-soft eighteenth fairway.

Danikov turned to the others and remarked, "So much for our supposed advantage on the tee shot. He hit it dead-center and only five yards shy of 300 yards."

The two non-factor players hit from the blue tees. Then Danikov's new player was up. He received the non-benefit of what Danikov could manage in the way of a subliminal swing suggestion. Randall said, "Partner, you aren't gonna let him try to outdrive the hustler just because he has a fifty yard advantage from the tee are you?"

"Of course not," Danikov dead-panned.

The golfer's words at addressing his ball were, "I'm gonna outdrive this s.o.b. one time if it's the last thing I ever do."

The player had a reasonably good swing, but it could not hold up under the extreme duress to which it would now be subjected. Pulling his right hand over the top of the club during his swing resulted in an ugly topped shot. The ball bounded and skimmed across the ground and ran left of center in managing to advance no more than a hundred and thirty yards. Exasperated, Clayman shouted, "Oh, no! A wounded worm-burner. We're dead."

"If we died every time you guys made the call," Danikov said, joking, "we'd be slow to answer Christ's call to resurrecting the dead. Relax. Our guy can still make four."

With work to do, Danikov first perched himself on top of his man's cart as he chased down the cart path after the terrible tee shot. After a moment he eased down into the player's space and began to utter a repetitive calming notion. "Trust your swing. Trust your swing. Trust your swing."

For the golfer's next stroke—and with his real-life cart partner witnessing—Danikov's player approached his ball this time with a very different attitude than on the tee. He pulled out his metal three 'wood' for the 230 yard shot to the green, saying, "My distance. Good lie. Stay within yourself and trust this old swing. Yup, gonna trust this swing."

The club brushed the grass and caught the ball flush at the precise low point of the swing's downward arc. The Maxfli slowly rose to its half-altitude before being influenced by the natural draw of the player's swing, carrying it at first toward the pine trees at the right of the fairway, then back towards the green. The ball lit on a slight ridge a few yards short and to the right of the green's front edge giving it a bigger bounce than normal. The ball leaped forward once, then again a second time before it touched down to roll up a slight incline to within ten feet short of the hole.

Of the total of eight spirit and flesh figures variously positioned on the hole, all but three leaped from their positions and shouted. The hustler and his playing partner slumped in their cart. Santan sulked too, but only for a moment.

Jumping up, Santan instantly began exhorting his man as he rode along for a distance with him saying, for probably no effect whatever, "You're a hundred yards closer than he was. Nothing but a pitching wedge! You can get inside of that! Keep your head!"

Randall was the first to arrive at the big hitter's ball, then Clayman and Danikov, followed by Santan. All of them were well ahead of the only two live players in which the spirits were interested. Santan was using a broom motion in the direction of the opposing spirit threesome as he cursed them shouting, "Get outta here. Tend to your own man. Don't be trying to influence mine." He added punctuation by snarling and saying to Randall, "You do anything to cause my man to falter and you'll be honoring a god of treachery."

Randall muttered, "Your guy isn't even here yet and he's been traveling for three days. Ought to be a law against hitting a ball so far. With his swing he could probably reach the green from here even if he chunked it. That's 'chunk' with a capital 'C,'" he said for Santan's benefit.

Danikov restrained his cheerleader. "Come on, Artie. Luke has enough problems without your help."

The spirit threesome left the scene. As Clayman and Danikov approached the green to watch the results of their opponent's shot, Clayman said, "I used to have a friend who regularly played a long knocker like this and he loved to say, 'Sure he hits it big off the tee, but on every hole you still get to put a wedge in his hands.'"

"Incoming," Danikov said. The hustler's wedge shot was hit solidly, but was pulled a little left of a right side pin placement. The ball ended up twenty-five feet away, but on the level.

Clayman was ecstatic, saying, "We've got him, Tommy Ray. Your guy can pop his right in and we'll waltz out of here with Matilda."

"You're as bad as Artie," Danikov said, chuckling. "You remind me of the farm boy checking the nest of one of his prize hens and seeing ten healthy eggs equates that with the number of chickens he thinks will hatch."

"I like the less creative, but original version better," Clayman said. "I'll try to remember the lesson though."

Santan was eyeing his player's putt from every angle he could think of. Clayman noticed that Santan seemed about to be unduly focused on his savior-of-the-moment, when the live player suddenly looked around nervously. Perhaps the hustler was anxious about a repeat of the earlier and crucial, but negative putting episode. Santan also seemed to notice the effect and retreated, leaving the player to his own devices.

The hustler's putt was struck purely and solidly and it rolled smoothly, drifting ever so slightly left-to-right less than a quarter of the width of the hole. The ball ran to its goal as if in a drainpipe to a rain barrel. Center splash. Birdie three.

Danikov looked at a dejected Clayman as if to say, "See what I mean?"

Randall scurried to his partners' sides. "We still have one chance of staying alive," he said. "What do we do?"

"Did you see what Santan did with his player?" asked Danikov. "He let him play his game. These other three guys play their own game pretty well. Besides, I overheard how much they have riding on the game. Our guy knows how much his shot counts. Let's back off."

Danikov's player walked up to his putt with the same kind of confidence he had exhibited prior to his magnificent fairway shot. He checked the line from below the hole, then from above it, then below it again, finally observing it from the side on his final approach. As he was about to stroke the ball the player said aloud to himself, "You've had this putt a thousand times, Max. Stroke it like you know that." He did. The ball went in and the spirits' match would go extra holes, still in a sudden death playoff.

THIRTY-TWO

THIS TIME, after having finished a hole, the three allied spirits hung around the green rather than dashing off to the presumed next tee. The foursome they had ridden for the past three holes had finished their round. The "next" tee could be any tee, given Santan's capriciousness. Clayman complained about that to Danikov and Randall. "We're under a distinct disadvantage. He picks the holes and the players. It's unfair."

"Right," Randall said. "Time for the worker spirits to unite against the tyranny of the capitalist spirit. What say we refuse to play any more vicarious golf?"

"O.K.," Clayman said, "you've made your point."

"We're playing the game precisely as I made it," Danikov said. "The fact is we're fortunate that two of two have gone our way. I can also tell you this: there's no guarantee for right over wrong."

"Why would God not recognize your battle and help you subdue Satan's emissary?" Clayman asked.

"Ah, the eternal question asked by the sanctified," answered Danikov, gently ushering the other two away from the green so as not to be distracted by the upcoming live foursome's shots, a group in which they had no interest. 'Why me,' you say? This question is among Satan's favorites. He loves the planting of that sort of seed for the productive fruit it bears in his fight to blind both the faithful and the skeptics. Man punishes himself trying to answer the question in light of man's own flawed sense of logic. Consider that if mankind were required to follow some sort of predetermined code, where would be the free will given to him that makes man what he is?"

"Well, O.K.," Clayman said, "Forget about requiring otherwise 'bad' men to do right, but still, doesn't God intervene once in a while to make terrible things right?"

"The book of Daniel makes it clear that if God always rescued those who were true to him, Christians would not need faith. God has a hand in everything, but His hand doesn't stay the mind or motives of his servants, let alone those who deny Him. That's our job."

At that moment, Santan, who had again momentarily whisked elsewhere returned and caught Randall's eye, motioning for the group to follow him. Clayman was trying to analyze the current situation. With Santan's golden boy having finished the eighteenth he had lost the horse he would otherwise have stayed with. Since their adversary was now handicapped in not being able to select from known players—both for himself and for Danikov—the next best thing to rely on for an advantage would likely be a hole with a handicap stroke for one player over another. Clayman thought that would probably mean a par five. But which one?

As the spirit foursome crossed over the embankment which housed the cart tunnel leading from the eighteenth green back to both the clubhouse and the tenth tee, Santan led them to the par five tenth hole. He appeared to be watching intently as the foursome which had only pulled up to the tee box unfolded themselves from their carts as they complained about a delay. As they walked out onto the tee itself, some taking practice swings, Santan said, "This is our group. Your man is wearing the green cap with the RiverTree logo on it, Danikov. Mine is the one with no hat."

Santan pointed to both Clayman and Randall and then gestured in the direction of the tenth green, saying, "Why don't you guys head out to keep an eye on the tee shots?"

"They may prefer to stay with the game," a suspicious Danikov said. "But I'm curious. Tell us what made you pick this particular hole and group?"

"You think I'm going to share my strategy with you, even if you can't do anything about it?" Santan was suddenly aware of the truth he had just stated. "O.K.," he said, retracting his position. "I might share at that. But first, reverend, what's *your* game plan?"

"To pray for my man to do his best and for your soul to be given up by Satan."

"Hah!" Santan roared defiantly with an unholy look of glee. "You asked me to prophesy, so I will." He threw up his hands as if in supplication, saying, "My God has already given me this hole! When it's over, I'll reign over this little corner of the spirit world and you'll be lucky if I don't blow you and your sidekicks off into the void."

Danikov shuddered and pulled himself together to stare straight into Santan's eyes, searching as he said, "Man, don't you see what's happening to you? You've become possessed by the devil. Ever since our arrival as spirits you've defended your position vigorously, but never with so much venom. You intend to 'reign' over us? Where did that come from?"

"Not from your Christ," Santan said, disdainfully. "From myself. I answer to no one. Not in life. Not in spirit. I have support, however, but he is a mentor, not a master."

"Santan, hear your words! They're not yours. They're alien. Even your blasphemy against Christ can be forgiven if you would only ask forgiveness. Those who aren't ignorant of what they do, however, and also refuse Christ, are in Satan's camp."

"It's you who are misled," Santan said. "Even more so Clayman and Randall by turning."

Clayman and Randall were upset by Santan's remarks and appealed to Danikov with looks that begged him to refute the antagonist.

Santan kept up his barrage, again directing his comments to the other two: "What difference does it really make whom one chooses to be his God? When it's over, dead is still dead, whether as decayed flesh or as emasculated spirit."

"I believe," said Clayman through his completely recast attitude, "that you may find there to be a much less desirable third alternative after death."

Danikov nodded in saddened agreement, saying, "In fact, Luke, I fear you're carrying around an engraved invitation. Tell me why you wouldn't be interested in life after death when life is so precious for so many reasons, and knowing firsthand that it can be taken from you in an instant?"

Santan was at first quiet. Then, after a moment's thought, he became defiant, jutting his chin and narrowing his eyes. "I've never found life to be so precious that I couldn't imagine it ending, even as it did," he said.

Danikov was incredulous. "Never? How about during your childhood?"

"Especially then."

"What happened to desensitize you?"

Santan hesitated before replying. "Religion!" he retorted.

"Religion without faith, a common malady. What could possibly have happened to hold your religion responsible?"

"A man died. A young man so committed to your almighty God that it cost him his family. His faith, and I mean faith, betrayed him."

"What happened?"

"I told you. He died."

"But how? Doing what?"

Clayman was amazed at the exchange between the two, that Danikov had for a second time actually engaged Santan in something resembling a personal dialogue.

"Drowned," Santan said. "He drowned saving a drunken speedboat driver who had just hit and capsized the preacher's small fishing boat." Santan was about to say more, but then held back, almost as if in disgust.

"Was the pastor your father?" Danikov asked softly, compassionately.

"Yes!" Santan blurted. "He not only lost his life, he left his family impoverished and vulnerable." Santan displayed no emotion in making the statement as he continued with his narrative, unable to refer to the pastor as his father. "His wife died a year later. With no family to take them in all three siblings found only abuse in one foster home after another. Two of them died in their teenage years. I ask you very simply and with no expectation whatever: 'What kind of God rewards selfless devotion by crushing his subjects? Better to either worship no God at all or name what you love most as your God."

"How old were you when you lost your father?"

"Thirteen."

"You blamed God?"

"No. There was no God to blame."

A revelation suddenly came to Danikov. "Santan," he said gently, "you don't realize it, but you were once in the Lord's camp. All children are. You simply let pride lead you away at an early age. You need desperately to return to Him for the same reason God's people have always needed to return."

"You're dead wrong. If I were to be arrested for being a Christian, there wouldn't be enough evidence to even bring me to trial, much less to convict me."

"Luke, what would you say is the most important event in the history of the universe?"

"I can't speak to that. But I do know that the most damning event in my life is what I just described."

"I pray you'll come to healing over that personal tragedy," Danikov said. "One of the most startling verses in the Bible for victims such as you is addressed to the apostles by James, who said to consider it pure joy when you face trials. He said those who persevere under trial are blessed, because when they've stood the test, they'll receive the crown of life that God has promised to those who love him."

"You're starting to talk like my father. What's your denomination?"

"It doesn't matter," Danikov said, giving himself a symbolic scratch on the back of his head, "because evangelicals united in the Gospel are one family. It's been said by many and for centuries—although often forgotten when men allow opinions to seep into theology—that in things necessary there must be unity, in things less than necessary there must be liberty, and in all things there must be charity."

"Well, that's quite a sermon. As for James, however, we didn't walk in the same shoes. I long ago gave up on a just God allowing so much suffering in the world."

"Luke, you have it backwards. Why doesn't the world suffer more? Given our unending work of great and small sin and destruction upon His planet, why does God even tolerate us?"

Now it was Santan's turn to reflect momentarily. He placed his interlocked hands behind his head and symbolically stretched. "I don't love God," he said, "simply because there is no God."

"But there is. And He loves you. He so loved the world that he sent his only son to give up his life for man's sins. He was pierced for our transgressions and crushed for our iniquities; the punishment that brought us peace was upon Him, and by his wounds we are healed. Luke, you have only to accept God's grace in order to gain salvation. Do that and you'll be healed of a lifetime of hurt and anger."

"Don't take this too personally," Santan said, sarcastically, "but I want to be clear on something. I don't like either you or your attitude. I find both intrusive. Why is it that Christians think they know how other people should live?"

That caught Danikov by surprise. He welcomed the question, but he didn't expect Santan to ask it. "Let's see if I can focus your complaint a little more sharply. You don't like having religion shoved down your throat and that's how you view the direction of our discourse. Right?"

"Dead right."

"I understand," Danikov said. "You don't want me hounding you to change your values. You feel you have the right to do what is right in your own mind."

It was Santan's turn to be surprised. "Well said," he responded warily.

"One of my favorite theologians, R. C. Sproul, Sr., addressed that question. He said essentially that if God is the Lord of the human race, the Creator of all of us, and if he holds us accountable to him—and he does and is—then there's an objective standard of what is right in his sight. He points out that God reveals very clearly that one of the great symptoms of our human fallenness is the idea that people have the right to do what is right in their own minds."

"Sproing!," Santan said, shaking his head. "I walked straight into the proselytizer's trap."

"Don't be so automatically defensive, Luke. Mathematics is a science of logic as well as absolutes. See the logic of Sproul's argument. The whole concept of the Judeo-Christian religion is that ultimate righteousness is declared, not by my personal preferences or by yours, but by God and his supreme character. If I as an individual come to an understanding of what God requires of people, then that means I am required to do certain things."

"Thank you very much, but I'll pass," Santan said, folding his arms over his chest. "I reject the notion of salvation by grace as absolutely as the Jews themselves rejected it two thousand years ago."

Clayman could not keep silent. "I'll remind you again, Luke, that not all Jews rejected Christ. I recognize that even more clearly now in reflecting on Sheila's argument that the Jews rejected Christ as the Messiah simply because they were expecting that the coming kingdom would be like that of the forty years of King David's leadership, not to mention the deliverer himself, who would free Israel from its enemies."

"That's correct," Danikov said. "Those were the popular Jewish messianic expectations, not that the messiah would be a humble servant. His coming was prophesied by Isaiah in the Old Testament. The Jews of the time did not have the benefit of reading the New Testament, but we have both Old Testament prophecy and New Testament fulfillment."

"As Tommy Ray has gently reminded me, Luke," Clayman said, "Let those who have ears, hear."

With that statement, Santan's heart was hardened even more. The three spirit allies could sense it at once. Santan raised his right hand and pointed his first finger skyward and then dashed it sharply downward saying, "I curse you all in name of my father's false God." Then, incredibly, he composed himself, and before the others could even react to his initial outrage Santan instantly shifted into debate format.

"Danikov, you've relentlessly battered a vulnerable skeptic with your incessant clamor about Christ fulfilling Old Testament prophesies. Then you used New Testament hellfire threats to hammer a happy agnostic into limp-rag submission. You know what you are? A sorry, pseudo-scholar attempting to justify a hypocritical life with a failed imitation of a saint."

"Your personal insults don't bother me," Danikov said, the barest of grins on his face, "although I will admit to its poetry. All I have to answer to is your challenge of Biblical truths."

"So prove your claims," Santan said.

"I have no proof. The proof of fulfillment of Old Testament messianic prophesies are exactly where you say they are: in the New Testament."

"All right, I'll cut you a little slack for the moment," Santan said, locking his hands behind his head, as if bored. "Be specific about these supposedly fulfilled prophesies."

"You'll only argue against each, regardless of their authority."

"Isn't that legitimate?"

"Of course it is, if the arguer is open to reason."

"I'm as open to reason as John Wesley."

"You greatly flatter yourself," Danikov said. "But I'll test that premise." He was delighted to have even this entree to possible meaningful discussion. "There's the Old Testament prophesy that the Messiah would be born in Bethlehem," he began.

"Prophesied by whom?"

"Micah."

"Coincidence. If your Christ happened not to have been born in Bethlehem, the prophesy would then have been either buried or rationalized."

Danikov took a symbolic deep breath to enable his motor to cool. Don't concede any shots in this verbal match, he thought. "You want something more substantive?" he said. "O.K. The messiah would be born of a virgin."

"The most suspicious of all of your so-called fulfillments. There is absolutely no way to prove such a birth actually happened outside your New Testament's interpretative history. Next prophesy."

"If you discount this particular multi-documented bit of biblical history, you're implying that all of written history is subject to challenge once actual witnesses have died. That's decidedly not Wesleyan."

"I don't agree. The fact is that you're simply being subjective in defense of your position. Have you any other prophesies?"

"The messiah was to be a prophet, like Moses."

"I can't argue that. Even the Jews concede that Jesus was a prophet. But big deal. Prophets were a Hebrew kopek a dozen."

"Again, I question your definition of being a 'reasonable' man," Danikov said. "I suppose you also find it coincidental that the Messiah was prophesied to be rejected by his own people."

"No. On the contrary, quite expected. Most leaders face rejection sooner or later."

"Would your broad theory-of-expectation also be extended to crucifixion?" Danikov asked.

Santan was enjoying this immensely, as evidenced by his enthusiasm for continuing. Clayman was squirming at Danikov's inability to score on Santan's mind—let alone close—on the issue. But ah, he thought, the crucifixion prophesy offered promise.

"Did Christ die on the cross alone?" Santan questioned.

"You know he didn't. Two others were crucified alongside him."

"Thank you for your testimony," Santan retorted, "that crucifixion was obviously common in those days."

Clayman was depressed. This is going nowhere, he thought.

"Your only intention is to simply deny that prophesy both happened and was fulfilled," Danikov said. "I can hardly wait to hear your argument against the prophesy that the messiah would be raised from the dead."

"Let's hear the exact nature of the prophesy."

"As it happens, I can oblige," Danikov said, glancing at Clayman. "Again, the psalmist David: 'Nor will you let your Holy one see decay.'"

"Interpretation. Nearly everything Biblical is subject to interpretation."

At this point, Randall, who had been totally outside the fray, struggled against saying something—anything—simply to be a participant. He gave in, saying, "Tommy Ray, back off a little. I think you're wearing him down." Randall lamely smiled at his effort.

"The sarcasm isn't necessary," Danikov said. "If I hadn't been advised by Barnabas to persist in this effort I would have long ago shaken off the dust from my feet as a testimony against Santan, but I'm not quite through."

THIRTY-THREE

Santan was in no rush to see the argument concluded. "And is it to Barnabas that I owe my saving?" he asked, savoring the conversation even more since he had cleverly managed to place Danikov in the witness chair.

"You're not saved," Danikov said with authority. "As a matter of fact I regret not having spent more time with you discussing the fundamental fact that man was created in the image of God."

"Point dismissed," Santan said with a wave of his hand. It looked to Clayman as if Santan were suddenly feeling superior about the argument. "Look," Santan continued, "man has to look like something. Now, let me get this straight. If I believed in your savior, I'd be saved from hell, and for all eternity. Correct?"

"That's only part of it. You would also have to repent of your sins."

"And as we speak now, exactly where is your savior?"

"At God's right hand."

"That, too, was prophesied?"

"Certainly. By no less a figure than King David, again in the Psalms: 'The Lord says to my Lord: sit at my right hand.'"

Santan swung his right hand in a downward, right to left motion, then from left to right, as if brushing everything away, and saying, "David this. David that. Simon says this. Simon says that."

"Whether you like the reference or not," countered Danikov, "your biblical namesake had much more to say about David. Luke was a physician, historian and a man of science. He was also a man of great detail and study, and he carefully wrote in the book of Acts that although the patriarch David died six generations before Christ, he—King David—was also an Old Testament prophet and knew that God had promised him on oath that he would see one of his descendants on his throne. That happened through Jesus Christ."

Santan shrugged and began drifting from the scene, his fun apparently ended. As he did so, he made a parting comment, "You make a wrongful assumption about me in your persistent arguments. I simply don't believe man has an eternal value. Therefore, I, atheist." With that Santan rushed off.

"Brother," Clayman said, whooshing over to Danikov and making the sort of arm motions he would if he could physically hug someone, "you've done a wonderful job of witnessing to a totally unrepentant sinner. Take heart in the fact that Randall and I are beginning our walks with the Lord as a result of your efforts, although I now understand that this could only come about as a result of God's grace. For my part, I've observed your own growth since our special circumstance began."

At that, Randall joined in. "Hear, hear. I wish I'd said it."

Danikov didn't know that he could agree with their assessment based on his success with Santan, but he was gratified with Randall's observation. He had actually been wondering about this very thing. "Thank you," he said. "While I may have failed to penetrate Santan's mind set, I have tried. I turn him over to the Lord." Danikov seemed tired.

"I think I know what effected the change in us," Randall said, apparently wanting to discuss the subject further. "But what about you?"

"The same as changed you," Danikov said. "The Holy Spirit. Before, when I tried to witness by my own power and authority, I failed. I tried to show what I could do for God rather than showing and telling what God had done for me. In other words I left the gate early."

"Men, don't look now," Clayman said, "but our antagonist must have left something here. He's back. My guess is he's itching to finish this critical hole, and with it the match."

Santan charged into their circle as Clayman was finishing his comment. "You're damned right I am," he said. "This is no summit meeting. Let's get back to play so we can—."

"—In due time," Clayman said with authority, interrupting Santan. "In the meantime, light somewhere, will 'ya"? I have a question I want to ask Tommy Ray, and you will probably do well to pay attention to his answer." He turned to Danikov and asked his question. "Exactly why did Jesus have to die?"

Danikov was instantly revitalized. "If Jesus had stayed on Earth," he said, "his physical presence would have limited the spread of the gospel, because physically he could be in only one place at a time. After Christ was taken up into heaven, he would be spiritually present everywhere through his Holy Spirit."

"I'm still having a hard time understanding the Holy Spirit," Clayman said. "For most Jews that's a vague concept of Godly activity or power."

"You're not alone, pardner," Randall said. "The Holy Spirit is not any part of the belief of most other major religions, so far as I know."

Danikov was decidedly a renewed spirit. "I'm glad you asked," he said. "Let me try to shed some light on that. Jesus made this very point about the Holy Spirit to his disciples during the period of more than forty days in which he came and went among them after his resurrection. In that process he was seen by more than five hundred eyewitnesses. He told them not to leave Jerusalem to witness, but to wait for the gift his Father had promised."

Clayman looked puzzled. "The gift?"

"Yes. Jesus explained that John the Baptist baptized with water, but in a few days the disciples would be baptized with the Holy Spirit."

"How'd that unfold? I mean, is this all in the Bible?" Clayman asked. "In the New Testament?"

"I'd give anything to present all of you with a Bible right now, or at least John's Gospel, but you'll have to accept my word on the subject. This story is what Pentecost is all about."

"When I hear the word Pentecost," Randall said, "it sounds mysterious."

Santan remained in the loose circle of the foursome, no longer participating, but with a strange, unsettled look about him.

Danikov answered Randall's query, acutely aware of Santan's momentarily diminished presence. "The story is short, but one of the most powerful in the New Testament. All the original twelve apostles were together in one place when a violent wind filled the whole house where they were sitting. They saw what seemed to be tongues of fire that separated and then came to rest on each of them as the apostles began to speak in other tongues."

Now Santan appeared even more unsettled by the conversation. Danikov continued with his explanation. "After the disciples themselves were filled with the Holy Spirit, God-fearing Jews from at least fifteen different nations were staying in Jerusalem during Pentecost, which was an annual festival of thanks giving for the harvested crops. Now we come to the punch line."

Clayman was nodding in anticipation and tried to clap his hands, surmising that all they lacked was some gospel music. Randall joined in with the spirit of the moment, saying, "Bring it on home, Brother!" Santan's eyes were darting, his mouth slack.

"First," Danikov said, close to his promised closure, "the Galilean disciples witnessed to the gathered crowd and then Peter spoke to his truly international audience. Each of those in attendance heard the disciples . . . speaking in the listener's *own* language."

At that, Santan inexplicably erupted. "Words piled upon words!" he shouted. "A Spirit who is yet a person! Speaking in tongues! What next? Will you handle snakes? Gibberish!" He faced Clayman and Randall, saying, "Don't you see what he's doing? You're like children soaking up every word simply because your misguided leader utters them." Turning now to Danikov he said, "Show me the results of your redemption!"

"If I do, will you believe in your redeemer?" said Danikov.

"I will believe what I believe."

"You're wasting your time," said a disgusted Randall. "I know him. Neither his heart nor his mind would entertain an appeal from Christ himself."

"I can't give up," Danikov said. "No one is impossible for God to reach and change. Even the most zealous and relentless of all the early persecutors of Jewish Christians, Saul—himself a Jew—was turned by the Lord. Jesus appeared to him on the road to Damascus as Saul was bound to capture Christians and return them to Jerusalem. First Jesus questioned him, then blinded him for three days, and finally delivered him. As the apostle Paul, he immediately began witnessing and ultimately shaped the history of Christianity."

"You hope to convert Santan in that fashion?" Randall asked in disbelief. "He hates you and sees you as evil. You're my friend and you believe, but you don't have that power."

Clayman had withdrawn from the conversation out of . . . what? . . . he thought. Fear? Fear *of* Santan or fear *for* Danikov? And now fear about what Randall had said. He could only add, "I pray for all us."

"Take heart," Danikov said. "My redemption is my belief. I'm not offended by what anyone says. I'm only encouraged by Jesus' words: 'Blessed are you when men hate you, when they exclude you and insult you and reject your name as evil, because of the Son of Man.'"

No one said anything. Moments passed. Then Danikov surprised everyone, most of all Santan, by simply saying, "Suppose we get back to the match. After all, that's what brought us here in the first place and that's why Santan returned. Let's take it to conclusion."

"Sanity returns," Santan said, slowly releasing the safety valve of his curiously overheated emotion. "O.K.," he continued. It's still my man against yours and your man is up." Now Santan pointed to Danikov's player on the tee. "See how I allow you an advantage?" he said, growling. "It's about over for you, anyway."

Clayman was trying to understand Santan's unpredictable mood swings, not unlike his own a few holes back. Randall hadn't made the adjustment very well either, being wrenched from participating in the Great Persecution to the return of vicarious golf. He reacted visibly, unexplainedly jumping up and down and raising his fists in protest. "No way!" he shouted, "Santan predicted your man was up before the group itself gave us any indication who would hit first. The only way he could know your player had the honors is for him to have checked their scorecard. That's a violation."

Danikov said, "Luke, did you see the group's scorecard?"

Santan didn't blink. Instead, he whisked himself over to face Danikov and said, "Firstly, you're persuaded by your henchman to accuse me, having no personal knowledge of anything. That's a sin of which I doubt your God would approve. Secondly, without proof, the former doesn't matter one whit. On that defense alone I flatly reject your caddy's charge. Thirdly, we made no rule prohibiting such scouting. That rule died with our acceptance of your own new proposition. You can't change the game simply because you're bound by your own sense of what's fair. Now," Santan said authoritatively, "your guy is up and the game is on."

"You may have denounced the charge, Luke," Danikov said, "but you didn't deny it. I believe you're guilty, but you're also correct on your point. If you only understood the ultimate consequences of your actions."

At that moment, a brilliant halo of light encircled them and the foursome found themselves suddenly transported to a totally unimagined locale having nothing whatever to do with either golf or life as they knew it.

THIRTY-FOUR

CLAYMAN IMMEDIATELY RESPONDED to their second recent change of venue with, "My God, where in hell are we?" A narrow river separated two distinct vistas. On one side all they could see was a wasteland of desolation and intense heat resulting from a multitude of smoldering fires. Thousands of profusely-sweating humans wandered about, each with the same hopeless countenance. Many were groaning under their apparently pointless, yet laborious tasks and all were driven by relentless overseers.

On the other side were as many individuals, but they appeared comfortable and contented, seemingly occupied with pleasant if minor tasks. These people looked robust and beaming and were without obvious supervision. Clayman was instantly confused and frightened as he looked around at the others for support. Instead of three besides himself, he counted four. The extra spirit looked familiar. "Barnabas?" he said, hope accompanying his question.

"Yes," Barnabas said. "Excuse me for again intruding unannounced."

Danikov spoke up, saying, "Not at all. We're delighted to see you again, especially under this surprising circumstance. We're the ones to apologize, however. Our brother Clayman unadvisedly, but unintentionally, managed to curse our arriv—."

Clayman interrupted. "Yes, I did," he said, "and I'm ashamed for it. Please accept my personal apologies."

"Not necessary," Barnabas said. "In any event, repentance must always be directed to the Lord."

"Barnabas," Danikov said, "what are we here for?"

Clayman took a deep breath and tried to hold it, anticipating the worst. Randall had a wild-eyed look. Santan was searching the landscape as he pondered possibilities.

"First of all," Barnabas said, "you're mistaken about having gone to Hell. One doesn't descend there for a mere visit under any circumstances. Only those whose souls are lost and who do not seek forgiveness from God will suffer from the torment of eternal separation from God. You're visiting Hades, from which place the resurrected, both saved and lost, await the final judgement. I've been asked to see that you get a brief glimpse."

"Asked?" Santan said. "Asked by whom?"

"I'm merely a messenger," he responded.

"If you're taking requests," Santan said, sarcastically, "I'd like to see the Master of the Fires."

"Your request will be carefully noted," Barnabas said.

"I have a thousand questions," said an impatient Randall, "but at least expound a little on what you just said about Hades. Are you speaking biblically?"

"The book of Revelation. Believers and unbelievers alike experience physical death and come directly here to visit when they die. That is both good and bad. All people will be resurrected, but believers will be resurrected to eternal life with God while unbelievers will be resurrected to be punished with a second death—eternal separation from God. Hades is very carefully segregated by the nature of one's living attitude. From here, ultimate departure is for either heaven or for hell, for better or for worse."

"Segregated by attitude, I believe," repeated Danikov, "rather than by ambition, position, achievement or even good works."

"Correct."

"But what," said Clayman, still fearful, "about those who struggled with their attitude, who struggled with accepting Christ?"

"The saved are saved. The unsaved are segregated by what they did with what they knew."

"You speak in riddles, spirit," said Santan. "Let us speak to someone who is an official."

"Foolishly said," Barnabas replied. "You are not here to negotiate. And I doubt if you, in your condition, want to meet The Master. At any rate, you cannot. When you have properly come here, Christ himself will greet you. I suggest you be ready at that time, which you now know could come at any moment."

"You're the biblical Barnabas, aren't you?" Danikov said, suddenly inspired. "I asked you once before, at the moment you left us. You lived and preached as an associate of the apostle Paul?"

"Yes," Barnabas acknowledged. "We worked together to build the church's foundation after Jesus ascended to heaven."

"You were also known as the Son of Encouragement," Danikov said. "Are you with us for that purpose?"

"Let me pose this question," Barnabas said. "Do you recall asking me during my last visit about the purpose of your spirit transformations?"

"I do," Danikov said.

Randall joined in with an observation. "You weren't very forthcoming at that time." Barnabas smiled. Danikov shook his head, a slight frown on his face as Barnabas said, "I don't know what you have gained since then, but I must inquire. Have you learned anything about the truth of your own lives?"

"Judged by what standards?" Randall asked, confused.

"By what standards would you think?" Barnabas returned the question.

"He means by the only one that counts," Danikov said. "By the standards of Jesus Christ."

"Well," Randall volunteered the lead, moved by the overwhelming events culminating in what he perceived as personal closure time. He spoke from his heart. "The truth about our lives—mine anyway—has been troubling."

"It is time to overcome your problems. The love and forgiveness of Jesus is all you need to correct and cleanse you."

"Are you speaking of the grace and truth of Christ that Danikov has been telling us about?" Randall asked.

"I am."

Randall was suddenly moved. Tears cascaded down his spirit face as he fell to his knees, hands upraised. "Heavenly Father," he said, "You know I've sinned greatly. You also know that I have quietly asked for your forgiveness." Then he added a personal request which he had wanted to bring up several times over the course of his gradual conversion, but hadn't known how to phrase. The question was born of his long-dwelling agnosticism. "Lord, If we could but see you we would know your glory. Amen."

Danikov was overjoyed by Randall's public confession but concerned for his yet-lingering doubt. He looked hopefully towards Barnabas, who slowly raised a hand in recognition of the situation. He said only, "My son, no one has ever seen God, except for . . ." He paused and nodded to Danikov, allowing him to finish the verse.

Through tears Danikov said, " . . . except for God the only Son, who is at his Father's side, and who made Him known."

Danikov regained his composure enough to say, "Thank you for asking about our welfare, Barnabas. In fact, I believe we've learned much about truth—Artie and Paul and I. About why and what Jesus came to Earth to teach us. And although Luke professes to have no interest, I don't think he can deny the growth the three of us have experienced. Can you, Luke?"

"*Your* growth?" Santan responded without empathy and with even less interest. "What do I care about that? This whole side trip is a sham, a set-up for my would-be benefit. Hell, for all I know the entire thing may be only a dream. I'm telling you, once and for all, that there simply *is* no God!" Santan practically shouted in protest. "I know this for an absolute fact because . . . I have proven it! I have proof!" he screamed.

Santan whisked back and forth over the dividing stream, first on one side, then the other, confused by the obviously great disparities on the two sides, but totally unmoved by Barnabas' explanation for it.

It was Danikov who asked the obvious question as Santan returned again from the other side of the stream. "You have proof? What are you talking about? Has your tortured soul gone mad?"

"No. No!" he said, now in control, defensive. "The algorithmic proof. *My* algorithmic proof." Pride was now manifestly evident in his voice. "I was widely recognized for it. If you were at all well read in mathematic circles you would have heard of the Santan Algorithm."

Danikov first looked at Clayman, who shrugged, then at Randall, who was even more expressive. Randall then qualified his initial reaction. "Well, I know something about algorithms, but I never heard of one preceded by the name Santan. As a matter of fact, we used quite a few algorithms in advertising." He was directing his comments to the other two. "Since Mr. Einstein asked, think of algorithms as systematic step-by-step sets of instructions for doing complex problems with lots of variables."

"You mean," Danikov said, "Santan is talking about using mathematical equations, but not for mathematical purposes?"

"Well," Randall replied, "that's a simplification, but it helps. Even simple software is essentially an algorithmic approach. On the more complex aspect, an algorithm can even make exact real-time models of atomic blasts. I think IBM actually did that."

Santan waved them off. "You fools. If you read anything but comics and the Bible, you would know. In the 1940s to 1980s, only one kind of algorithm existed: the Simplex algorithm. In 1985, the Karmarkar algorithm was developed. Compared to the Simplex, the difference was like flying from one distant city to another rather than driving. I took that accelerated approach in 1995 and designed my algorithmic proof around one of the newest Karmarkar types called pattern recognition."

"Pattern recognition?" Clayman asked in sarcastic protest. "What are you going with this? Are you daft? We're on the brink of eternal judgment here, and you're dancing with mathematics?"

"Yes," snapped Santan as if to a remedial undergraduate student, "This is hardly trivial since it totally refutes the hell-and-damnation guise in which our dream guide has somehow placed us all. Try to follow this." Santan had gathered himself fully and would sell his point as hard as he could.

"Pattern recognition algorithms sort through massive amounts of data looking for obscure, but repeated patterns. I fed my algorithm both biblical and scientific data over several years of input. The object was simply to determine the existence, or not, of God. I tried to remain open to the absolute answer."

"Bless you for crumbs, oh wizard!" said Randall.

Santan was becoming increasingly annoyed with his former ally Randall's belligerent tone, but he stored his hostility. "If I may continue," he said. "Granted, I went for a near-perfect solution, rather than a perfect one, because the speed difference of the calculations is huge. Even at that the calculations still required three years and I had the best software of any university. My algorithm was able to achieve its result within 98% of the optimal conclusion. Not surprisingly, I was hailed for the epic completeness of the research."

"That self-congratulatory praise notwithstanding," said Danikov, "you think you actually came up with a provable equation whose answer to the question, 'Does God exist?' was 'No?'"

"Precisely. Irrefutable proof," Santan said, as if he were back at his credentials consideration review board and defending a thesis with all the vigor of someone who has spent so much time at one project that his very identity was tied to it. "God does not exist. Cannot exist. My algorithm proves it. Therefore, you waste your time evangelizing me and others."

"All you've proven," Danikov said, "is that you're a slave in defense of your own warped logic. Let me give you a fundamental truth to ponder. And Barnabas, feel free to correct me on this. If eternity can be represented as an unending straight line and man's life in the flesh as represented on that line is no greater than the width of a pencil point, then why would you not choose eternal life beginning with that pencil point? And that choice, Professor Santan, is eminently yours."

"I spit on both your line and your lie!" Santan said, angrily, spitting nothing but air, but nevertheless punctuating his point.

"Santan," Danikov said, "until a moment ago I feared you had committed the unpardonable sin in your deliberate refusal to acknowledge God's power in Christ. Jesus said those people cannot be forgiven—not because their sin is worse than any other, but because they will never ask for forgiveness. I was wrong in my earlier assessment."

Danikov paused, then added. "There *is* hope for you. You aren't evil by nature. You're simply and incredibly disillusioned."

"Gentlemen! Gentlemen!" Barnabas said, "This is no time for bickering. I can't argue Danikov's illustration. All of you are keen observers. I compliment you on that. And as a group I believe you've made wonderful progress, although one of you seems to think Man has concocted God as a salve for his mortality." Randall winked at Clayman.

"But before you depart this site," Barnabas continued, "let me answer the one question you have all been searching for since you arrived."

At that the foursome leaned forward in anticipation.

"This should surprise you, but all of you may yet survive the lightning strike that felled you. That survival remains your choice. I beg you not to lose the opportunity."

"What does that mean?" Clayman asked, both incredible hope and agonizing despair trying to register on his face. "You speak as if we ascend or fall as a group. What's the wild card here?"

"You misunderstand," Barnabas said. "God Himself said that when the time has come, even the dead will hear the voice of the Son of God, and those who hear will live. A time is coming when even all who are in their graves will hear his voice and come out. Much less the task for you who are on a special journey. Those who have done good will rise to live and those who have done evil will rise to be condemned."

"And will we all recognize one another when we make it up yonder?" Randall said, trying to take the edge off something that continued to worry him. Clayman frowned, considering Randall's response to be flippant.

"There's a pretty good clue in the Bible, Artie," Danikov said. "When Moses and Elijah appeared to Jesus on the mountaintop there's no scriptural mention of anyone saying, 'Who's that?'"

293

"This is nonsense!" Santan said, again wild-eyed. "The four of you are two of a kind. Two pair of deuces. Strong on appearance, but not a winning hand in a tough game . . . Judge."

"We don't judge you," Barnabas said. "Moreover, even the Father judges no one. He entrusts all judgement to the Son. If you do not honor the Son, however, you do not honor the Father, who sent him."

"Amen," Danikov said.

"Amen," echoed Barnabas. "God wants all men not simply to be their best, but to be perfect little Christs. Of course you won't meet his goal, only One has, but that is nevertheless, your maker's expectation."

"I'm still afraid that it may be too late for me," Randall said.

"It is not too late so long as you still have being," Barnabas said. "As Tommy Ray knows, one day each of you will stand before God and each of you will then be asked to give an account of your life. Your only answer can be that you're a sinner. You can add, however, 'But, God, I am saved by grace through Jesus Christ.' You will have said the only thing possible to mitigate your sin and allow you to rest with the Lord through eternity."

In the next instant the spirit foursome found themselves back on the tenth tee at RiverTree.

THIRTY-FIVE

THE SPIRITS WERE MOMENTARILY IN SHOCK over their experience, but by now had become used to sudden, changing venues and they quickly re-focused. Danikov's previously assigned player was about to hit. "Golf rules!" shouted an exuberant Santan as he moved in tightly to the live players to observe the action. The others joined him.

Danikov's player hit a little squibber of a shot to the right, but it didn't reach the parallel creek hazard. Santan's player's shot was much better, but still only about 200 yards off the tee of the 488-yard par five white (senior) tee. The spirit foursome again ignored the other two players simply because their scores didn't matter.

This was one of Clayman's favorite holes. He liked it for its compound layout. The hole was a rare double dog-leg, combining both a starting left to right line with second-shot alignment nearly opposite. In addition, the hole started out being slightly uphill and ended up being downhill, with a water hazard bordering portions of each side. Beyond that, the hole was graded such that it fell from right to left to-wards both trees and water from about two hundred yards out.

Danikov's player hit a decent recovery shot to the right middle of the fairway. He wouldn't be able to hit the green in three and, in fact, found his next shot in a green side bunker which was short and to the right. Santan's power hitter nearly equaled the length of his tee shot and had only about a hundred yards remaining to the center of the green, which for him would require a sand wedge.

As that shot struck the green from a great enough angle to easily hold, the air was immediately punctuated by Santan's shout: "Dance-time!" The ball was still a good thirty feet from the pin, but it was on the green in regulation and the player would at least have a putter in his hands for his birdie attempt.

Randall and Clayman were camped at the far side of the bunker, uphill and just off the green. They were watching both Danikov and his man as the player approached the results of his previous shot. The player's doubts over the upcoming shot were not apparent, but they existed. With mock humor the sand-locked player shouted to his opponent who had reached the green in regulation. "Give up?" he said in humor.

In response the intended victim tried his own version of a mind game. "You have a stroke," he said, but you're gonna need it to get up and down from deep, damp sand to tie me. Deee-p sand. Daaam-p sand," he said, trying to both plant and water a seed of anxiety.

Instead, the worry appeared to sprout for Danikov as he shook his head three or four times, but said nothing. Clayman noticed and commented to Randall, "Tommy Ray is carrying the weight of his world on his shoulders right now, but I think he's actually more concerned with *losing* Santan than losing *to* him."

"What do you mean?" Randall asked.

"Well, if 'trapper' here can't pull off a career shot Danikov will lose his already long shot at softening Santan's hardened heart."

"Yeah, well, don't count out either of those yet," Randall countered.

Danikov tried to prepare his player to be both positive in his attitude and firm with his sand wedge swing. The practice swing without club touching sand was O.K., but not of much value. The swing that immediately followed, however, met too much sand. Sand easily flew to the green, but not the ball. Instead, the ball was merely advanced to within a foot of the bottom lip of the bunker. Before Danikov, Clayman and Randall could fully grasp the significance of the missed shot, the player--disgusted with his previous effort—quickly moved to hit the next shot. Intending to definitively blast it out of the bunker he swung overly hard and nearly topped the ball. It managed to skitter clear of the sand, however, and raced dead on-line towards the pin. The spirit threesome, hope instantly rescued, watched nervously as the ball belatedly began braking against the up hill force. "Whoa, whoa, whoa," Randall shouted. Thud! The ball struck the pin and seemed to poise for an instant in mid-air. Clayman and Randall had been practically on top of the ball as it had winged its way toward the hole, exhorting it to do exactly what it did, but to also drop dead. Half of their hopes were met, but the ball bounded away to come to a stop three feet to the left of the hole. The two spirits seemed to lose theirs.

Santan carefully studied them and Danikov who was had remained standing to the side, taking it all in. He relished in Clayman's and Randall's emotional reactions. Danikov's was nothing like theirs, but he knew the bottom line had to be the same: bitter disappointment. His take on their collective perception of the hole's certain outcome was clear. The hole was Santan's. The match was won! Two putts by Santan's man would formalize it. Only a three-putter from thirty feet could cost him the win, and only then in the event Danikov's player dropped a pressure-laden, side-hill slider from three feet.

Santan paced alongside his player as both reckoned the putt's line and speed. Then Santan began a series of odd movements with his hands, as if weaving a spell over his player, who was now about to putt.

Randall was now lying prone in resignation. Danikov remained merely watching. Clayman had recovered from his dashed hope and was trying to measure every nuance of action, spirit or live. Their opposing live player didn't exhibit much animation. Was he thinking 'lag it' or 'bag it'? If I were Santan, he analyzed, I'd leave him alone. Hopefully, he thought, Santan might not be able to manage that. Ultimately, Clayman reasoned, he could only hope that Santan's player would totally miss-hit the putt."

No such thing. The ball left the putter head on a fast, but fairly flat track. The stroke was a commercial one as the player wanted to assure himself of par. If Santan could have applied for adoption of his player, he would have done so the instant putter struck ball. By the time the ball had come to rest eighteen inches short of the hole, Santan would have been delighted to actually sign the adoption document. The ball lay marginally within the length of the leather grip. The player quickly looked around for a 'gimme' sign, which wasn't actually necessary in their game, but was still always appreciated.

Randall propped himself up for one last pro-active, if symbolic, effort. "Make him putt it!" he shouted, but not with a great deal of enthusiasm. One of the putter's opponents looked at his playing partner, who shrugged. One of them said simply, "Pick it up."

Clayman slumped in dejection. Santan's reaction was predictable: joyful eruption! Clayman looked around, stunned by the apparent finality of things. "Is that it?" he said to Danikov. "It's over? We lose?"

As far as the spirit foursome was concerned, Danikov's player didn't need to finish playing the hole. He couldn't beat or tie Santan's player. The spirits naturally had no interest in the live players themselves, only in their play. Danikov, head raised after a deep sigh, briskly whooshed to Santan and offered him a rueful smile along with a congratulatory, if symbolic handshake. "You win the match, Luke," he said.

Santan matched the symbolism of the non-material handshake, but he wanted to revel in the reality of his victory. He said with exaggerated emphasis, "The real success is that I'm spared the sermon you used to corrupt my former cohorts." Santan then turned to the others, saying, "But as for you gentlemen, my door is still wide open. After all, we may still have some 'time' to do. After all, what else do we have except golf and talk?"

Clayman waved him off. Randall responded by saying, "I don't know, but there has to be more to life than golf, vicarious or not."

"Luke," Danikov said, "I know you believe you've won everything, but I think you may have actually lost far more than you've gained."

"Thanks for the sour grapes, counselor, but I'll pass. I have a busy agenda now that I've managed to cast a seed of doubt onto your vacillating entourage."

"I have confidence in them," Danikov said. "But now that you've clearly won the vicarious golf match, humor me with answers to a few questions."

"Concerning golf, or do you want my recipe for living also?" Santan said, flushed with himself. "Certainly. Be glad to tutor you."

"Thank you. Philosophically, wouldn't you admit that the flesh and blood beings of our previous existence were miraculous?"

"Can't argue with that, professor. Matter of fact, that seems precious given our current circumstances."

"O.K., so you put a single human life in context with incredible complexity. Right?"

"What's your point?"

"Simply this. Since you agree that such a marvelously-engineered being couldn't possibly happen by sheer accident, then don't we owe our allegiance to that creative reservoir from which we sprang?"

Santan looked amusingly around at Randall and Clayman and then back to Danikov, saying, "Sproinggg goes the trap! I follow the logic. *Your* logic, anyway. But I don't concede the point."

"O.K., I accept that," Danikov said.

Clayman marveled at Danikov's persistence. Here he had been soundly defeated at their all-consuming spirit-game activity, yet he instantly rebounds to challenge the victor, who was still full of himself. Maybe that was why. Perhaps Santan was most vulnerable in his most prideful moment.

"Remain for a moment in your newly-found logic," Danikov said. "Man lives. Man sins. Man needs redemption. Prophets prophesy. The Creator responds. The Savior arrives. Man kills Savior. Hundreds witness the Savior resurrected. Savior ascends to heaven and offers man the same option. Who are we to deny this incredible gift?"

Santan smiled. With arms outstretched he said, "Behold, the master spinner. He takes a little of this from here and a little of that from there. He spins his web from here to there to make a fragile bridge. Suddenly the spinner argues that now a truck can be driven across it."

Clayman shook his head in appreciation of both Danikov's challenge and conviction. How would this ever play out? he wondered.

"Look," Danikov said, "the reason your concept of a God doesn't work is simply because your God is too small."

"Tsk, tsk, my God-fearing man," Santan said. "Is that any way to encourage discipleship?"

Pausing for a moment in reflection, Danikov said, "No, it isn't. Let me make amends." He bowed his head, saying, "Father, even my enemy laughs at my efforts, recognizing that I have indeed sinned for not loving my brother whom I see. How then can I please God whom I have not seen? Rebuke me so that I may gain knowledge."

"Stop it, man," Santan said, arrogantly, "You're embarrassing us all. I could call down some nasty stuff on you if I didn't think you were already whipped on both fronts."

Danikov blinked twice at Santan's inexplicable boast-fulness. Again, he took a moment to reflect on developments. "Let me make another, very different observation," he said. "Its logic is unarguable and even though I've addressed the subject before, things have progressed considerably."

"You mean the difference between being a winner and a loser?" Santan said, taunting him.

"No. More like the root of that sort of thinking. Increasingly, you've been speaking and reacting in ways that haven't been quite like you. You don't seem to be in control of yourself, Luke. For example, how do you think you came to grow from merely passive to hostile atheism?"

"What are you talking about? Santan asked, apparently surprised by the question.

"I don't know how else to put it except to say I believe you may have had some ungodly help. Now don't be upset by something I'm about to do. It won't harm you. We have no substance, remember. All I'm going to do is place my hands near your spiritual sphere."

Santan stepped back, but Danikov persisted, placing his hands as near to Santan's head as their two spirit forms allowed. Then he spoke forcefully. "In the name of Christ, demon within Luke Santan, name yourself!"

With only a moment's hesitation, a deep-throated growl issued forth from a snarling Santan, his eyes an orange blaze seen quite visibly through his otherwise misty presence. "I am Pride," the voice said. "Go away from me for I have lived here a very long time."

"Then you will be homeless!" Danikov said, stepping back from Santan, but pointing directly towards him. "Pride, I command you leave this spirit now. In the name of Christ Jesus and by the authority He entrusts to true disciples, I cast you out!"

A hideous spirit form slowly, as if reluctantly, slipped from the top of Santan's misty presence, visible to all but Santan himself. As it exited, it spoke in the same throaty growl as before. "If I choose to leave, I will not go far. My presence within this host is welcome. In fact, when I return I will bring others worse then me."

"Name them as well," Danikov said with commanding authority. "In the name of Jesus Christ, whom you know to be the Prince of Peace, I command you to name them!"

Again came the darkly echoing voice from the demon, "Among them are Arrogance, Evil Behavior and Perverse Speech."

"Go now and take them with you, and do not return." Danikov commanded. "Love for God and love of sin cannot coexist."

"This man does not love God," the demon responded, "He honors the fallen angel. You cannot prevent my return." With that, the demon disappeared.

Clayman said nothing as he was trying to assess what he just witnessed. An unnerved Randall, struggling to retain his emotional balance, spoke. "Man, I don't know what that was all about. I'm freaking out. But what's with the 'fallen angel.' You mentioned that once before. What does that mean?'"

"He was simply raising his flag," Danikov said with disgust. "A demon is a fallen angel who has joined Satan in his own proud rebellion against God. Because they're corrupt and degenerate, their appearance reflects the distortion of their spirits."

"How do demons come about and what's their agenda?" Clayman said now, at first as frightened as Randall, but now with Danikov's reassurance feeling a little relieved.

"Unbelief binds the hands of God and releases the demons of Hell," Danikov explained. "As for their agenda, it's to prevent, distort or destroy people's relationships with God. That simple."

"But what's with the threat?" asked a nervous Randall.

"Jesus tells us about that in St. Luke's gospel," Danikov explained. "When an unclean spirit goes out of a man he goes through dry places, seeking rest. Finding none, he vows to return to the house from which he came. But when he comes he finds it swept and put in order, so he goes and takes with him seven other spirits more wicked than himself."

Santan made an unintelligible noise. Then he blinked his eyes and rubbed them with both hands, backing off a little from the group. "What happened?" he said. "Danikov, have you been tinkering again? I resent your efforts at spiritual conversion."

"You still think you're your own man, eh?" Danikov said. "You put far too much faith in yourself and none where most of it ought to be—in the Lord, our God."

Clayman, still rocked by this most recent of events in their never-ending odyssey, said, "I witnessed what just happened, but I'm not certain I believe it." Increasingly intrigued and yet bewildered by the unfolding events, he thought he sensed Danikov going in the other direction, his faith and authority appearing to grow stronger by the event.

Randall was still visibly shaken by both the match's loss and the incredible encounter with Santan's demon, but his resolution, too, was bolstered by Danikov's confidence. "What next?" he asked.

"Gentlemen," Danikov said, "I believe we have come to a turning point. I have a sense that this foursome may finally be prepared to continue its journey. I don't know exactly what that means, but I praise God, from whom all blessings and mercy flow."

"Something is suddenly weird," Clayman said. He looked around quizzically. Then he raised one arm, hand and index finger above his head as if testing for the direction of a strong breeze, "I have a strange feeling. And this isn't the first time. In fact, I've had it every time we experienced one of our paradigm shifts. I think the first time I felt it was a split second before we were struck by lightning. It happened again when we shipped out to the Middle East, and a third time right before our visit to Hades. Now with the appearance of a sure 'nuff demon I have to tell you I'm flat scared. What if we're bound for a more permanent destination?"

Thirty-Six

Moments later Clayman observed that something was indeed different. It was raining. He wondered about that for a second. *Surely they hadn't returned to Hades!* Then the connection with rain in Hades brought him an inward smile. All four of them were still together, he thought, but in looking around he could tell they were no longer just off the tenth green. No, they were on the . . . eighteenth tee. *But what was different?*

Then something clicked and Clayman stammered, "Look! Randall's clothing is—." Pause. "Clothing!" he shouted. "Hey, we're not spirits anymore! We're wearing clothes!" He put his right hand on his chest and . . . . felt something. *Felt! What a foreign sensation.* He looked around for a second time. He could see that the others had on the same clothes as when they were struck by lightning. "My God," he said, "has the unimaginable happened a second time?"

Randall spoke through tears, patting himself all over as if he were on fire, "We're not dead! We're not dead! We're not even spirits. We're flesh and blood. Oh, my God, we're alive! We've returned from the dead, or . . . from wherever!"

Santan was jumping up and down and pumping his fists in the air as Danikov turned and wildly ran the thirty yards or so from the eighteenth tee back up to the seventeenth green. Once there he faced up the canyon-like hill and—as he had done when they first became spirits—shouted at the top of his lungs, "God loves you!" Within a second or two he heard the faint echo, "'God loves you!'"

"There," he said, "that's what I wanted to hear." He returned to the group and all four of them, including Santan, took turns embracing and pounding each other's back. As Danikov, Clayman and Randall then kneeled and bowed their heads, Santan dashed the few yards to the carts to inspect his golf clubs, which were exactly where they had been left. Danikov prayed, "Merciful God, we confess that we have not loved you with our whole heart. We have failed to be obedient. We have not done your will, we have broken your law, we have rebelled against your love, we have not loved each other, and we are unworthy of your grace. Forgive us, we pray. Free us for joyful obedience, through Jesus Christ our Lord. Amen."

"Amen," said the other two in unison.

Danikov then prayed silently, praising the Lord and asking forgiveness for each of the foursome, himself included. He also remembered to thank God for returning him safely to Marilee and fervently asked the Holy Spirit for spiritual reconciliation between Paul and Sheila. He then exclaimed aloud, "We are indeed alive. Frankly, I'm more surprised than you guys, but I can assure you we haven't returned from the dead. Only one man has ever done that . . . well, and lived to never die again. Maybe our experience was merely some sort of alternative life flash."

"What makes you think we weren't dreaming?" said Santan, who was wearing the broadest grin of them all as he marveled at what he considered to be unbelievably good fortune. He inspected his driver, holding it with reverence.

"Because," Danikov said, "I would be willing to bet that we all had precisely the same dream with the same people and participation. And as I think about it, it occurs to me that the conversion of two souls in our foursome by the Holy Spirit through our vicarious golf match has a biblical precedent, though obviously not in the same league."

"What's that?" asked Clayman.

"Christ's sacrifice on the cross," Danikov said.

"Clayman had an incredulous look on his face. "What?" he exclaimed.

"Don't you see?" Danikov said. "The substitutionary atonement of human sin by Christ's sacrifice on the cross was accomplished for believers *vicariously*."

"Wait a minute," Randall said with a mischievous twinkle in his eye, "I think I see what he means. In other words, God sometimes works his wonders in vicarious ways."

Danikov shook his head. "That's too close to being a pun to suit me."

"I swear," Santan said, "you three would give credit to your God if you were cured of Cancer."

"We certainly would," Danikov said.

"Hold on a minute," Clayman said, "we need to pass a test. Quick, Luke, throw me four golf balls."

Santan questioned the request, but obliged him by un-zipping a huge pocket on his golf bag and flipped Clayman two unopened sleeves of balls. Clayman easily caught them and ripped them open. He pulled out all three balls from one sleeve and added a fourth from the second sleeve. He began to juggle them in a side-by-side pattern resembling a fountain's flow. He smiled as he juggled, saying, "I wanted to see if our physical skills had deteriorated in the hundred or so years we were in limbo. They haven't!"

"I don't believe we were away quite that long, men," Danikov said, pointing in the direction of the seventeenth tee. "Look! What do you see coming down the cart path in the rain?"

"Well, I'll be a son-of-a——" Santan said, then interrupted his own sentence with, "It's the same foursome that was playing behind us when we took our lightning hit." Feeling almost giddy, he again did a little jump, shouting, "We are definitely back into 'grip it-and-rip it', men!'"

"We may be back," Randall said as he sat down in one of the carts, feeling suddenly introspective, "but personally I'm a lot worse for wear."

At that moment, the driver of the first cart hit the brakes and slid on the wet path to an abrupt stop behind one of the foursome's carts. The second cart nearly crashed into the lead cart. All four of the enthusiastically-arriving play-ers jumped out as someone said, "I don't believe it! We were standing on the tee when the siren sounded a second before the two biggest lightning bolts I've ever seen struck you and your carts simultaneously."

Another of the visitors was even more animated, wav-ing his arms and saying, "We saw you guys take a direct hit and then fall. We jumped into our carts to come down the hill. Halfway down we heard two 'God loves yous' and now here you are, standing on the tee—and in the rain—like nothing happened. I don't get it."

"We don't get it either," Danikov said, shaking his head, "but plenty happened. And you'd be right not to believe it. But look, it's raining too hard to play. You guys go on into the clubhouse and we'll be along as soon as we can collect ourselves."

"Shall we call 911?" asked another of the players. He pulled a cellular phone from his golf bag in anticipation.

"No, thanks," Danikov said as he waved off the offer, not bothering to check with the others. "We're fine. That burnt odor you smell is either from our clothes or our souls. We're not certain which, but it isn't from our flesh. Please. We're fine. Go on to the clubhouse before you get any wetter. Tell those at the 19th hole what you saw. You'll be big hits. We won't be long."

"Yeah," said Santan, "but cut us a little slack. It's not that big a deal." Santan's three golf mates looked at him wryly.

They all watched the hand-waving, head-shaking two-cart foursome disappear down the eighteenth hole cart path. "Would anyone like to get in out of the rain?" Clayman asked. As if on cue, all of them dashed for their carts, with no one giving any thought to popping open either of the two remaining untrashed umbrellas.

As they scrambled into the carts, the two drivers hesitated momentarily in depressing the accelerator pedals. At that instant, several surprising things happened almost simultaneously. The sun abruptly broke through a lone blue patch of sky and the rain stopped. For the barest of moments a rainbow appeared, even though it was apparently still early afternoon and the sun wasn't low in the sky as is normally the case for rainbows.

Before anyone could comment Santan had stuck one up-raised hand out of his cart, checking for rain. Then, with his other hand, he symbolically zipped his lips and shook his head. The other three laughed in unison.

The foursome watched in amazement as the rainbow quickly faded and was immediately followed by a cloud-clearing breeze which in turn warmed their faces. They all sat in silence as if frozen to their seats, confounded at the dramatic weather reversal. After some seconds, all four climbed back out of their carts and stood, arms and palms upward as if to say, "Oh, to be alive!"

Santan verbalized his thinking. "You know boys, we got ourselves an open hole of golf. I won the last hole and with it the match we thought we died for. But that was in an-other world. I have an idea—." Before he could finish his sentence Santan winced sharply, followed by a second, even stronger wince.

"What's the matter?" Clayman asked. "Are you ill? Maybe your system hasn't yet caught up with being put back together."

"No," said Santan, regrouping. "I'm fine. Just an odd twinge . . . no, like . . . well, I don't know exactly. Almost like a . . . a . . . foreboding. No, that's stupid. But I've never felt anything like it. Oh, well. Like you say, probably just an adjustment to a miracle."

"Miracle?" said Danikov, puzzled. "That's not a word I've heard you use before."

"I said that? I doubt it. Anyway, here's my idea. Let's make one last game. I'm gonna cut you some serious slack. We play this hole all over again, but this time as players, not spooks. And it'll be for the *real* win, not just the virtual win." Santan winced again, this time with some obvious pain as he went to his knees.

Danikov said, "You may need a doctor, Luke. Let's give it up."

"No," he said, straightening up and shaking his head several times. "I'm fine. Whatever it was has passed." He squeezed his eyes tightly and then shook his head once more like a dog shaking off water. He pulled out his driver, gripped it, and took a couple of practice strokes.

Clayman stepped forward. "Before you go to work with that stick, Luke," Clayman said, "I assume we've returned to the same democratic society we left. How about a vote? Artie?"

"Are you kidding?" Randall said. "I think I'm the luckiest man alive. And I'm anxious to share the details of this experience with anyone who'll listen. That is, if I can first sort it out for myself. But I'm good to go one mo'."

"Tommy Ray," Clayman said, "you haven't had much to say since we landed, but you've obviously had a profound impact on both Randall and me during this incredible journey. This is inadequately said, but we owe you a great deal. Are you up for playing a final hole and a second chance to hogtie Santan?"

Before Danikov could respond Randall said, "I keep chiming in late, Paul, but your sentiment goes double for me. We owe you, big-time, Tommy Ray. Could I get an 'Amen?'"

Clayman smiled and obliged. Danikov was not quick to respond. After a moment, he did so in deliberate fashion. "Brothers, thank you, but I'm the beneficiary here. If the Lord hadn't sent you how could I have learned the lesson of a more serious compassion for Man?" As he spoke he slumped against his golf cart, allowing tears to roll down his cheeks. "I think we desperately need to pray once more before we finish." As he bowed his head, both Randall and Clayman followed suit, but not before each glanced at Santan, urging him to join them. He was clearly not about to make it unanimous.

"Dear Lord," Danikov began, "I don't know what your plan for us was in all this, but I thank you for safely bringing us through it and back to our families. I especially thank you for guiding me in my trust of your divine will, and we especially thank you for coming into the spiritual lives of these two men. We praise you for the grace Paul and Artie have both accepted. As for Luke, don't give up on him. His heart has been hardened, but you've done that to others before him and still brought them to the fold. In Christ's name, Amen."

Clayman was moved to a Christian embrace of Danikov and then of Randall before saying, "You know what I missed most, now that I think about it? The sense of touch."

"Really?" Randall said. "For me it's the sense of smell. Food, man. The palate. I wasn't hungry while we were in spiritville, but now I'm never gonna miss another meal."

Danikov laughed. "You stay with that attitude and we'll have to tether you." Then Danikov turned sober. "Since we're baring our souls in our brave new world, I rejoice in two things in particular. First and most importantly, that I'll again be able to read God's Word. Secondly, that my Marilee is not lost to me, as I had feared. Now that we're back I think we all must realize how much more important certain things are."

"Amen to that," Clayman said as he turned to Santan. "Sorry we didn't offer you a hug, Luke. Do you still feel like you have to bury us?"

"Thanks for sparing me the touchy-feely bit," Santan said, waving to dismiss it. "But bury you?" he said, "I merely come to beat you. Look, I don't know what's happened either, but my partial recollection of certain deeds and words are at odds with who I think I am. Maybe I . . . ow! That hurts!"

He swatted himself twice on the back of his head and neck. "Ow! There it is again. Maybe I picked up a rash. Feels like someone's trying to peel off my skin an inch at a time. C'mon, guys," he said, trying to ignore the pinpoint pain. "Let's finish the game. See if you guys have the guts and talent to put your rhetorical religion up for grabs. You say your God is a God of second chances. I'm gonna do as much for you myself."

"You're still mightily confused," Danikov said. "So before we hit our last tee shots of the match, I want to address that issue. Jesus doesn't call us to religion, but to faith. The world insists that religion is a good thing and that it doesn't matter what religion one holds as long as one holds it sincerely. That's not what the Bible says. The prophets of Baal were religious, but they were purely evil. The people who hounded Jesus from the start of his evangelistic course were the religious people of his day. They did everything they could to discredit his ministry and bring him down."

"If not to religion, then," said a puzzled Clayman, "to what does God call us?"

"To faith. To faith in Him."

"Yeah, yeah," Santan said, sarcastically. "I've heard all this before. Let's cut to *my* chase. Here's the deal. You'll admit that I own the Vicarious Open. That's not enough. I want the live version, too. We don't need to put any money on this. Same teams we started with. If my team wins you put the clamps on about salvation. If we lose I put up with it. You with me, Artie?"

Randall hadn't been thinking about team play and he was surprised and a bit slow to react to the invitation. After a moment's pause, he said, "OK, count me in . . . partner, but that doesn't mean on the spiritual side. This formerly bouncing ball knows exactly where he's going to light."

"Fair enough," Santan said. "In other words, I'm makin' you guys whole for another chance at the big enchilada. Ow!" he said, twitching his head. A sudden sharp pain shot through him. He looked around as if trying to identify a tormentor. "I have a monumental migraine coming and going like a pendulum," he said. "But I can play through it."

Before he could take another practice swing, however, Santan staggered back a half-step and then folded forward at the waist, wailing. "Oh, my God!"

"Now I know you must be hurting," Danikov said, "but I don't think the cause is natural. I've been expecting your demon to return."

"Why do you think that?" Clayman asked.

"Because," Danikov said as he cupped his mouth and chin with his right hand, "when we returned from our spiritual experience Satan's 'house' was not only unoccupied, its doors were left wide open. Satan is trying to re-establish residency. Resist him with every fiber and nerve in your body and mind, Luke, and I may be able to help you. Is that O.K. with you?"

At that Santan fell to the ground, writhing and moaning. He could not respond to the question.

"Good," said Danikov to the others. "That's implied consent." He knelt on one knee as he carefully and methodically placed both his hands on Santan's head, saying, "Demon Pride, hear me! You and your brethren will not take back this man's soul. He no longer has need of you. By the authority Jesus gives believers, I call upon the Lord God to cast out each of these demons. Depart from this man's presence, now!" Nothing happened. Danikov brought into play the Jesus card. "In Christ's Holy name, I command you to obey!"

With another even more violent spasm and then a double, twisting shake of his head, Santan sat upright. His tortured expression slowly faded to one of somberness. He said weakly, "It's gone: the headache . . . the pain . . . them. I heard what you said, Danikov. Was that voodoo or exorcism? I don't buy into it, regardless, but certainly something worked."

"It was not me, but the Lord working through me," Danikov said. "It's time for you to come to faith."

Santan shook his head, then got up. "Look," he said, "I appreciate your help with the headache and the bogeys, but I won't accept yours or anyone else's faith."

Clayman jumped in, amazed at Santan's persistent denial. "Luke, now that I see things clearly I have to ask how you can say you have no need of *some* faith? After all, Man is only man. We didn't create ourselves. We're all mortal sinners, born that way."

"Well," Santan said, "get a load of you."

"Luke," Danikov said, "He's right. You're no different than any of us. Before our common spiritual experience you worked, you ate and drank, you played, you loved.

You may not have prayed for a very long time, but you lived life. Then for a period—along with us—you lost every one of those precious abilities you had taken for granted."

"He's telling it straight, partner," Randall said. "That little spiritual side trip had to be for a greater purpose than we imagine."

"God took his precious gifts from us," Danikov said. "And now they've been miraculously returned. At the end of this day each of us will have to face ourselves concerning these matters. Surely you now realize that tomorrow is promised to no one. This may be your last opportunity to get right with your maker. Don't pass it up."

Santan was not moved. "Now it's threats, is it?"

"Threats?" said an incredulous Danikov. "How can you ignore what we've just been through? What are you holding out for? We live but a second in God's time. At most, a few more years remain to you before your body will be fodder for worms. That's how little time you have to prepare. Eternity is a long time when you're not a part of it; or worse, suffering without end. You can't actually desire that when all you have to do is simply accept God's Grace."

Santan's nostrils flared, his eyes widened, and his hands flew up in front of his face which was contorted with rage and a sudden loss of self-control. Through clenched teeth he managed to say, "Damn you. I wanted to be civil, but you leave me no choice. Everything about your cursed faith is hinged upon Jesus' actual resurrection. You have no absolute proof! You and your holier-than-thou religion are caught up in the greatest fraud in the history of mankind. I can't trade logic for groundless faith."

Clayman wondered, first of all, what Danikov would make of Santan's outburst and secondly, how he would respond.

"You're absolutely correct," Danikov said, calmly, "in that Jesus' resurrection is the key to the Christian faith."

There he goes again, thought Clayman, shaking his head. Danikov was treating Santan's boilerplate reaction as if it were a simple request for more information.

Danikov continued. "And why is His resurrection so important? Because not only the Old Testament prophets—but Jesus Himself—prophesied it."

"I've heard the claim for eyewitnesses," Santan said, calming himself, "but that, too, could have been part of the fraud."

"How would you explain His grave clothes being left in the tomb as if Jesus had passed right through them?" Danikov queried. "The headpiece was still rolled up in the shape of a head, and it was at about the right distance from the linens that had wrapped Jesus' body. Even your stubborn mind set and brilliant imagination couldn't explain how the Christians—or even a grave robber—could have stolen his body and left the wrappings as if they were still shaped around it."

"And you'll no doubt tell me the proof of that is—?"

"Found in the Gospel according to John."

"Again the Bible," Santan said with a dismissive gesture. He thought for a moment and then said, "Tell me, witness, would you describe your religion as a compassionate one?"

"I would," Danikov replied.

"Then how do you square compassion with a group that abominates other groups?"

"Which groups?"

"For one, homosexuals."

Where was all this coming from? Clayman wondered. The demon had already been driven out. What had sparked this latest outburst?

Danikov was up to the task. "Both the Old Testament and the New Testament clearly prohibit a man or a woman from lying with someone of the same gender," he said. "It's simplistic to refute this with the argument that 'God loves all people'. He does, and unconditionally, but that doesn't imply that He will also affirm the act of homosexuality, which sin He pronounced as unclean and a perversion of His will."

Santan reacted with a smug expression, saying, "Ah, but you Christians classify sin by degrees. For example, if I were to commit adultery—which easily makes your top ten sin list— most Christians would still not be predisposed to prejudice. Point them to a little homosexuality, however, and Christians become vocal prohibitionists."

"Sin is the intentional choice to think, choose, and behave contrary to the ways of God," Danikov argued. "But even given your argument, unlike homosexuals— adulterers or thieves or even profaners—are not seeking to have their status elevated to a public norm."

"Then you think sin is relative."

"Absolutely not. Sin is sin. Sinners are sinners. That's why they call the church a 'hospital for sinners.' We're all guilty. But we can't leave it there. God clearly states that we need to admit our sins and then work to avoid them."

"But Christians still don't seem to mind judging others," Santan turned to tack in another direction.

"I can't speak for individuals, but being a Christian means *not* judging others. The reason for that is simple: only the Lord knows what's actually in people's hearts. When someone tries to *defend* his sin, however, he's judging himself."

"Look, I'm not defending homosexuality," Santan retorted. "But it *has* been around for a while. Fourteen of the first fifteen Roman emperors were reportedly homosexuals."

"*All* sins have been around for a long time. And you make my point. Homosexuality was, and is, one of the marks of a degrading society. Look, Luke, I don't know why you're on this kick, but homosexuality is not an illness, it's a sin, and because it's a sin, it can be forgiven. And that gets us back to you. Even with your blasphemies, God still loves you."

"Dammit, man, I don't want your melon-headed pap! That's for losers. I'm my own man and proud of it. Leave me alone. Let's play golf."

"I've known some proud men in my time, Luke, but you're right up there with the best. By doing what is right in your own eyes and not relying on God, in reality you're doing what is evil in the sight of God. And here's the proof you're always asking for. There are countless examples of this in the Bible. It's called apostasy, or falling away from God. Not learning from our past mistakes seems to be a fundamental failure of man."

"You have an answer for everything, don't you?"

"Hardly. But there are parts of the Bible that are easy to understand and God's unconditional love for Man is one of them."

"O.K., so your faith is your passion," Santan said as he picked up his driver and took several practice swings with it. "Mine is golf. My question is, do you want to play golf or talk religion? My offer to play this hole for final bragging rights is still on the table, but not for long. What's it gonna be, boys, the born-again Christian and the Messianic Jew against the Christian spy and the match champion, or do you want to walk?"

"Tee it up!" Danikov replied.

Thirty-Seven

" O.K.," Santan said, itching to play, "the game is for
two points, low ball against low ball and high ball against
high ball. You win both points you win the match and the
day. If my team wins *either* point, you're bagged. Any problems with that?"

Randall had essentially sat out the most recent sparring
round and at this he said, "It's up to you guys. I've already
been drafted."

"Well, I haven't," Clayman said. "Your partner wants us
to put up fresh cornbread against a hot knife. Forget it.
When this foursome was zapped in-the-flesh after seventeen holes we were dead even. All the golf after that isn't
merely spiritual history, it's irrelevant. Let's just play it
straight up, Luke. You win, you win. You lose, you lose.
We're not giving you odds."

"Handicaps included, of course," Danikov said, chipping in with a big smile at Clayman's assertiveness.

"OK, crybabies," said Santan, again taking a healthy cut with his driver. "Draw your weapons."

Clayman turned to Danikov and said, "Well, captain, how do we play it? It's the eighth handicap hole so the four stroke difference between you and Santan nets you nothing, but Randall and I each get a stroke."

"Then it's simple," Danikov said. "We both post par. One of them will have to do better to beat us. If they do worse, our cup runneth over."

"Brilliant," Clayman said. "Have you forgotten something? I'm an 18-handicapper. That means during eighteen holes of golf I'm usually busy making bogey or worse."

"Now that's positive thinking," Danikov chided. "Remember what the nonagenarian managed with a little attitude adjustment?"

"I heard that," Randall said, smiling. Turning to his temporary partner, Santan, he said, "Pars for the captains and bogeys for the grunts. But that would be a push wouldn't it?" He sighed. "You guys lead off. Luke, you O.K. with that?" Santan nodded.

"I'll lead off," Clayman said. He checked the wind with a tuft of grass, which fell straight down. "Good. No complications." Before he stepped up to the ball, however, he stopped to breathe deeply and savor precious life. As he did he offered a brief Hebrew prayer in surrender to the Lord, "*Adonai Elohaynoo.*"

Danikov heard him and nodded in silence.

Clayman swung at the ball and made full contact, but pulled the shot well left. The result of his 230-yard drive was problematic: rough, trees, a broad stretch of pond water, one bunker and 190 yards to the center of the green.

"It's in play, partner," was the extent to which Danikov felt he could encourage Clayman.

Santan wasn't quite as impressed. "You may as well put that one in your pocket," he said. "Long grass, hard wood, deep water and soft sand are all that remain between you and the short grass."

It was Danikov's turn. After getting his line and taking one more routine practice swing than usual, he stepped up to the ball. With a compact back swing he then started his down swing. He allowed his hips to lead the way, muscle memory insisting his arms and hands follow in a positive, rhythmic tempo. His hands and wrists came powerfully to the fore with his left side braced to allow his body's coil to work its dynamics.

The ball was swept from the tee with a slight and powerful up-swing. The ball took an immediate high road and then his usual fade kicked in moving the sphere to just left of center to a perfect landing and a short hop on the always-soft fairway. What remained was a straight-away eight iron with no forestry in between.

Clayman couldn't suppress either a broad grin or the urge to try applying a little pressure to their kindred opponent, Randall. "Well, at least we have two balls in play. You'll have to knock this one into Cherokee County to keep up."

"I don't think so," Santan said. "He'll settle for slow and go."

Randall teed up with a determined expression, but then rushed his swing in spite of his partner's suggestion to stay on an even keel. The three-wood caught turf before sphere and the result was a high fly ball that would have hit the ceiling of any domed baseball stadium in the country. "I'm dead!" he said.

"Randall," Santan said, "as a Christian pilgrim you wouldn't think of going into the tank on me, would you?"

Randall was embarrassed and stammered, "Luh . . . look, big dog, that was a 22-handicapper's testimonial to his game, nothin' else. I don't have the talent to screw up a shot deliberately. I'll try my best, but you're right about one thing: I'm sure not pullin' for us."

Santan stepped up to the tee and without hesitation drove his ball hard. Before the ball had even reached its apogee Santan quickly bent over to pluck his tee from its newly-prone position. It took off on a medium trajectory that drew slightly back to center and got a surprisingly good bounce before stopping, leaving him with no more a soft nine-iron to the green. By the time he had straightened up he still had time to watch the shot's satisfying finish. Randall whistled as the other two added more articulate compliments.

As they all left the tee box to mount their golf carts which were nearly ten yards away, Santan lagged behind the others to take a final survey of the four shots. As he started forward he abruptly stopped, his jaw sagging and his eyes widening. Sitting atop one of the golf carts for Santan's eyes only was the same horrific-looking creature that had first been driven from his spiritual form by Danikov. Santan had not seen the monster before and could only stare, while the others, seeing nothing, went about replacing their tee clubs in their golf bags.

By any other name, Santan's "demon" had a near-classic appearance with a scaled body, pointed ears, chin with body hair, and brilliantly reddened eyes. In one of its two long-nailed hands it grasped not a trident, but a huge-headed driving club. His legs and two hooves were dangling to the side of the cart facing the players while the demon distractedly balanced the club on one finger, club head up. A yellowish mist exuded from and surrounded the creature's entire body.

The other three momentarily arrested their progress at the carts when they noticed Santan still on the tee and acting peculiar as he pointed to one of the carts. They shook their heads. Danikov's and Clayman's cart was first in line and Clayman hit the accelerator without bothering to first release the brake. They drove off with a sudden lurch.

Before Randall could step into their cart Santan said, "You don't see anything?"

"Where?" asked Randall.

"Right there. On top of the cart."

"Uh, come on Luke, today's been a long year. Let's finish this thing."

"Stand aside, then. I'm gonna take another practice swing here." Santan took two steps forward, leveling his driver as if it were a baseball bat. He drew it back to the right and parallel to the ground before bringing it back in a powerful arc that whistled through the air toward the creature, skimming the top of the cart. The only result was the demon's look of surprise as he instinctively, but unnecessarily tried to parry the blow with his own immaterial club.

Santan said as he swung, "If I don't need God, I sure as hell don't need demons!" His swing having met nothing of substance, Santan quickly jumped into the cart and motioned for Randall to do the same. They raced down the cart path's twisting route clipping the wooden sign that read "Cart paths only on this hole." Randall carried his own look of surprise all the way to their first stop.

Santan hit the brakes a little past parallel of where Randall's skied tee shot had come to rest near the middle of the fairway. Santan was about to drive Randall over to his ball when Randall said, a little unnerved by Santan's antics back on the tee, "Uh, uh, remember the sign you shot down on the flyover?"

"Oh, yeah," Santan said. "I'm still a little preoccupied."

"Here," Randall said, "I'll take all the sticks I'll need to finish and you can have the cart. And keep one thing in mind, will you? If you should shank your iron shot into the woods it could be the stroke you'll treasure for the rest of your life . . . and for the next one."

Santan frowned and ignored the comment as he drove forward leaving Randall with his three clubs. The demon, having remained perched atop the cart, now swung down and into the vacated seat, totally surprising Santan and nearly causing him to roll the vehicle. He was even more surprised to hear the creature speak.

"Look," the demon said in a low, rumbling voice. "I've been with you for a long time and have helped you when-ever you called. We both know it's important for you to win this final hole from your accuser. I can help you once again."

"I can't believe this," Santan said, his eyes blinking rap-idly. "Why can't the others see you?"

"They don't want to. Would their God attend to you personally as I've been sent to do? Tell you what. Let me make a little adjustment and then you can hear me out." No sooner had the demon said the word "adjustment" than he looked like any forty-year old club golfer wearing golf shorts and a visor. "Is that better? he asked.

"It has to be better for you," he said. "I must still be hallucinating as well as talking to myself. Maybe it's all from the pain I felt in my gut. Is that your specialty?"

"Never mind," the demon said. 'Look, Danikov has an extra club in his bag for a total of fifteen. Call him on it and he'll concede the hole and the match."

Santan could barely believe that he was actually conversing with the . . . *something* . . . riding next to him in his cart. "He isn't the kind of player to make that sort of mistake," he said.

The demon's voice now sounded not only testy, but also as if it were speaking through a wet stocking cap pulled over its mouth. "I just counted them," it gurgled. "Fifteen! The point is to call him on it and claim the hole." The demon then fled the moving cart.

Santan stopped the cart parallel to Clayman's ball and watched Randall strike his second shot. It was hardly better than his tee effort. The shot still left him a good hundred yards or so to the green on the par four hole. Even with the handicap stroke, he wouldn't likely be much help to Santan, unless Clayman messed up.

As Clayman approached his ball he raised his arms in frustration at his shot predicament. Leaving the cart on the path Danikov had walked over to Clayman's ball with him and was silently assessing the situation.

In the meantime Santan slipped quietly out of his cart and casually strolled the three steps over to the other twosome's empty cart. He successively tapped his forefinger on each of Danikov's clubs, his lips moving slightly as he counted. The demon was correct.

"Give it your best stroke, Paul," Danikov said, encouraging Clayman. "That's all you can do. Don't worry about it."

That little gesture of recognition and support served to re-energize Clayman. It suddenly came to him that he very much had a chance to help Danikov win the ultimate golf match. Randall already lay two and he was still a hundred yards short of the green. Make a good shot, he told himself. *But how?*

Clayman continued the situation analysis. The lie was all right. He could get the club head on the ball since the sparse rough was not really a factor. For starters he would need to slice his favorite club—a metal seven-wood—past the small tree which was forty yards away and the only tree defending the green from his left side position. The shot, however, would have to be hit hard enough to sail over most of the length of the pond's myriad fish, snapping turtles and geese-laden population before he could possibly end up a little right of the bunker and just short of the green. He had shaped the shot perfectly in his mind's eye. If he could only accomplish it in reality, he *might* be able to get up and down for par. O.K., that's it, he thought, the immaculate execution!

Clayman was nearly ready to attempt the shot of his life. Danikov was watching intently as the other two only casually glanced in Clayman's direction, giving him no chance to put the ball into serious play. Clayman stepped boldly to the task and swung. The club struck the ball solidly from a slice stance as it began its perilous—perhaps quite short—journey. After a forty-yard start, the ball brushed a few grasping leaves on the left side of the 150-yard marker tree and then launched itself out over water.

Gaining altitude, the ball's initial straight flight was quickly overridden by the slice. The ball looked to easily carry the waterway, however, as the shot seemed to be perfectly duplicating Clayman's imaginative vision. The brush with the fresh flora, however, began to evidence its toll as the little white sphere's velocity was impacted.

This caused it to break out of the ball's arc and begin plunging perilously toward the water's surface mere yards from dry land. The demon, again perched on top of Santan's cart leaned forward, intently observing the shot's progress. A smirk spread across his countenance with the shot's mortality quickly closing.

While still at a relatively low angle and with some force yet driving it, the ball dropped even lower to the water's surface. At that moment a foot-long snapping turtle broke the water line at that precise point in following through with his lunge towards a meal of minnow. When surlyn ball met turtle carapace the result caused the projectile to catapult forward from the pond and safely into the first cut of rough. The turtle quickly returned to the bottom of the pond in order to digest a meal and ponder a back ache.

The demon sat high enough off the ground to see exactly what had happened and reacted by whipping an incongruously yellow-misted, but humanized head back and forth in rage, finally glaring in the direction of Danikov, suspecting duplicity.

Neither Danikov nor Clayman—nor even Santan, for that matter—were in a position to actually witness the turtle's reluctant interference. Each could see, however, that the ball had somehow bounced out of the hazard. "Poor plan. Great execution," said Danikov as he shook his head and grinned. Clayman jumped up and down, straining to see the shot's final result. "Yeaaah!" he shouted in both disbelief and excitement.

While Clayman continued to celebrate his good fortune, Danikov turned his thoughts to his own shot. There was nothing difficult about this, he reasoned. Pin's at the back and no measurable breeze, he thought. He had been thinking eight-iron all the way to his ball. But how to compensate for the effect of adrenalin pumping endorphins through his body like a fire hose carrying a rush of water? One way was to actually go to a longer club, but use a more relaxed swing. Not the norm, but he chose it anyway, putting away the eight-iron and pulling the seven.

Santan was nearby and watched the club switch, followed by Danikov's several practice swings. He realized that his opponent was uncertain about the shot. To contribute to Danikov's confusion he tried a little applied psychology by calling out to him, "Give me something to shoot at, hot shot."

Danikov swung. It was beautifully timed and perfectly struck. "Come on, be the right club," he said aloud. By the time the ball began its descent, however, he knew the shot had been too solidly hit for the less elevated club. "Get down!" he suddenly pleaded. The ball lit softly enough at the back of the green and took only a small first hop onto the back, but level tier. By then, however, it was too late for perfection. The ball trickled to the green's back edge and then onto the first-cut fringe by no more than an inch. Still a fine shot, but not what it might have been.

"No luck!" said Santan in mock empathy. He, too, had at first pulled out an eight-iron, though he was ten yards closer to the green than Danikov had been. Seeing his opponent's adrenalin working overtime he didn't think he could rein in his shot any more successfully. "O.K.," he said aloud, "let's go the other way and let it all out."

He plucked a nine-iron from its nest and settled in for his address. His back swing reached away and just short of parallel and then crashed down through the golf ball and up, carrying eight inches of green-topped orange-red turf in short flight behind the ball. The perfect shot, however, would have required only seven inches of turf. The ball ended up fifteen feet short of the pin, but on nearly the same line as Danikov's. Santan used several choice epithets in cursing the results, but they were more for theatric's sake.

Danikov stopped his cart parallel to the eighteenth green. He saw that Clayman appeared distressed. "Don't worry, partner," Danikov said. "We're in the thick of this thing."

But as they left the cart Clayman surprised Danikov, saying, "That isn't it. My greatest fear is that I may already have lost Sheila. No matter what I say or do now, she'll think our past problems predict our future."

"You're premature in making that judgement," Danikov said. "Besides, I told you I've been praying for you. I believe that God always answers prayers, even though we don't always recognize it."

As they stepped out of the cart both of them suddenly realized that dozens of people were standing on the roadside hill behind and well above the eighteenth green, watching the play. Even more were continuing to crowd in and some were waving while others began to applaud. As Santan and Randall pulled up behind them Randall said, "Gentlemen, news of our miraculous survival, and I presume our finishing-the-match-at-any-cost credo, has reached the clubhouse."

At that moment as Danikov and Clayman began walking towards their respective balls, Clayman saw something that caused him to squint in its direction. "Tommy Ray," he said excitedly, his eyes misting, "That's . . . that's Sheila standing at the far left of the crowd." He let that fact sink in before he continued. "She has never come to see me on the golf course. Do you think, that despite our problems, she really cares?" He swatted at a tear as if it were an insect.

Danikov said nothing, but he smiled at Clayman and clapped him on the back. In response Clayman dropped his head and shook it in gratitude for both Sheila and Danikov. At the same time he pulled his handkerchief from his back pocket.

As Danikov looked up in the direction of where Clayman had indicated Sheila was standing, he was surprised by the crowd's rapidly increasing size. By now he was at the back of the green and much closer to the crowd on the bank than were the other three players. As he glanced up and then back he was forced to do a double-take. From his partner's previous description he thought he recognized Sheila, but who was standing next to her at the very end?

"Marilee!" Danikov said, moving his lips, but not making enough sound for anyone to hear him. He bit his lower lip in an attempt to hold back tears as he waved in her direction. She enthusiastically returned his wave.

Clayman looked up at the bank again and noticed that both Sheila and the woman standing next to her were waving. Danikov was waving back. Clayman immediately assumed the connection. He wondered how it could be that Marilee and Sheila were together. They didn't know each other. Then he understood. *Joey!* She must have called each of them from the clubhouse. She's the only person who knew both players, knew that they were playing together, *and* that they would have worried mates. The two women must have found each other as they were watching and waiting for their half of the already fabled foursome to finish.

As Marilee again enthusiastically waved to Danikov he had to turn away to maintain his emotional calm. Clayman was intently watching this subtle interaction. He felt the same sort of emotion for Sheila and his lower lip quivered at the thought of her and how much he wanted to share with her everything that had happened to him.

Both Randall and Clayman were readying themselves for their approach shots. Even without the presence of the fast-growing gallery either one or both of them might easily succumb to the final-hole pressures of the biggest match of their lives. With a boisterous and cheering gallery scrutinizing their play, who could be certain that either of them would even be able to make contact with the ball?

Randall was much further from the green than Clayman so he prepared to hit his third shot. He made a good three-quarter back swing with his pitching wedge, but as he started his down swing he simultaneously rotated his head forward, if ever so slightly. The club head struck the ground before the swing had bottomed out and sliced its way into the soft turf. The club head remained buried, the ball untouched. A quick, sympathetic groan came from the gallery.

Santan said, "Have you no shame, Randall?" Instead of going into a rage as he normally would have, however, Santan kept his head, the greater need for success on the hole helping to keep his temper in check. In fact, he switched from more characteristic chastisement to actual encouragement. "Try it again, but this time keep your head still and your eyes on the ball. And remember, it won't move until you hit it." Randall swung again, this time keeping Santan's tips in mind. The ball flew beautifully and plopped right down onto the middle of the green. "Bravo!" Santan exclaimed. The crowd let out a tremendous cheer and Randall doffed his cap in both relief and exaggerated recognition.

Clayman's "turtle bouncer" had left him only twenty yards short of the green and to the right of the bunker. Except for being in light rough he was in perfect position for his third shot on the par four hole. Santan's creative gamesmanship, which no one had actually objected to during all their holes, was designed this time to recreate for Clayman a vision of Randall's recent failure. With mock sincerity Santan said, "Now don't *you* stick your 'pick' in the ground."

Clayman had intended to bring his loftiest wedge from the cart, but couldn't seem to locate it. Oh well, he thought, better off not to tempt fate. Instead, he determined to chip with the seven-iron. In doing so his ball landed short of the green and bounced up, but well right of the pin, perhaps twenty feet from the hole. Clayman had avoided Santan's subconscious snare and he lay three while Randall was four. Each of them had a handicap stroke coming.

Clayman was the first to putt and pulled his ball so far left that the right-to-left roll resulted in his closing only half the total distance to the hole. He was so embarrassed he couldn't look up towards where Sheila had to be watching.

It was Randall's turn and with Santan's tutoring he lost no time in stepping up to stroke a level lag putt from fifteen feet to within a foot and a half of the objective. "Pick it up," Danikov said. "That's double bogey six, for a net five, but a good recovery." Randall was happy to accept.

"Now, brother Paul," Danikov said, turning to Clayman, "knock yours right into the hole for a point, and all I have to do is tie Mr. Santan. Then we can sing all the way up the hill to embrace our deeply missed mates."

Clayman was already focused on Sheila's presence. What could that really mean? Was it that difficult for him to believe she truly cared enough about him to trudge to the dreaded "hobby-field?" Even if she'd been told he was playing hurt and in the rain? That wasn't very sensitive of him. Bottom line is she was here. He peeked a look in her direction. He could see her smile. What a beautiful smile.

"You waitin' for a team photo?" said Santan, taunting Clayman.

The player refocused. Taking another look at his line he observed no distinct impression as to break, or the lack of it. He again paused, then glanced at Danikov. Joking, Clayman said, "For all I can see it's gonna break *up* hill. Whad'ya think?"

"Putt it like it was on a string," Danikov said. Straight and up the hill. Stroke it hard enough to finish a foot and a half directly behind the hole. It's your kind of putt, Paul." Clayman again bent to the task. He sighted, drew back the putter, then returned the blade to meet the ball squarely. Rolling, rolling, rolling . . . right on target . . . closing in on the front lip of the hole now and still moving. The ball teetered on the lower edge and would have plunged to the bottom of the cup with a clatter if both gravity and friction hadn't triumphed. The last motion of the ball was backward half an inch.

Clayman stood watching, still expectant as Santan interjected a comment. "Yo, Pauli" he said. "I don't think that sucker's gonna restart and roll uphill from a dead stop. Pick it up for six. Neither yours nor Randall's strokes matter, but you tied the high ball. Looks like your captain's gonna have to row after all."

The demon Pride loitered hungrily near the flagstick, which still lay on the green.

Clayman approached Danikov shaking his head, trying to shake off his failed effort. He continued past him and interestedly eyed his partner's line. "You know," he said, "If I could have found my pitching wedge for that approach shot, I might have gotten it closer. I hope my club is in your bag."

The demon slumped momentarily in reaction to the obviously lost opportunity. Santan gave him a look that implied absolute stupidity on the demon's part. Randall said, "Luke, you're away. Shall I replace the pin or can you see the hole?"

"I don't need it," Santan said.

"Don't go too far with that flagpole, Randall," Danikov said. "I'll want it for a backstop when he's finished." Clayman picked up the pin from its prone position and stepped well out of the way.

With the club-count tactic now a moot point, Santan noticed the demon standing near Danikov while curiously holding up his hands about ten inches apart and parallel to one another. He appeared to be absorbed by something, as if scanning some invisible file.

Santan didn't know or care what that was all about. He knew he needed to drain his twelve-foot putt. By making it he could probably assure himself of the win he desperately wanted. Even if he missed, he still had an outside shot at a win, if Danikov were to miss.. He wanted this putt more than any other in his life. He needed this win more than any thing in his life. As he stepped up to address his putt he said loudly without bothering to look up, "Hear any school bells, boys?" No one bothered to answer him.

Carefully assessing the side-hill line and speed he then performed his ritual pre-putt routine: two dry-run swings a half-step away from the ball, but on a parallel line.

He stepped up to the real-time position and stared at the ball for a full ten seconds. Following that he rotated his head slightly in looking at the hole, then looked back at his ball. Once more he stared at the hole, then again looked back at his ball.

Now he drew back his putter. Without hesitation he returned the putter softly and smoothly on the same line. The ball was struck with just enough force to send it firmly across the slight downhill grade. He could not afford to be either short or on the low side of the hole. Looking good so far. Not right. Not left. Surely not short. Maybe perfect, providing the relatively fast-moving ball hit the hole squarely.

The ball was rolling dead on line for the center of the hole. It remained on line . . . only another five feet . . . still rolling . . . still tracking perfectly. Now only a single metal spike mark remained between the ball and the hole. The spike mark had such a fractional impact on the ball's roll that although the sphere would reach the hole, it was with the barest margin, slightly right of center, and on the high side. Santan started walking toward the hole, believing he had holed it. Even with the tiny angle of deflection imparted by the spike mark the ball nevertheless dipped into the hole. But only temporary entrance was gained.

Although the ball actually dropped below the hole's surface, its velocity and angle combined to cause it to instantly and dramatically reemerge at a 45-degree angle. It went into a new orbit, spinning two feet down the hill. Santan immediately stopped his advance, stunned.

As quickly as a pitcher thinking he has thrown a call-strike to end an inning steps towards the dugout before the plate umpire can fully make up his mind, Clayman and Randall simultaneously moved to high five one another, with Clayman shouting, "Yessss!"

Randall offered false condolences to his playing partner, saying, "Tough luck, pal!"

Danikov moved to quell the premature uprising. "You guys mind holding off for a bit?" he said. "We still have some golf to be played here."

Now the demon rushed to Santan's side, growling in his bottom-of-the-barrel voice, "You can still claim the match!" he said, defiantly, "Listen to me."

An exasperated Santan muttered softly, but sarcastically, "Right, you ex-horned freak. Chances are really good a 12-handicapper will take three from ten feet away. The best I can hope for is two putts and a tie."

"No," said the demon in his deep, but rasping voice. "We have an option even if he should hole the putt. Watch Randall."

"Watch Randall?" Santan whispered again in irritation. "He's already holed out. It's Santan we're worried about, fish breath."

"Don't trifle with me," said Pride, his tone of voice now as menacing as his former decaying appearance was offensive. "I have the power of life or death over you."

"Excuse me," Danikov said, distracted by Santan's mumbling, "I doubt you're praying that I make this, so if you can hold off your incantations for a moment."

Santan waved off Danikov's objections, but he was intently watching both him and Randall. Santan hadn't yet marked his two-footer and was about to when Danikov motioned, saying, "Good try, Luke. Pick it up," conceding his par four. Both Clayman and Randall frowned as Randall quickly replaced the pin for Danikov and then moved in Danikov's direction.

"Now's the time, partner!" Clayman said as he moved out of Danikov's line of sight.

Danikov moved to address his ball as Randall crouched down behind both Danikov and his ball, offering a rare opinion about a putt's line. "I know you're a good putter," he said, "but did you see how Santan's ball was breaking right as it died?"

"I did," Danikov said, smiling as if he were thoroughly enjoying himself and totally mindless of the pressure. "But I'm going the opposite way, so I'm just gonna put it out a cup's width to the right and stroke it just hard enough to drop into that huge, gaping sinkhole."

Randall loved it and signaled his approval as he moved straight back several paces before gluing himself to a spot to watch the result.

Danikov took several perfect grass top-brushing, short strokes before stepping up to the ball. A third pendulum-smooth swing resulted and the ball rolled firmly through the planned minor arc. The fivesome was frozen in place. The ball was center cut and did not stop until it was dead inside the hole. It could not, however, find the bottom of the cup.

The ball made a metallic clink as it came to rest against Randall's carelessly placed, slightly forward-leaning pin. The ball was in the hole, but not below the surface, therefore it had not yet been successfully holed. No matter, the three-some erupted in roars.

Santan, at the demon's incessant urging, screamed above the din. "Don't move, Randall! You were improperly positioned on an extension of the line of putt behind the ball while your partner stroked his putt. In match play that's a penalty of loss of hole. The point is tied."

Randall looked bewildered. He turned up his palms and shook his head as everyone was looking at him. He said, "I'm sorry. I didn't know you couldn't—."

Danikov interrupted, putting up a reassuring hand towards Randall and then turned to Santan, saying, "Your water is being turned on and off like a faucet, Luke. You know USGA rules better than that. The rule only applies to balls lying on the green. I was clearly off, if only by an inch. That's why I called for the pin to be replaced. Your guardian demon, if he's still somewhere around, has been run over by a Mack truck."

As Danikov defused the claim he stepped forward several paces and bent the flagstick slightly back and away from the edge of the cup where the ball was delicately lodged. As he did so the ball fell loose and to the bottom of the hole.

Randall yelled at Santan, "Smoke that!"

Danikov, Randall and Clayman low-fived each other before offering handshakes to Santan, who refused all. As the threesome walked towards their carts. Santan hung back, glancing in the opposite direction at the scowling demon and giving him a jerking thumb movement. "Power of life and death, huh?" he said quietly to the creature. "You're the sorriest excuse for a partner I've ever seen. Go to Hell."

With Luke Santan, however, the demon Pride was well pleased.

As all walked the rest of the way to their carts Danikov again offered his hand to Santan, saying, "Take it, Luke. No hard feelings. And another thing. I'm letting you off the hook with the walk. I know you by now and I think you'll give all of this some serious thought. Sooner or later I hope you'll come to the conclusion that it takes more faith to *deny* Christianity than it does to actually *embrace* it."

"The greatest motivation for winning," Santan said, "is simply to avoid having to take the winner's crap."

Danikov hesitated, but then decided to continue. "Look," he said, "I understand how bitter you were after losing your father as a child, but you still owned the free will you talk about. By not giving your will to God, however, you lost the opportunity to draw close to Him at a critical time in your life. The good news is it's not too late to do that."

"What?" Santan replied incredulously. "Not then. Not now. Not ever. I wish I hadn't shared that personal story with you. It died long ago."

"No, it didn't. If it had died, you wouldn't have brought it up. But you *can* lay it to rest once and for all simply by letting God know you hated the moment of your father's death, and that the suffering caused you to subvert His will. Admit that sin and you can come to know profound peace and love you have never known."

Santan glared at his antagonist. "What would you know about how I suffered?" he asked.

"You're right," Danikov said, "I never lost a parent as a child, but when Marilee and I lost our first child to Cancer I was just as devastated as you must have been. Children are not supposed to die before their parents."

"Well, I'm sorry about that," Santan said. "I didn't know. But I do know I was bitter to the point of despair."

"So was I full of bitterness and self-pity. Even hate," Danikov said. "But my wife convinced me to wrap up all those negative and self-defeating thoughts in one simple response."

"Yeah," he said. "And what was that?"

"She led me to embrace our daughter's death."

"*Embrace* it?"

"I know," Danikov said, tenderly, "That was my first reaction, too. But Marilee convinced me that by damning the tragedy I was really questioning God's will rather than submitting to it."

"That's not for me," Santan said. "I never came to accept my overwhelming loss with such timidity."

"There's a better word than that for what we were filled with," Danikov said. The afternoon sunlight reflected off his moist eyes. "It's called grace. As a result of the peace and love we found in accepting God's will, we were so filled with grace that when others came to us to offer consolation, we found ourselves actually healing those who came to console us."

Santan blinked twice at Danikov's words, but said nothing. Danikov again offered his hand. This time Santan responded by offering to shake hands, certainly not warmly, but nevertheless a handshake. After shaking with Danikov he repeated the effort with each of the other two, who by then had gathered around. All remained on the green since no other group was behind them.

Danikov said, "Men, when we get through the tunnel this crowd is going to be all over us. Before that happens, how about your quick wrap-up thoughts about our little adventure? Artie?"

"That's easy," he said. "Starting tomorrow I'm gonna' prioritize. God, family, job. I lost joy in my life. I think I can find it again. At least I discovered truth."

"My friend," Danikov said, embracing Randall, "you never discover truth. Truth is revealed. And you had a revelation."

"You're absolutely right about that. I guess I have a lot yet to learn."

"So do I, Artie. I want to be a part of your Bible study and accountability group. Glowing coals glow only as long as they remain in a group."

"First things first for me," Clayman said. "If Sheila still wants me, I'm not only going to join her on her walk, I'm going to propose marriage."

Danikov embraced Clayman also and said, "And think about making this little reunion group a threesome."

"That comment makes me curious about something," Clayman said, swinging his putter with one hand as he looked away for a moment. You already have your salvation well in hand. Where do you go from here?"

"You're right about our salvation coming from faith alone. That is, we are justified by our faith. But only as we *grow* in Christ do we become sanctified." Both Clayman and Randall said "Amen."

Before Danikov could ask for Luke's final take, Clayman preempted him. "How about you, Tommy Ray? What do you make of all this? For without your efforts Artie and I would have ended up with nothing but unplayable lies."

Randall laughed and nodded. Santan made no comment as he remained about a foot out of the others' circle, practicing his putting stroke but listening to everything.

"Thank you, but all credit is due the Lord," Danikov said in response. "I, too, have learned a great deal. I thank God for placing the three of you in my life. I thank Him for sending me Barnabas. That encourager told me that if I should ever again hear a voice within me saying, 'You're not a witness, then by all means witness . . . and that voice will be silenced.' I still have one overriding need though, and that's church."

"Any particular reason?" Clayman asked, not questioning, merely curious.

"Because," Danikov said, "while I have much to study and learn, I also need a retreat."

Clayman simply nodded, smiling. He would let Danikov close things with Santan.

Danikov turned to face the estranged member of the foursome. "Luke," he said, placing one hand on his shoulder, "you get the last word before we're mobbed. Will you re-run your numbers? God will always, always, be with us. I know you don't want to hear it, but we love you too."

Santan was not ready to ask why. "Look," he said, "we shared a unique experience so I suppose we have a common bond, but . . ." he hesitated. "That doesn't include our views about religion, faith or the lack of it. I merely grant that you won the golf match. I remain self-reliant." He looked away and then back to Danikov and said, "My truth remains as before."

"I agree with you," Danikov said, "about the importance of truth. It is more important than tolerance. But opinions don't count, only truth does. Otherwise you're dwelling in ignorance. And since the Bible is saturated with God's Word, that's where we need to meet God and truth."

"Look, Danikov," Santan said, "believe it or not I understand that all Christians are called to evangelize. But that's your problem, not mine." Then he added with a grin, "I *do*, however, want a rematch."

If you, dear reader, are interested in how you can accept the gift of God's incredible grace, all you have to do is take to heart five basic points of Christian belief :

* God has a wonderful plan for our lives because He loves each and every one of us.
* Each of us was created by God *in order* to have a personal relationship with Him.
* Because we are all born sinners we are separated from God through that sin.
* God so loved us that he sent Jesus to be sacrificed on the cross for our sin.
* Each of us must be willing to confess our sin in agreeing with God about the awful nature of our wrongs, to turn from them, and to ask Jesus into our hearts.

If you want to accept Christ (or Yeshua, the Hebrew word for Jesus, the Messiah) as your Lord and Savior, pray the following prayer, and trust that god will answer it:

"Lord Jesus, thank You for loving me and giving me Your life on the cross in my place. I now receive you as my Savior. Thank you for forgiving my sin, for sharing with me Your eternal life, and for making me a new creature. Help me now to live for You as I continue the journey of eternal life in Christ. In Your name I pray, AMEN."

Give a Novel of Christian Faith and Golf
to Family, Friends and Colleagues!

Yes, I want _____ copies of The Foursome at $16.95 each, plus $3.05 shipping per book. (Georgia residents please include 7% state sales tax.) Canadian orders must be accompanied by a postal money order in U.S. funds. Allow two to four weeks for delivery.

The Foursome by Terry Dodd

Name _____

E-mail _____

Address _____

City _____ State _____ Zip _____

Daytime Phone _____

Evening Phone _____

Quantity Ordered: _____

Total Cost of Book(s): _____

Shipping and Handling: _____

Tax: _____

Total: _____

Please make your check payable and return to:
Dodd Consulting Group
1425 Market Blvd. Suite 330-235
Roswell, GA 30076